MY WIFE, MY LOVER

By Robert Donmayr

Published in United Kingdom by Julian Estelle Press, 38 Hewitt Avenue, London N22 6QD

Cover Designed by James Keary

Printed in bound by Biddles Ltd, King's Lynn, Norfolk

Dedicated to Estelle my soulmate

Also by Robert Donmayr

Toto The Outsider: a biography

And being prepared:

The Whirling Soul

Chapter One

Jon Tolman was standing by the window at his office in San Francisco. He had an athletic body and was over six feet tall, with brown eyes and dark hair. He was well groomed and carried with him the smell of expensive after-shave. He was looking at the street which was being flooded by a torrential rain that afternoon. The streets were empty, except for a few people running to cross the road. As usual he had his cigar in his mouth, but for some reason it was not lit. He stood there pensive with a smile on his face. He could still remember the first time he met his wife Sarah Sanders. It was at an evening art class. She was standing tall and slim by her easel painting some fruit put there on a table. She was dressed casually, just blue jeans and an open collar shirt. He became attracted to her, as soon as he saw her sky blue eyes shaped like almonds, and her long blond hair falling over her shoulders. Just by chance there was an empty space to her right and Jon rushed to fill that place. They hit it off as soon as their eyes met. It was love at first sight for both of them. And from that evening they became inseparable.

Now Sarah was carrying his twins, and was expecting them in a week or two. They had a room ready for them and decorated by Sarah, for she was an artist in every sense. Jon stopped looking at the rain and with a sense of regret went back to his desk. In the corner there was a replica of a high rise building, which he had designed and was proud of. Everybody in the firm liked him and within a few short years he had become the executive director of this well known architect firm.

That evening after leaving his office, he met with some colleagues to have a drink in the well known bar round the corner; that was where most of his associates and friends ended up at the end of the day. It was a habit, a kind of 'pilgrimage' one might say.

But tonight as he was trying to listen to one of his friends talking about some issue of the day, he found himself very absent minded as he could not concentrate on any subject that was being mentioned: something was bothering him, but what? he could not tell. Suddenly he emptied his glass in one go, and in a hurry, wished everybody goodnight and instead of walking out, he found himself running through the door and toward his car. He stopped by the pizza restaurant which was not far from his apartment and ordered Sarah's favourite which was pepperoni and anchovy: she kept having a crave for it since she became pregnant.

As soon as he opened the door to the apartment, he heard Sarah's voice anxious and distressed:
"Why are you late", said Sarah, "especially to-night".
"Why?", asked Jon, "what is special to-night darling?" then he realised that Sarah was not herself at all. She was anxious and restless; she was not relaxed at all and her breathing was faster than usual. He guessed that the babies were due for that night. Sarah wanted to go to the hospital right away.
"Do you think we could have a bite of the pizza first", said Jon?
"No, not now", replied Sarah holding her stomach, "can't you see that our princesses are due for tonight? Let us go, I can not waste any more time: I have my bag ready in the bedroom, will you fetch it darling".
Jon was rushing around. He brought the bag and was going to phone his parents when Sarah screamed with pain.

"Please take me now Jon", said Sarah, "they are coming".

Jon helped his wife down the few steps towards the car and drove so fast that he wished he was a racing driver.

At the hospital they quickly wheeled Sarah to the delivery room just on time, as her waters were breaking: Jon held Sarah's hand all the way trying to comfort her: then one cry came out loud and clear, followed three minutes later by another one. That is how the two princesses made their entries into this world.
"Look how beautiful they are" said Jon, "they are just like you Sarah, and I am so proud of you, for you have made me the happiest man on earth" and he kissed his wife.

I am a father said Jon to himself again and again, wait until I tell the whole world about my two angels.

Chapter 2

That night after kissing his wife good night, he left the hospital and drove home very excited and proud to be a father. He was so thrilled that he could not sleep at all. It was two o'clock in the morning when, fed up of turning and tossing restlessly, at long last, he got up and went to the kitchen to make himself a hot chocolate; while opening a box of biscuits, an idea came to his head; he rushed to the living room picked up the phone and called his parents.

Brr… Brr… Brr…

"Hello" answered a sleepy voice, "who is calling?"

"Hello mom" said Jon excitedly:

"Is that you Jon?", said Jane, "what is the matter, what time is it and why can't you sleep?"

"Mom", said Jon, "you have become a grandma".

"What a grandma", said Jane, "who is a grandma?"

"Mom", said Jon, "wake up now: it is three o'clock …"

"Three o'clock", said Jane, "and you are ringing me at that time; it better be important".

"Mom", said Jon, "Sarah gave birth to two lovely princesses, do you hear me?"

"How could she", said Jane, "she is not due for another two weeks; have you been drinking again son?"

"Mom", said Jon, "we have two beautiful princesses and they were born last night at eleven o'clock precisely; the spitting image of you; they were two weeks premature but they are healthy and well."

"Wow, I am a grandma" screamed Jane, "do you hear that Georges?"

"Georges, wake up" shouted Jane. "You are a grandpa, isn't it exciting?"

"Are you sure, here"; said Georges, "pass me that phone"; and he snatched the receiver out of her hand.

"Is that you son?", said Georges, "is this true? since eleven o'clock last night?"

"Yes dad it is true", said Jon, "you are a grandpa now."

"Congratulations are in order son", said Georges, "and how is Sarah?"

"She is doing fine", said Jon, "but I will call you to-night and tell you all about it; bye for now".

Jon sat on the couch and poured himself a large whisky. He dreamt of his two girls, and how he was going to give them the best that money can buy, especially education. He could see himself and Sarah at their graduation ceremony being so proud of their daughters. They looked so beautiful, and all the family was fussing around them; and with these lovely thoughts he fell deeply asleep on the sofa.

It was ten o'clock when he woke up. He had not changed into his pyjamas that night, so he felt dirty and smelly in his suit. He quickly took his clothes off, and hit the shower. Then he put on a pair of jeans and a jumper. He made himself some coffee and picked up some mail off the floor. But he was not interested. He drank his coffee as quickly as he could and ran out of the apartment: he stopped by the coffee bar where he ordered a large breakfast washed down with an orange juice and a large coffee. Then he stopped by the florist, and got Sarah a large bouquet: coming out from the florist he went to a sweetshop and bought his wife her favourite dark chocolates.

When he arrived at the hospital, Sarah was already feeding one of the babies. Jon looked so happy: he kissed his wife, and took the other baby in his arms.

"How did you sleep sweetheart?", said Jon

"I was tired", said Sarah, "but I wanted to have the babies with me

all night; and now I feel great and very proud to be a mother".
"I am so happy Sarah", said Jon, "that to-day I am going to skip work. I shall ring the office and tell them that I have become the proud father of two lovely princesses. Right now, all I want to do is to be with you" and he kissed his wife and gave her a big hug.

After Sarah finished breastfeeding the twins, Jon helped to put them in their cots; he sat by her side and put his arms around her and said "have you decided what to call them now?"
"Oh yes definitely", said Sarah, "it will be Holly and Jessica".
"I like those names", said Jon, "they are perfect, and we are going to be a very happy family". But Jon noticed some sadness in Sarah's face and asked "What is the matter, do I sense some kind of regrets in your eyes?"
"I wished my parents were alive just now; they would have been so proud of the girls".
Alas it was not meant to be, for they were killed in a car accident when Sarah was just fifteen.

Chapter 3

The days went by smoothly and Jon's parents came to look after the twins everyday and take them to the park near by.

Sarah resumed her artistic studies and was accepted as a full time teacher at the college; she was well loved by her colleagues. Sometimes she had to stay late for some student meetings and Jon found himself babysitting his daughters: but he did not mind, on the contrary he enjoyed it, and gave Sarah a rest.

One night, as he was reading a story to Jessica and Holly who were already half asleep, the phone rang and a voice he knew quite well said "Hi Jon, I am sorry to call you at home, are you doing something?"
"Hi Paul", said Jon, "what is up that cannot wait till tomorrow?"
"Jon", said Paul, "listen, I have very good news: A firm in Vancouver wants to see our designs; they want to build a high rise office and they have invited some directors with their wives to meet for a week or so, to discuss their project".
"It sounds grand", said Jon, "but what is in it for us, and why are you telling me all this?".
"This is the point Jon", said Paul, "would you like to represent our firm there? you will take Sarah with you, it will be a break for both of you - a kind of working holiday - what do you say?"
"Thank you Paul it is a lovely idea", said Jon, "but first I have to discuss it with Sarah. I will tell her as soon as she comes back from the college".
"That is great Jon", said Paul, "let me know tomorrow of your joint decision".

That evening, Sarah arrived just in time to hear Jon say good night to his mother on the phone.

"Hi darling what is up?", said Sarah, "you look a bit excited: how were the princesses? Anything happen this evening?"

"Oh yes darling" said Jon, kissing his wife; "and you are going to love it". And he told Sarah about the trip to Vancouver. "It will be like a second honeymoon for us, what do you think?"

"I look forward to it", said Sarah, "but what about the girls?"

"It has been fixed with mom", said Jon.

"Wow", said Sarah, "tell me quickly how you arranged that with mother?"

"Well, mom knows a neighbour called Marion who used to be a nanny. She will ask her tomorrow whether she would consider taking care of the girls for a week: what do you think?"

"It is an excellent idea Jon", said Sarah, "I can't wait for tomorrow".

The next day, Georges rang Sarah enquiring about the princesses.

"They are doing fine dad", said Sarah, "and do you know what I found?"

"What is it Sarah", said Georges, "what have you found?"

"Well", said Sarah, "the other day, while they were having their bath, I noticed on one of them a birthmark on the right side of the navel and funny enough, her sister had it as well and at the same place. It looks and has the shape of a tiny half a moon, and they are both identical. Is it not extraordinary?"

"Wow", said Georges, "wow, that is something; by the way Sarah and before I forget, I have a message for you from Jane: it is about Marion our neighbour. She will be delighted to take care of the girls while you are away. She cannot wait to see them".

"Thank you dad", said Sarah, "that is great news".

At work, Jon was being briefed about his trip to Vancouver.

They talked about it over a meal as well, and Paul was proud to be able to advise him.

"Well Jon I wish you good luck on your trip", said Paul, "and make sure that you come back with a contract".

"I will"; said Jon, "have no doubts about it".

Sarah took a week off from work; actually, she was due two weeks vacation, so there was no problem on that account. Jon came home a bit earlier that night to prepare for the trip.

"I spoke to Georges this morning Jon", said Sarah, "and at any time now, I expect the door bell to ring and Marion to appear" … She had hardly finished her sentence when the door bell rang and Marion opened the door carrying a suitcase: she was of average height with hair going grey; she stood there at the entrance with a big smile on her face.

"How did you do it Sarah?" asked Jon, "you must be a witch". Sarah laughed and went to welcome Marion who was still waiting at the entrance.

"You are Marion I presume, remarked Sarah, welcome to our home. I am Sarah and this is my husband Jon; we have been expecting you" and she shook hands with Marion, while Jon took her suitcase.

"We are both happy that you agreed to look after our children at such short notice", said Sarah.

"The pleasure is mine Sarah and actually I am completely free right now", said Marion. Straight away, the couple liked Marion. They knew that she would be ideal for the kids. "Come have some coffee before we show you around" said Sarah.

"Let me give you my references first", said Marion, "they are in my bag".

"No need for that Marion", said Sarah, "it is enough that you are Jane's friend; this is worth more than any references".

"Oh thank you", said Marion, "you know how to make people feel

at home; I am glad to have found you; it was meant to be".
"Are you psychic as well", said Jon, "like my wife?"

Marion smiled and said nothing. Sarah and Jon relied on their instincts and somehow knew that Marion would stay with them much longer than anticipated; she was shown to her room, which was adjacent to that of the twins. Marion left her suitcase on the bed and said: "I already feel at home here, I shall sleep here to-night so the girls will get used to me as soon as they wake up".

Jon and Sarah burst out laughing. Sarah got hold of Marion's hand and entered the bedroom where Jessica and Holly were fast asleep.
"Oh the little angels" said Marion.
"yeah, yeah,"repeated Jon behind her.
That night, every one in the household slept soundly, knowing the twins were in good hands.

Chapter 4

The next day was a hectic one. Everybody was rushing around preparing for the trip. Sarah was taking care of her two princesses with special maternal feelings. It would be the very first time that they would be separated, and she was reluctant to be away for a whole week: although she knew that deep in her heart they were in excellent hands with Marion. Already the twins were happy playing with her; they hit it off right away.

The week before, they had had their first birthday party and everything went very well: Sarah felt happy and fulfilled in every sense of the word. She enjoyed being a mother and a wife; but to-day she had an awful premonition: she felt as if the girls were being taken away from her and into Marion's arms. She could not explain the emotion and felt uncomfortable. That night she told Jon of her fears.
" It is mother's instinct darling, remember it is the first time that you will be separated"; said Jon, "there is nothing to worry about sweetheart". He hugged her lovingly against him.

Early next morning, reluctantly, they kissed their children goodbye and promised to bring them lots of presents.
"Write to me or phone", said Sarah, "if anything goes wrong Marion".
"Do not worry Sarah", said Marion, "just go and have a good time: you deserve it".
"Bye Marion", said Jon, "I know they are in good hands with you. I shall see you when I come back".

They kissed Jane and Georges who came early to see them

off, and made their way to the airport where a company plane was waiting for them. It came all the way from Vancouver to pick them up. When they boarded it, they were surprised to find it almost full. Most of the group and their wives were in a party mood. "Come and join us here" said a couple, "we have saved you those two seats".

When the plane took off, every one cheered, then a stewardess brought some sandwiches and coffee. "The champagne will be served later" said the air hostess.

Two hours later, they landed in Vancouver where a welcoming committee was waiting for them. They were driven straight to their hotel and shown to their rooms. That evening, the firm threw a party in their honour. They all had a lovely time: Jon and Sarah danced together most of the night and were teased by some colleagues who called them "the young lovers of the night".

Next morning, Jon and his colleagues went to their business meeting, while the wives got together and went for a shopping spree.

The meeting went on till late in the evening. They had to face tough negotiation and competition from other firms. Jon was exhausted when he arrived late at his hotel. While Sarah ran him a bath, she told him how she and her new friends spent their day shopping and dining. When they were ready, they went down to the dining room and joined the rest of the team. That evening was appreciated by every one; they discussed business and shopping. As soon as they went to bed, Jon and Sarah fell deeply asleep in each other arms exhausted.

The next day was another hectic day for the team. Their

meeting was long and laborious; after long hours and studying and discussing their projects, at long last, they came to an agreement and signed a contract. There were lots of handshakes with all parties smiling and happy. Every one was delighted to have endorsed the contract so soon. They all ended up in the bar for celebrations. That evening, there was another get together with lots of food, drinks and dancing.

Next morning after breakfast Sarah told Jon: "don't you think that we ought to go back to our little girls to-day, instead of sightseeing for the rest of the week?"
"You have read my mind Sarah", said Jon, "but first let me tell the rest of our team of our decision".
"While you discuss it on the phone with your friends, I will get our luggage ready", said Sarah.
Brr …Brr … Brr …
"Hello" said a voice:
"Is that you Mike?" asked Jon.
"Yes Jon, what can I do for you?", said Mike;
"Listen Mike", said Jon, "Sarah and I cannot wait to see our princesses; we have missed them so much, that we have decided to make our own way home today, and not wait for the end of the week as expected. So say good bye to everyone for me and I shall see you next week at work".
"Fine Jon, kiss Sarah for us", said Mike, "and have a safe journey".

After that, Jon rang the airport to book two seats back to San Francisco. Alas all the planes were full except for a small two engine aircraft which was only half booked "shall I reserve two seats for you sir?" asked the clerk.
"Oh yes please", said Jon, "I shall pay with American Express, if that is all right?"
"The take off is at seven o'clock this evening sir"; the clerk said,

"will you make sure that you come an hour earlier to fill some forms?".

"You bet any amount", said Jon, "we will be there on time".

"I don't bet", said the clerk.

"Listen Sarah", said Jon, "as we have a few hours to spare, let's go to a store and treat our girls with some more presents: I also want to buy something for mom and dad and may be Marion".

"What an excellent suggestion Jon, after shopping I will treat you to a nice meal in some posh restaurant".

"You are on Sarah", Jon said, "just lead the way".

Hand in hand, they strolled along the avenues teasing each other and looking at the shop windows.

"This", said Sarah, "reminds me of our first week when we met".

"And I was holding the hand of the prettiest girl in town".

"You do know how to pay a compliment darling", Sarah said, "and until now, I always thank God for attending my art classes. It was the best decision of my life..."

- "And of mine" interrupted Jon. "At long last, that evening, I could not take my eyes off you".

They arrived at the airport with lots of luggage and toys and made their way straight to the airline desk. After filling the forms, they were given their boarding tickets. The engines were already running as they entered the plane. There were around fifteen people sitting and waiting for their arrival and as soon as Sarah and Jon sat, the plane started taxiing towards the runway, where it gathered speed and climbed steeply towards the black clouds which were accumulating that evening.

Chapter 5

"How are my angels this morning" said Georges to his wife Jane. "They are just coming down with Marion, she has finished bathing them", Jane said.

They all ate a hearty breakfast with Holly and Jessica learning to feed themselves. They were over one year old now and trying to copy their parents, but half of the food ended up on the floor.
" Whoever finishes first will help me with the washing up girls", Marion said. They nodded their heads and tried to hurry up.
Georges was reading the papers when he saw the picture of a small plane smashed against some trees in a forest.
"It looks like there has been an awful plane crash Jane and some twenty people seemed to have died, can you see that?"
Just by chance Marion switched on the television in time to hear the news flash: "A small plane with eighteen passengers aboard and four crew members crashed into the forest" no reasons were given yet, but a storm could have been the culprit.
"What a waste of lives", Georges said.
"When are Jon and Sarah due back?", Marion asked.
"Not before two or three days I reckon", Georges said.
"Thank the Lord for that: at least they are flying in a big plane; it is much safer than a small one, especially in a storm".
"You are right there Marion", said Jane, "I agree with you".
Brr .. Brr ..
"Hi" said Marion picking up the receiver, "who is it".
"Hi, this is Paul, Paul Goodman, who is on the line?"
"It is Marion", said Marion, "the children's nanny".
"Is Jon's father or mother there?" asked Paul.

"One moment Paul", Marion said, "I pass you Jane".

"Hi", Jane said, "this is Jon's mother; who is calling?"

"My name is Paul Goodman, and I am a friend of Jon", said Paul.

"Oh hello Paul what is the matter? and how can I help you?"

"Well Jane, I do not know how to say it, but have you heard the news flash about a plane crash?"

"Oddly enough we were just talking about it, the three of us. Anyway, what has it go to do with Jon?"

"Well, well …"

"What is it Paul"?, Jane said, "what is the matter, Jon is due back in three days".

"It was supposed to be in three days", Paul said, "but for some reason Jon and Sarah changed their minds and boarded a small plane last night and …" He was interrupted by a scream from Jane.

"It cannot be, it is not possible, please tell me that it is not true". And she dropped the phone and collapsed on the couch crying and screaming.

"What is the matter Jane what is it?", Marion said, "you are frightening the princesses". Jane was speechless and kept crying and shouting: "no, no, it can not be true".

"What happened Jane", Georges said, "what is it; why are you screaming woman and who is on that phone?"

"Hello, who is it?"

"Are you Jon's father?" asked Paul.

"Yes, what happened", Georges said, "why is my wife so upset, what did you tell her?"

"I am sorry", Paul said, "but Jon and Sarah were in that little plane which crashed in the woods".

"Are you sure?", said Georges, "they were not due back for another three days".

"I am afraid my colleagues in Vancouver rang me to say that they changed their minds and shortened their trip to be with their princesses sooner", Paul said, "because they missed them. The plane was caught in an awful storm and for some reason one engine caught fire. I will call you later when I find out more about it. I am awfully sorry to bring you the bad news, but Jon was my friend". But there was no response for Georges stood there speechless as if struck by lightning. He dropped the receiver shaking and trembling, his eyes were fixed on the picture in the paper showing the accident. Marion was speechless as well; she replaced the receiver and said; "I am taking the children to the park, they looked frightened, you two stay by the phone in case you hear more about it". Georges came out of his daze and switched on the television waiting for some more news about the crash.

" Why on earth did they change their minds?", Georges said, "Why could they not have come back with the others: it cannot be right, that Paul is telling lies, it is not impossible, it cannot be".

Suddenly another news bulletin appeared on the screen: this time they gave the list of passengers who boarded the plane. A telephone number was given to the relatives who wanted to confirm the names. The crash was definitely due to an electric malfunction leading to the disaster: no one survived the tragedy. Georges kept on looking at the list; alas Jon and Sarah were on it. There was no mistake of identities. He picked up the phone but it was engaged. He banged the receiver and went to the kitchen to make some coffee.

During all that time Jane stayed speechless: her hands were still shaking and she looked stunned. Georges came back, and offered her a cup of coffee, but she would not respond; she went to her bedroom without a word. Georges drank his coffee believing that at any moment now the door would open and Jon and Sarah would come in: it was just a bad dream, and soon he would wake up. He rang the emergency number again and this time he got through. Alas he was not dreaming. The names of his children were on the list of people who boarded that plane. There was no mistake.

When Marion came back with the twins, her eyes were red, for she had been crying all the way to the park, although she tried to hide her distress from the kids. Georges picked them up in his arms repeating: "I shall always be here for you my little princesses, do not worry".

Next morning at the office, the news of the accident spread all around the departments; people could not believe or understand why it had to happen to such a nice couple, if not at all? As a gesture of respect they closed early and went to the bar to drown their sorrow.

Chapter 6

That morning San Francisco was basking in a warm sun and not a single cloud was to be seen, except for the Tolman family whose whole life was plunged into a complete darkness. Friends and family attended the funeral. Marion stayed at home seeing to the food and drinks for the guests who arrived after the service in a sombre mood.

As soon as Georges came back, he picked up Jessica in his arms while Jane was holding Holly; everybody was talking about the departed while helping themselves to food and drinks. It did not take too long before the congregation turned into some kind of business gathering: some of Jon's associates were already discussing about who was going to replace him.

A few weeks later Georges and Jane sold their house and moved into Jon and Sarah's residence which was much bigger. Marion was invited to stay with them for as long as she liked; she was so please with the offer, that she refused to be paid for her services. She became so much attached to the children that one day out of the blue she told Jane and Georges; "from now on and with your consent, I declare myself the children's godmother." Georges and Jane showed no surprise at all. They hugged her with tears in their eyes.

They started their new life with the grandparents doing their best to replace Jon and Sarah. Life went by slowly at the beginning but soon became hectic with the two girls becoming more demanding.

It was their second anniversary now, and Jessica and Holly

were growing healthy and beautiful. Holly inherited her mom's looks with her blond hair and almond shaped blue eyes; while Jessica took after her father with light brown hair and soft brown eyes shaped like Holly's. They somehow looked very much alike. Jessica was the quiet and peaceful one, listening more and talking less, while Holly was just the opposite, loud and restless.

"I think that Holly will turn into a tomboy soon", Georges said.
"Why, what makes you think so?" said Jane.
"Oh yes, she already plays rough with her sister"; Marion said, "she would rather kick a ball than play with dolls like Jessica".

One day the five of them went to a pantomime. It was packed with children of all ages and their parents. They were having a good time eating sweets and drinking, while watching a ballerina dancing on the stage: she looked as if she was floating on air and her feet hardly touched the ground.

Suddenly in the middle of the show, while everyone was watching quietly, mesmerized by the beautiful dancer doing a "Pas de deux", two little voices sounded loud and clear: "I want to do that granddad,I want to do that nanny."
Everything stopped at that moment while all the heads turned towards where the noise came from.
"Sshht", said the audience all around.
"Sshht", said Marion to the twins pulling them towards her, "tell us later what you want".

After leaving the theatre Marion told Jane and Georges: "Tomorrow I will go and see a friend of mine who is a ballet teacher and runs her own school; I will take my darlings with me and let them watch a class".
"What an excellent idea", Jane said, "I wish I could come with

you…"

"And why couldn't you?" Marion said. "We will make a day out of it: will you join us Georges?"

"No, not tomorrow for I have some business to attend to, but you go and enjoy yourselves and have fun".

Next morning Jessica and Holly woke up earlier than usual, for they were excited at the prospect of watching a ballet class. They got Marion out of bed although it was too early; she got up rubbing her eyes and mumbling something still half asleep. She ran them a bath and fetched them clean clothes. She helped them get dressed but for some reason this morning, it took them twice as long, for they were too excited and kept changing their mind about what to wear.

When at long last they came to the kitchen, breakfast was waiting for them prepared by Jane who was as excited as the girls. They ate heartily and left all the washing up in the sink; they were too much in a hurry that morning to be bothered about it.

Jessica and Holly were introduced to Marion's friend whose name was Imogen. She was in her fifties and of medium height, but still slim, and good humoured. She welcomed the twins and shook hands with them, then they all sat in a corner of a large hall. They watched children of different ages doing different exercises: some were stretching on the floor, others were rehearsing with a teacher, and further away some were doing bar work. There was a lovely atmosphere in the room and the twins could not take their eyes away from the class. They were mesmerized by all those young bodies flowing with grace. At the end of the session, they told Marion and Imogen how much they would like to join a class, and asked how soon it could be.

"First tell me your ages", Imogen said.

"They are not far from reaching the lovely age of three",
Marion said.

"To be honest Marion, I usually do not take children before the age
of three, but just this once and only because I have fallen in love
with them", Imogen said, "I will make an exception; I will enrol
them right away. What do you think children?"

"Yes aunty Marion, please say yes; we want to be ballet dancers like
all those children".

"All right children you win", Marion said, "now calm down and
please speak one at a time, but first let us ask what nanny thinks of
it".

"It is all right by me Marion", said Jane, "I am pleased to see that
they would like to be ballet dancers; so let us go and buy them their
outfits".

"No need for that, for I have my own little shop at the back of the
school. Come with me children and let me take your
measurements".

And so at the tender age of two and three quarters, the
twins started what might be their future careers. The whole family
was proud of their enthusiasm. Next day Marion took a photo of
them in their beautiful leotards and watched them starting their first
lesson; soon, they proved to be natural and relaxed.

A month later Imogen was so impressed with them, that she
offered to give them extra tuition at no extra cost, to the delight of
Jessica and Holly: the twins seemed to enjoy hard work and went
through all the elaborate and difficult training with enjoyment. They
never seemed to complain.

Chapter 7

Danny was a sixteen year old boy. He was above average height and very strong physically. He had broad shoulders and was blond with blue eyes. Something in his looks made people laugh, and those who knew him liked his funny side. Actually his IQ was that of a seven year old child. He did so badly at school that his teachers gave up on him very quickly.

Most of the time he played truant and his mother Emily abandoned all hope about his future. She was a barmaid and had no time for his antics; she had to work long hours to be able to survive; so most of the time, Danny was all alone to do what he wanted without being disturbed. As a matter of fact he was a kleptomaniac: whatever he fancied in shops or stores, he stole without giving it a second thought. It did not matter to him what he took, and he filled his room with all kind of objects. There was toys everywhere, empty bottles, cans and bags and all kinds of unnecessary items. Most of the time, Emily put them in the dustbin but not long after they were being replaced. Poor Emily gave up on him as well, and did not know how to react. She remembered that when he was as young as five when she went into a shop to buy him some sweets , she caught him taking a toy from a shelf and hiding it under his shirt; when she told him to put it back, he went into a tantrum and laid on the floor screaming and shouting: but Emily would not fall for his nonsense. She picked him up and left the shop apologizing for her son's behaviour. After leaving, he seemed to have quietened down. On the way home Emily felt a bit guilty about it; that night as she went to his room to tuck him in and kiss him good night, she saw that same toy on his sideboard.
"Where did you get that toy from, Danny?" asked Emily.

"From the shop mom", said Danny.

"But I told you that you could not have it", Emily said, "and I saw you putting it back".

"I just wanted it mom" Danny said.

"But that is stealing Danny, and thieves are put behind bars" said Emily, "do you know what that means?"

But Danny did not seem to worry or care about the consequence of his actions; and from then on, his bedroom became more crowded than ever. Emily took him to a doctor who referred him to a psychiatrist for tests; but that did not help either: he was put on medication for a while, but it did not put Emily's mind at rest.

Time went by and Danny grew up to be a strong teenager. At sixteen he was already bored with his life and was talking about suicide. His mother found him a job clearing tables and washing up; but soon he got bored with it and packed it up to the despair of his mother. She gave up on him completely and decided to enjoy her life while she was still young and attractive. At the bar, she was still attracting the attention of some customers, who were giving her the eye. But she was cautious now, for she had enough of those men who stayed with her for a week or two at the outmost and then disappeared without trace. She still remembered the longest relationship she ever had; it lasted just over six months and then as soon as her lover found out that she was bearing his child, he left without notice. Three months later Danny was born.

Chapter 8

Jessica and Holly, who just reached their third birthday, were showing some artistic signs which must have come from their late mother. Georges bought each of them a box of oil paints and some colouring pencils. They loved it and showed their pleasure by splashing it on the walls of their room. Marion went after them cleaning and washing the mess they made. She vented her anger on Georges.

"Why don't you get them some books on ballet instead, then you could read for them" said Marion.

"I agree with Marion, they are too young for painting and this will interfere with their ballet", said Jane.

"I am sorry, for you are both right" Georges said.

One day on a foggy after noon Marion forgot to fetch the children on time from school: so she took the car and drove as quickly as she could. She was lucky to arrive just on time to see their teacher taking them back inside. She apologised for being late and made her way back home: half way, she stopped by a shop next to the park.

" Would you like to come with me to get your favourite sweet?" said Marion.

But there was no reply from the twins; Marion looked back and saw them in deep sleep; never mind said Marion, I will not wake them up, I shall not be long my lovely angels, for when you wake up, your favourite sweets will be on your laps. She ran out of the car and into the shop, forgetting to lock the door of the car. She picked up the sweets and when she came to pay she found herself stuck in a small queue. And old lady was in front counting her cents to the cashier, who was very patient.

"I shall not be long maam".

"Please hurry it up, for I left my children in the car". Suddenly she felt guilty at leaving Jessica and Holly alone even if it was for a very short time: what if they woke up and found themselves alone in the car, what would be their reaction. When the old lady finished counting her money, Marion quickly paid for her goodies and rushed to the door; she ran to her car and opened the back door to wake up the girls; she stood still for a moment not believing her eyes: what she saw, frightened her. One of the twins was missing and it was Jessica. She dropped the sweets that were in her hands, looked around the car, and then screamed like mad; a passerby rushed to see why she was screaming : Marion, still crying, managed to explain what had happened: one of her twins was gone, nothing else was missing. Some people came out of the shop, wondering what all the noise was about. When it was explained that one of the girls had been kidnapped, one of them ran back to the shop and rang the police. Others looked around for the missing little girl. Meanwhile, Marion's screams woke Holly who looked frightened: she started crying, and not seeing her sister around, started screaming. Marion, still in a state of shock, picked her up in her arms and covered her with kisses and tears.

"Oh my baby, we have lost Jessica, she has just disappeared" repeated Marion holding Holly tightly against her: everybody was running in different directions looking for a child, but in vain; the park was empty.

The police arrived within minutes and everyone ran to them trying to explain all at once what had happened. They tried to calm Marion down but she was hysterical: she and Holly were still screaming and crying. The police tried to find out exactly what had happened, but without success and no one could give them specific details of the missing child. A police car drove around the park to see if something unusual was going on, while another officer drove Marion and Holly to the station: there, a policewoman took Holly in her arms to calm her down, while someone else brought a glass of water to Marion: then she was asked to phone home.

"Is that you…Jane?" asked Marion.

"No Marion, Georges, here"; said Georges.

"Please Georges, call Jane quickly, for something awful has happened…"

"What is it Marion, why are you crying and what happened, tell me".

"It was only two minutes, I swear…" Marion said.

"What are you talking about, what two minutes?…"

"I have just left them for two minutes, I swear…"

"Where are you now?"

"I am at the police station…" Marion said.

"The police station? what for, what have you done? pass me an officer so I can make sense of what is going on".

An officer took the phone from Marion and explained to Georges what had taken place in the park. Georges was speechless for a while; he stood in the middle of the living room, shocked and dismayed, then shouted: "we are coming, officer, right away."

He called Jane who was just preparing the evening meal:

"Leave everything and come with me to the police station".

"The station? why, what is it Georges? Tell me what has happened?"

"I will tell you in the car…"

"No tell me now, I want to know…"

"Well, well, it seems that Jessica has been kidnapped…"

"Kidnapped? how could it be, there must be some mistake, how could she have disappeared, Marion was with her".

"Let us take a photo of the twins, the police might want to see one".

Jane went all white like a ghost: she stood there in the middle of the room mumbling something about Jessica and Holly. "It does not make sense to me, why somebody would want to snatch a toddler, I do not believe it." She wanted to hear for herself what had occurred, so she picked up the phone and dialled the station, just to be told once again that Jessica was definitely missing.

" We are coming presently officer", and she put the phone down.

With panic in their eyes, they left home and managed to call a taxi that took them to the station. There, they found Marion very agitated and out of control. Georges took Holly from the policewoman's arms, and did his best to calm her as well.

" I only left them in the car for two minutes to buy them some sweets, I swear it was no more than two minutes: they were asleep and exhausted, that is why I did not want to wake them up..."

"Do you mean that you have left them alone in the car?"

"Just for two minutes I swear, it was only two minutes..."

"How irresponsible of you Marion, how could you leave them alone in the car, even for two minutes, how could you?"

Marion was sobbing, mumbling and repeating to herself, that it was only for two minutes.

"Please calm down the lot of you," said an officer; "I have sent for a doctor to come and check Marion and Holly: meanwhile everybody sit down, and let us look at the facts"

The police sent more officers at the scene of the crime, to find out if they could follow some traces of find some tracks that could lead them to the kidnapper. They asked around if anyone had noticed somebody acting suspiciously: but no, no one saw anything out of the ordinary. It was unthinkable that someone would dare commit such a crime in the middle of the day.

After being told that everything would be taken good care of, Georges drove everyone back home: not a word was uttered on the way back. A heavy silence fell over them for the rest of the day. They sat around the telephone in case someone would ring with news of Jessica. Marion could not stay still, so she fed Holly and prepared her for bed; but Holly showed signs of distress at not seeing her sister. Marion sensed it and held her close to her heart, as if not to lose her as well. On the evening news, the abduction of Jessica was mentioned and a photo of the twins was shown on the screen, in case it jogged someone's memory. Alas, no one came forward that day or any other day; it was a complete mystery. That night the family slept next to the phone, hoping it would ring.

Chapter 9

That day Danny was feeling very lonely. He left home and went for a walk, he was restless and edgy. Emily was working in the bar and would not be home till late: she told Danny to warm the pizza she bought him as a treat knowing that it was his favourite take away. That evening, she had a date with a guy she met in the bar.

So in the afternoon Danny went to the park for a stroll; but it was getting hazy and dark, so he headed towards the small store across the park; a few cars were parked and as a matter of fact he tried to break into some of them without success; and then just across the road and next to a shop, he saw a car with a window slightly opened; he could not believe his luck. As he approached the car, he looked all around him, but no one was to be seen. As he reached the car and to his amazement, he saw two toddlers sleeping at the back: without any hesitation Danny managed to open the door and very quietly took one of the toddlers out of the car and into his arms: he shut the door quietly behind him and slowly walked away without being noticed.

Danny was very happy and proud; he had found himself a baby, he found it, and from now on he would be a big brother for the infant. He would be in charge and would not allow any one to touch it. It was his, and his alone. He made his way home, and every so often he looked around to see if he was being followed. Before entering his apartment he paused for a few seconds and then quickly opened the door and dashed in: he shut the door slowly behind him so as not to wake up the child; but it was too late, for Jessica was awake and looking around her for Marion and Holly. She looked at the stranger who was holding her and smiling at her, and she started crying. "Hey, hey, my little Lucy" said Danny, "don't cry, what is the matter, don't you recognize your big brother? You have been sick in hospital for a while, but now they let you out for you have recovered; so stop crying; there. Now you are back home with me Danny and I am going to take good care of you, my little sister".

Jessica stopped crying and managed to ask for a drink. As he put her down on the sofa and went to fetch her a glass of milk, he heard Emily coming in carrying a shopping bag.
" Hi Danny, come and give me a hand with the groceries". Danny put the glass of milk on the table and went to help Emily.
" What is that glass of milk doing there Danny?" asked Emily.
"I felt thirsty momsy" said Danny.
"But you hate milk".
"I have changed my mind…"

Before he could finish his sentence, the door to his bedroom opened and Emily got the shock of her life; there stood a beautiful little girl who was smiling at Danny and saying: "I want my drink Danny". Emily could not believe her eyes, she dropped what she was holding and looked at Jessica with astonishment.
"Who on earth is that little girl? can some one tell me who she is?"
"She is Lucy my little sister who just came back from the hospital: is that not so Lu …Lucy?"
"I am Jessi."
"No, you are Lucy: you woke up from your bad dream now, where you were someone else. Now you are Lucy, and I am your brother Danny, and this is your mother Momsy".
"Can some one please tell me what is going on? because I am going out of my mind right now; Can some one please pinch me and tell me that it is not true".

"She is my little sister, and I brought her back home, she is mine and mine only".

Emily realised that Danny must have kidnapped the little girl and now, she had to persuade him to take her back to her poor parents who must be worrying to death. Jessica seemed to like Danny; she smiled at him whenever he talked to her. She found him funny and wanted to play with him. She walked to Emily and raised her arms to be picked up. Emily could not resist her and took her in her arms, kissed her and made a fuss of her. It brought her back memories when Danny was her age and how cuddly he was. Jessica put her arms around her and kissed her.

"My little sister loves you already momsy ; you can tell by the way she looks at you".

"What we are doing here Danny is completely wrong. Think of her mom and dad, how they must be suffering right now".

"No, they are not suffering momsy because they have another baby."

"How do you know, have you seen them? and how on earth did you manage to take her?"

"She is mine, and I just took her back, why can't you understand that?"

"Because Danny, what you have done is called kidnapping, and it is severely punished by law.I do not want to see you going to prison my son".

"I do not care for she is mine, mine, mine".

Jessica who was watching those two strangers arguing and could not understand what it was all about, seemed to like them, especially Danny: she would have to tell Holly about him. She would like him. Jessica kept smiling at him, for there was something funny about him that made her laugh.

Emily was panicking: what was she going to do about Lucy? What if the law came and took Danny away from her. She could not bear the thought of it. He was the only family she had, and no way she would let him go to prison; although he was simple, but he needed her and she loved him to bits, and she only lived for him: so how could she turn him over to the police?

" All right Danny tell me where you found her?" said Emily.

"In the park momsy, by the little store" Danny said.

"Take Lucy Danny, I am going for a stroll to air my mind; I think I am going to explode, I need some fresh air: meanwhile see if you can give her something to eat. I shall not be long".

Danny was alone with Lucy. He looked at her and noticed how pretty she was; he was proud of having her for his little sister.

"Would you like some chocolate Lucy?"

Lucy looked at him without answering.

"What is the matter now Lucy, why are you not talking to me?"

"I am not Lucy, I am Jessica".

"No no, darling, may be in your dream you were Jessica, but now that you are awake, your real name is Lucy, do you understand".

"Yes please". Lucy said.

"What, yes please?"

"I want some chocolate now".

Danny smiled, at long last he had managed to make friends with her. He gave her half the packet he had in his hand and brought her another glass of milk.

Emily was walking in the park and was miles away dreaming: she looked around her and saw nothing abnormal; some couples were hurrying home from work in the dark, for the fog was coming down. She returned home and as she opened the door, an idea sprang into her mind: but first she switched on the television set to listen to the evening news ; and there was a photo of Lucy with her sister appearing on the screen: their names were Jessica and Holly. They looked so very much alike.

" SSHH, be quiet you two. Danny take Lucy to the kitchen For a moment: I must listen to the news to find out what it says about the disappearance. The TV pictures showed the twins in swimwear and pointed out their birth marks which were identical, and just above the navel. Summing up the report, the commentator said to look for a girl with a birth mark. "how silly can they be" said Emily to herself: how on earth are people going to look for a birthmark above the navel. While still listening to the news, Emily was getting agitated; she switched off the television, and called Danny back. Lucy was in his arms playing with his hair: she took Lucy in her arms and noticed that she was wet. She undressed her and washed her and put one of her vests on her. While doing so, she noticed the birthmark and quickly covered it. "I shall have to buy some clothes" she said.

"Danny, here is some money, go to the store and get Lucy two pairs of pants, get the smallest size possible and make sure that you don't speak to any one".

"Cross my heart momsy, I promise not to say a word about my baby sister". Danny said.

"Make sure that you pay for them and please be very discreet: please do not get into trouble, especially now".

Danny seemed worried now: it was unusual for him; normally he would not care, but today he could sense the seriousness of the situation. The fate of his baby sister was at stake, and he was already used to her: he loved her and did not want to lose her. So he did exactly what he was told, bought the pants and some bread and ran back home; he already missed Lucy. When he got home, Emily was cutting Lucy's hair: she looked like a boy now, and Danny with a laugh said: "I have a baby brother now" I am so happy.

" I have decided that we should leave this town right away. We have not got a minute to waste. So Danny go and get your suitcase ready, while I finish cutting her hair".

After that, she changed once more the child's underpants and once again noticed the beauty spot on her navel. It looked like a tiny mole: she covered it with some cream hoping that it would disappear. She tickled Lucy and kissed her stomach: she too was getting used to her, and she was so cuddly. She found some pyjamas which she managed to shorten to fit Lucy for the night. She covered her head with a hat belonging to Danny. It was too big, and covered her ears; but it did the trick for the time being. When Danny came back with his suitcase, he laughed his head off for he could not believe that the child hiding under his hat was actually his darling Lucy.

"There is a place in San Diego where I used to live. I think we should go there as soon as possible. We will leave tonight not to attract attention. I am sure that I can find a job there, while you Danny will take good care of your sister".

"Oh yes momsy, I will take good care of her: just tell me what I have to do".

"I am going to get my things packed as well, meanwhile take good care of Lucy".

She put her things in her suitcase and wrote a note to her landlord and put some money in an envelope. She told him that she had received a telegram from her sister telling her that her dad was dying and that she had better come home as soon as possible as he had only a few days to live. She added, that she was sorry that she could not say goodbye to him personally, And she locked the door of what had been her home for the last twenty years for the last time.

Meanwhile, Danny managed to put the suitcases in the car

and sat while Lucy was sleeping in his arms: they were in the back seat so as not to attract attention. Emily glanced for the last time at her home with some tears in her eyes. She made sure that Danny and Lucy were comfortably seated at the back, and drove into the night.

Chapter 10

Georges, Jane and Marion tried to cope with their loss as well as possible, especially Georges who could not believe and would not accept the disappearance of Jessica. Where was she? Why had she been abducted? Was she still alive? Did someone want a ransom? like one sees in detective films. The police had no answers to any of these questions. Not only had the vanishing of Jessica taken its toll on Georges, but Holly was also very disorientated for a while. Unlike Jessica, she had no one to play with and became very demanding. Even Imogen and all her ballet class were missing Jessica. They were so used to seeing the twins working together, that they felt sorry for Holly: she seemed so lonely that Imogen kept a motherly eye on her. Georges kept telling whoever wanted to hear him, that they had been sent a spell of bad luck by some witch who wanted them destroyed. First it was the plane crash which killed his children, and now his grand daughter has gone; who was next? Why were they being punished? And what God was doing about it?

"Tell me Jane, why our life is turning sour? and what have we done to deserve it" said Georges.

"I have no answer to that Georges, maybe…"

"Yes may be it is part of that famous plan of God …" Marion said.

"Plan? what plan, why does God have to make us suffer, what is the purpose of it and why? What did we do?"

"Just forget about God for a moment: we have to accept it and be philosophical about it.

"I can't, I miss my Jessica…"

Jane and Marion said in concert : "We have missed her as well and as much as you: but now we must concentrate on Holly who needs us most.

"This conversation is leading us nowhere; come on now Marion and let us bake Holly's favourite cake, so she will have a nice surprise when she comes home".

"The poor little soul must be missing her sister badly".

Time went slowly and painfully, but it was a healer as well. Holly was growing into a pretty teenager now. Her blond hair and blue eyes kept reminding the family of the daughter they lost years before. Holly was acquiring her mother's habits and mannerisms; lately Sarah was reappearing as Holly somehow.

"I wonder what Jessica would look like now, would she be like Holly? Would we recognize her if we came across her in the street?

"Of course we would, how could we forget her?"

One day Marion went jogging with Holly and found it very hard to keep pace with her: since the kidnapping, she never let Holly out of her sight whatever the reasons; but this was becoming too much for her, and even Holly was complaining about being slowed down. Still whatever the reason, there was Marion following her. One day Marion met with Imogen for a coffee.

"You know that your Holly is a natural dancer; she is a born ballerina and is very gifted in this art; she feels and lives every single movement she makes. I will not be surprised to see her turning professional later in life".

"She feels lonely since the disappearance of Jessica, I am sure that she did not come to terms with it yet: not even now.

"Poor Holly, but I can tell you now that she has made friends with a girl called Kyle who is of the same age. She is a cute girl with red hair, and is as gifted and flexible as Holly. They have become inseparable at school".

"I shall have to invite her for a meal one day after school, but funny enough Holly has never mentioned Kyle to me before, I wonder why?"

"Maybe she does not want to upset you", said Imogen.

"Upset me, how could she upset me?" Marion asked.

"Maybe she does not want you to think that Kyle could replace Jessica".

"Oh that is nonsense, I shall talk to her". Marion said.

That afternoon when Marion came to the school to drive Holly home, she met with Kyle and her mother: she invited them for supper to the next evening, to the delight of the two girls. The next day, they were all excited at meeting Holly's new friend with her mother. Jane was doing the cooking while Marion was laying the table; as usual, Georges was reading the papers. After school, Kyle's mother drove the children home and came in to meet the family.

"Please take a seat, I am Georges, Holly's grandpa".

"I am Jennifer and here is my Kyle".

"We are pleased to meet you both, I hope that from now on, we shall see more of each other", Jane said.

"Oh we will, I am sure, let us eat now", said Georges, "shall we? The kids must be starving".

They all sat around a well dressed table and Georges opened a bottle of wine and filled the glasses, while Jane gave the young girls orange juice to drink. To the delight of everyone, they found out that they were neighbours, and lived just two blocks away from each other.

"What a lovely coincidence", Marion said.

"It is a lovely surprise I must say, and I admit that I am very pleased about it; especially since my husband left me two years ago for a younger woman. It has been a very lonely life and my Kyle has missed him".

"Does he pay you alimony?" Georges asked.

"Oh yes, there is no problem on that issue, and once a week he takes Kyle out", Jennifer said.

"What do you do for a living; it must be hard for you?" asked Marion.

"Not at all, I am an artist; I paint and my work is much in demand", Jennifer said.

"Holly's mother was an artist as well: alas her life was shortened by a plane crash", Jane said.

"How awful it must have been for all of you: I am so sorry".

And so started a lovely relationship between the two families, Holly and Kyle became like two sisters to the delight of their parents; Kyle somehow replaced Jessica and the two girls became inseparable.

Chapter 11

That night when Emily drove away with Danny and Lucy, she headed on the highway towards San-Diego. She stopped by a gas station to refill the car and went to a nearby store which was open all night. She bought some food and clothes for Lucy and left the store carrying lots of bags. It was as if they were going on holiday. Half way toward their destination, Emily felt tired and Lucy became restless in Danny's arms: only he was happy and pleased with himself. He had a beautiful little sister whom he was in charge of, and even his momsy now seemed to have accepted "the fait accompli". He felt that deep down, she welcomed the change in her life which had been becoming too dull for her liking. Lucy already seemed to have brought with her a taste of early spring in their lives. She stopped by a motel for the night and ate heartily in a restaurant near by. After a good night's sleep and a very welcoming shower, they ate a copious breakfast, especially Lucy who for some reason did not stop eating.

"I think, my little sister, that travelling gives you a good appetite. We are so proud of you: aren't we momsy?"
"Of course we are, and it will help you grow big and strong", Emily said.
And on they traveled toward their destination.
"When I start work you will stay at home Danny and look after your sister that is what she is to you from now on. Do not forget it".
"Do not worry momsy for I shall take good care of her, and I will protect her with my own life if I have to; she is mine and rest assured that no one will harm her" and he hugged her so hard that the poor child nearly suffocated.

"I am very proud of you Danny, after all you have turned out to be a responsible young man".

Emily drove most of the day and stopped only once at a restaurant and strolled for a while to stretch her legs. Late at night they reached their destination. It was a caravan park with few mobile homes.

They spent the rest of the night sleeping in the car as it was too early to go to the renting office. As soon as the sun came out, they went to a nearby café which was opened all night and was full of truck drivers stopping for their breakfast.

When they went inside, Emily saw an advert on the door asking for a helper. While she sat Lucy at a table with Danny holding her, she went to the counter to order their breakfast;

"What kind of help are you looking for?" said Emily.

"I need a bright waitress, are you interested?" said the owner.

"You bet I am, when can I start?" said Emily.

"Right now if you can", said the owner.

"I have just arrived with my children; I shall have to rent a mobile home first, and then I shall start tomorrow morning: is that alright with you?"

"Welcome to our café" and he shook hands with her; "by the way, your breakfast is on the house".

"Oh thank you boss: by the way my name is Emily".

"Call me Jack".

"OK Jack, thanks a lot; this job means so much to me, and I shall be here first thing in the morning".

After breakfast while Danny and Lucy waited in the car, Emily went to the letting office which was just opening, and as, by chance, there was a medium size mobile home which could accommodate easily a family of Emily's size; she could move in right away, providing she paid a month in advance. Emily was very pleased with herself: she told Danny that Lucy had brought them luck; and that a beautiful beginning was dawning on them. They went to their new home happy to start their new life.

Life went on smoothly for Emily and the children; Danny was very happy to have Lucy. She loved him and called him "Daddy" sometimes, but he had to correct her by reminding her that he was her big brother. Lucy was about four years old when Emily took her to see a circus which had just arrived at the other side of the park. It was ten minutes walk from their home. The circus was just back from a world tour. They ate popcorn and drank pepsi. They watched the clowns making a fool of themselves, while the animals were being paraded in the center of the big tent. But what attracted the attention of Lucy most, was the high flying trapeze, which required courage and trust. Her eyes followed the artists from one platform to the other while she was licking her ice cream. Lucy was in a trance just looking at them. She loved it so much that day that when it was all over, she jumped on Danny's shoulders, put her arms around his neck and told him that she would love him always. She also kissed Emily and copied Danny by calling her momsy as well, for the first time, to the delight of Emily.

One morning when Emily had left for work, Lucy told Danny: "Let us go and visit the circus Dan Dan".
"But it will not be open till the afternoon" said Danny.
"But we could go to find out what they do in the morning under the tent", said Lucy.
"They must be practicing for their evening performance, and I do not think they will let us watch".
"Please Dan Dan please,I will give you an extra kiss; we could hide some place and watch without being seen".
"O K, let us go: but first let me have that kiss you promised", said

Danny. After kissing him Lucy climbed on top of his shoulders and they made their way across the park and through a narrow alley surrounded by tall trees and bushes. When they reached the big tent, they went in and were surprised by its size; it was the first time that they noticed how big it was. They found a corner which was badly lit and hid there.

There was so much activity going on that it looked like a festival. In one corner were some clowns with their mesmerizing mimes, their stunts included human levitation and the marvellous magic ladder. Lucy could not take her eyes off them; in another corner some dancers were exploring through classical and contemporary dance, the poetry of the eternal love affair. Further away some kids were practicing challenging street dance movements. Girls and boys of all ages were juggling, unicycling, and walking on stilts and high wires. But what attracted Lucy most was the high flying trapeze: she wanted to be up there with the artists and fly with them. Danny and Lucy were so captivated by the whole thing that they never heard the master of ceremonies approaching.

They were startled by his presence and wanted to run away: but it was too late, for they heard him saying; "Hi folks, are you enjoying yourselves, I am Peter and this is my circus; how do you like it?"
"It is very nice", and he tried to pull Lucy back. "I am Danny and this is my little sister Lucy".
"I love this place, may I stay a bit longer?" asked Lucy.
"Why, of course you can: I tell you what: give me a hand and I will take you on a tour and I will show you the animals at the back; you too Danny come with us as well, what do you say?"

Peter very proudly showed them around and introduced them to some of the acrobats who put on a show for them. Peter was tall and powerful; he seemed so proud to be holding Lucy's hand, but he had to lean on one side, and that made him uncomfortable.

" Do you mind Danny if I picked up Lucy on my shoulders, for this will help me walk much more comfortably". Hardly had he finished his sentence than Lucy jumped into his arms and on to his shoulders. Danny walked beside them, a bit embarassed by Lucy's familiarity. At the end of the tour he stopped by the trapeze corner and looked up, and shouted; "Robert come on down and say hello to our guests": a young boy of about eight years old shouted back: "I am coming father" and he went into a somersault and landed on the safety net beneath, to the astonishment of the guests. He was of an average height for his age, and had curly hair with dark blue eyes: he was proud of himself and gave the impression that the world was at his feet.

"Hi folks" said Robert, and he shook hands with Danny and Lucy, but did not let go of Lucy's hand. "Would you like to climb up there on the trapeze"?

"No, no way, it is too dangerous for my Lucy", said Danny.

"Do not worry Danny, I will be there with her to protect her", said Robert.

"How about you Lucy, would you like to climb up there?" Peter asked.

"Oh yes please, I would love to: and Robert said that he would protect me", said Lucy.

"Go on Danny, let her try, I assure you she is in excellent hands", Peter said.

"Well O.K., but Robert make sure to look after her: momsy will kill me if anything happened to my little sister".

Robert disappeared for a few minutes and came back with a pair of ballet shoes for Lucy.

"Change into these shoes Lucy; I will show you how to strap

them…"

"Thank you Robert, but I wore ballet shoes before…"

Danny who seemed worried, quickly said: "Yes, momsy sent her to some ballet classes ages ago." Lucy looked at him somehow bewildered and said nothing. She put on the shoes and held Robert's hand very tightly: she was apprehensive, but somehow knew that she could rely on Robert and climb up the ladder to the top platform. Robert followed her right behind.

"Danny look at me, I am on top look at me Danny", said Lucy. Robert was tightening the safety belt around her waist.

" To-day Lucy, I am going to show you how to swing on the bar: Put your hands on it and for the first time I shall swing with you, and then you will have to do it all on your own; do you understand that?"

"Oh yes", said Lucy rather calmly, and so she unwittingly started her first lesson to what was going to become her future career as a trapeze artist.

When it was over Robert lowered her down on to the safety net to the relief of Danny who had been worried all the time. Peter helped Lucy down to the floor, she looked at Robert who just let himself fall on the safety net. Poor Danny was feeling sick and miserable; he breathed a sight of relief when she came to him and kissed him.

Lucy's face was red with excitement. "I did it Danny, I did it". And she kissed him again and again: she also thanked Robert for looking after her, and whispered something to Danny.

"What is it Lucy?"

"She wants to invite Robert for tea, if that is all right with you Peter".

"I am sure that Robert is delighted to hear that, am I right son?"

"I would love to: when?" said Robert.

"We live at the caravan park just on the other side, we are at number twenty seven, it is ten minutes walk from here: will you come about five o'clock , will you come Robert?"

"I will make sure that he goes Lucy, he will be there around that time, if that is O K with you Danny?"

"Oh yes, that will be fine" said Lucy.

Peter was smiling discreetly, for Robert was a bit lonely and shy: Lucy would be an ideal friend for him: with a bit of luck she could make a good trapeze partner for him; "fingers crossed" he muttered under his moustache.

Chapter 12

On the way home Lucy, who was on Danny's shoulders, was singing and he was happy for her.

" Let us go and see momsy instead of going home. We shall tell her all about it" said Danny.

"Oh yes what a good idea Dan Dan, let us go and see momsy and tell her all about it and about Robert and what I did on the trapeze".

At the café Emily was busy taking some orders but was happy to see them.

"Go and sit at a table, I shall be with you in a moment", said Emily. As Emily took a break, she came back with a tray full of sandwiches and drinks.

"Momsy, momsy, we went to the circus and guess what momsy?" said Lucy.

"Yes momsy we went to the circus", but his mouth was so full that he could not talk any more.

Lucy took over and recounted what had happened that morning at the circus, adding "and I met Robert who is my new friend and he showed me how to swing on the bar. I am going to be a trapeze artist like him; I like him, and he also going to teach me how to be as flexible as he is. Peter invited all of us at the circus to-morrow; and to-night we have invited Robert for tea. He will come around five o'clock . Peter will fetch him because he is only eight years old and he is not allowed outside the circus by himself".

"Hold it, hold it, stop that natter for a moment for heaven's sake, and slowly tell me what have you done this morning".

"Danny, you go first and tell me what have you done to-day, and you Lucy please do not interrupt darling". Danny slowly recounted their adventure at the circus, but kept being disturbed by Lucy. "Tell momsy how I climbed the ladder to the top platform, and how I swung from one side to the other. What could have been told in a few minutes took twice as long.

"Go home now, I shall see if I can finish early to-night and meet your Robert".

That evening Emily was too busy, and could not take some time off to meet Robert and his father but Lucy and Danny had lots of fun with Robert; Peter left them earlier and went for a walk; and when he came back to collect Robert, he had an idea. "You are all invited to the circus tomorrow, and bring your mom as well; I shall have the best seats reserved for you". "I have already told momsy that you have invited us to the circus tomorrow Peter…" "How did you know in advance that I was going to invite you?" asked Peter. "You must be psychic Lucy". And they all left, happy at the prospect of meeting again.

The next evening Emily took some time off and went to the circus with the children. She took extra time for her make up and was complimented by her kids. "You look especially beautiful to-night momsy, I have not seen you like that for a long time". "Yes momsy you are extra gorgeous to-night why is that?" asked Lucy. "Thank you children for your compliments, you know how to make me feel good: but enough of that and we better make a move.

Emily was pleased to meet Peter and Robert and liked them right away. They sat together watching the acrobats and the clowns while eating and drinking. Peter told Emily that he had been a widower for quite a while and bringing Robert by himself was tough enough, but it had its rewards; just watching him growing up healthy and strong made him happy. But Robert missed at not having a mother like all children of his age. He could still remember his mother, for he was just three years old when she was taken away by cancer was a blow to both of them; and at the beginning they found it very hard to cope with it. Everywhere he went, he had to take Robert with him. The boy grew up in the circus and that was why he was so dedicated to it.

While Peter was telling his life story, Emily found herself unwittingly holding his hands: she was getting fond of this strong man with a soft heart; he looked like a rock on the outside but on the inside he was very warm and welcoming. Some how they had a lot in common, for both of them were bringing their offspring on their own.

Emily too told him that she was all alone, and bringing up her children all by herself. She was free as well and had no friends in this town: "so you see Peter, that you and I have a lot in common." "I work at the café at the other side of the park, you are very welcome to drop in at any time that you feel like. Coffee will be on me".

While Emily was holding his hand, Peter too felt the warmth of her touch and knew somehow that she was there for him; he seemed to enjoy the idea. At the end of the show and before leaving Peter came up with an idea.
"Danny, what do you do all day with Lucy?" said Peter.
"Nothing much Peter, we do a lot of walking together".
"Well I have a proposition to put to you and Lucy; but first Emily must agree to it".
"What is it Peter?" Emily said.

"Well, instead of those two doing nothing much during the day, I would suggest they come and work for me at the circus…

"Oh yes Peter, yes, yes, and yes; we would love to…" Danny said.

"Yes, yes, yes me too" Lucy said.

"Let Peter finish what he had to say Luce : I know that you are both excited, so am I actually: yes, yes; but let see what Peter has in mind.

"Here is my plan: Lucy will start training with Robert at the circus, and I am sure that I can find something to do for Danny".

"There is so much work to do in a circus, that you can choose whatever you like to do".

"Can I help with the animals, especially the horses?" asked Danny.

"There you are Danny. I shall have a word with the trainer first thing in the morning".

"Will I go on the trapeze?" Lucy said.

"Robert will take good care of you", said Peter.

"I am so happy to have met you Peter and you too Robert" said Emily. "I am sure that from now on, we are going to see a lot of each other. You already mean so much to me". And so started between them a beautiful friendship.

One week end, while strolling in the park Robert and Lucy were teasing Danny who did not mind actually, while behind them followed Emily and Peter holding hands like two lovers.

"Why don't you and the children move in with us, we have ample space in our home, and I could add an extra room if necessary".

"Do you mean that? Do you know what that implies?" Emily said.

"Oh yes I do, and it is with all my heart that I offer to share my home with you".

"Let us ask the children what they think" said Emily. Everyone thought that it was a brilliant idea.

"From now on I shall see you all day long Lucy, and I will take care of you as my little sister" said Robert. "As to you Danny, I shall be your little brother and you will come to my rescue when I need you".

"I would love to do this for you my little brother", said Danny.
And the same day, they all moved in together.

Chapter 13

Holly was sixteen now and growing into a beautiful young lady, she was tall and slim and doing very well at ballet. Actually she was a very talented dancer, not just at ballet but at all other aspects of dance. At school she and Kyle joined the gymnastic team and they both excelled in this demanding sport. They did very well academically and passed all their exams with flying colours.

One evening, Holly and Kyle went to a college dance. A young man asked Holly for a dance and she eagerly said yes: he said his name was Henry and he was eighteen years old: he was leaving college at the end of the term, and decided to become a doctor. He was starting his medical studies late next term, so he would be enjoying some rest from the college. Holly liked him the first time she set eyes on him: to her it was love at first sight. They danced together all night staring into each other's eyes. She felt very comfortable in his arms and as if she had known him for ever. He was a good dancer and was so much taller than her, that she promised to wear high heeled shoes whenever she was with him. When they danced too close, she could feel the rippling of his muscles; she liked his soft brown eyes and black hair. He happened to be the captain of the college football team. She found him sweet and easy to talk to. As for Henry, he fell in love with her blue eyes and blond hair. That evening after a lingering kiss, they parted company and he promised to call her the next morning. On their way home, Kyle who had also made a conquest could not stop talking about her new love, and began comparing the two men. They were both in love that night. Next morning Holly told her parents that she was madly in love, and that she had found the prince with whom she was going to spend her life. She was so ecstatic about it that she told them he came from another dimension.

"And how do we approach this prince of yours: with a reverence I suppose? Said Georges.

"You are already making fun of him granddad, but it is no use". Holly said.

"Yeah, yeah, yeah, how many times before have we heard that same tune Holly?" Jane said.

"Yes, but this one is for real grandma, and you will all love him like I do" said Holly.

"Oh yes, tell us more", Georges said.

"Stop teasing the poor child both of you: can you not tell that this time, it is the real thing?" and she smiled quietly.

"I thought of him all night long granddad, so I can not be wrong this time: can I? And from now on I have decided that we shall do everything together" Holly said.

"Is that right darling, I am ever so happy for you"; but a look of sadness appeared in his eyes: he was thinking about Jessica, and how they would have shared their ups and downs together. She would have been a dancer like Holly and talking about their respective boy friends, like now. Alas it was not to be, for some evil person decided otherwise. A tear appeared, but he quickly wiped his eyes not to upset his Holly. But it was too late, she saw his eyes and came to him putting her arms around him; for she knew he was hurting because of Jessica.

That morning Henry called as promised and they decided to go to the movies in the evening, when he arrived and to the amusement of her parents Holly made him a coffee. It was the very first time that Holly used the kitchen.

"How beautiful is love; it makes one do unusual things", said Georges.

"I hear that you are studying to be a doctor?" Jane said.

"As a matter of fact it is right, but I hope later on to become a neuro surgeon. I want to make my late parents proud of me".
"We are sorry to hear about your late parents Henry" Jane said.

Henry was upset and was holding Holly's hands tightly. When the young couple left, Marion said "What a lovely young man is Henry, I am sure that they will make a lovely couple in the future."
"I hope so for the sake of Holly. I would not like to see her hurt" said Jane.
"Yes, she is a very sensitive young girl and God knows that she needs happiness".

Early next day, the phone rang:
"Hi, this is Marion, who is on the phone?"
"Hi Marion, this is Imogen your friend, how are you doing?"
"Hi Imogen, how nice to hear from you. How are things with you?"
"I have excellent news for Holly: let us meet at the restaurant round the corner in an hour: we shall have some tea and cakes before I tell you the good news; I can not wait to tell you what it is: it is a miracle, so hurry up".
"Give me a hint Imogen".
"No, No, I am sorry Marion, it will spoil the fun. I want to see your face when you hear what I have to say".
"O.K. then, three o'clock sharp: but do not be late". Marion repeated the conversation to Jane and Georges who were playing cards.
"What do you think it is?" asked Jane.
"Why could she not give you a hint, what is the big secret?" Georges complained.
"I am on tenterhooks could I not call her back and find out what it is all about?" Jane said.
"Why on earth could she not tell you: I can not bear the suspense: I

do not feel like playing any more".

"Calm down you two, my guess is as good as yours; I am also impatient to know what it is all about, so here you are, carry on playing your game until I come back with the good news".

"No Marion, do not wait until you come back: this excitement will give me a heart attack; so you better ring us, as soon as you hear the good news".

"Georges: are we still playing or what?"

"All right you two, calm down. I promise to call as soon as I hear about it: are you satisfied now? at long last, so stop fretting, there".

When Marion arrived at the restaurant, Imogen had already ordered some tea and cakes ; she wore a big smile. "Hi darling", said she, and she got up to kiss Marion.

"Hi darling", and she returned her kiss. "Tell me the good news, what is it?" said Marion.

"First sit down and let us have some tea to calm you down" said Imogen.

"Please Imogen please, tell me now what it is all about: I promised my friends to let them know as soon as I hear from you. So tell me now".

"Well", said Imogen reclining back on her chair, and taking a quick sip from her cup:

"Well, Well.". said Marion.

"Well, last week when Holly and the rest of the class were rehearsing for the end of the term show, who do you think dropped in uninvited, and sat in a corner and watched the show?

"I don't know: who, who?"

"Well Marion, are you listening?"

"Yes, yes, please carry on".

"Well Marion, the director of San Francisco ballet society, the top man in person invited himself, and from my office watched the show, and guess what?"

"Please do not stop, what happened next".

"Well, he was searching for a girl, to be his "Prima Donna" for his Christmas show Cinderella, and if it is successful, they will not only be touring the U.S.A., but England, also Europe. The chosen girl will have the ballet world at her feet; she will be much in demands for the rest of her working life.

"All that is very nice Imogen, but what has it got to do with us?" Imogen for a moment seemed to be losing patience.

"Don't you see Marion, that out of all the pupils, who do you think he chose but Holly.

"Oh my God, is this true? our Holly a professional ballerina?"

"Not just a ballerina, but also a Prima Donna".

"Oh my goodness I am so happy: please Imogen pinch me to see if I am not dreaming".

"Yes, yes, it is true; you better believe me. Now that you know everything, let us eat".

In her joy and excitement Marion forgot the promise she made to Georges and Jane, and she tucked into the cakes and tea. When she got back late in the afternoon, and as soon as she opened the door, she heard Jane and Georges voices shouting all at once; "Where have you been, and what happened"?

"Were you not supposed to ring us and put us in the picture? And also tell us what was going on, have you forgotten?

"Yes why did you not call? What was so urgent that made you forget to call us right away? What excuse have you got?" Marion's face changed from joy to solemnity.

"I am awfully sorry I have just forgotten: with all the excitements and the news, I just forgot...Please forgive me for it was really selfish of me.

"Forget all that and tell us, is it about our Holly?"

"Holly was rehearsing a dance for the end of term show, when guess who dropped in?"

"Who, who?"

"The head of the national ballet society of San Francisco, and do you know what?"

"What?" said Jane.

"Out of all the school, he chose Holly to play the part of Cinderella for his Christmas show".

"Does that mean what I think?"

"Yes it does, and there is more" Marion said.

"Will somebody tell me what is going on".

"It means that Holly is going to be a professional ballet society dancer; and one of the best on top of that".

"Wow, my little princess is getting somewhere in this world" Georges said.

"I am going to cook Holly her favourite meal…"

"And I am going to bake Holly her favourite cake…"

"And I am going to lay the table".

That night there was a party at Holly's home, and Henry was invited too: they all enjoyed a memorable evening till late. So Holly signed a contract, making her an important member of the San Francisco national ballet society. soon she was joined by her best friend Kyle, to the delight of their families.

Holly started studying and working very hard, and soon it paid dividends. She reached in a very short time the pinnacle of her profession for she was a born dancer. Henry for his part became a doctor, and decided to continue further afield to become a brain surgeon.

When Holly turned twenty one, a big party was thrown in her honour by the ballet society. All the dancers and directors were around to wish her luck. At the end of the evening, Henry who was invited, popped up the question to Holly and in front of the guests; she said yes and they kissed to the delight of every one.

Chapter 14

Meanwhile back in San Diego there was a wedding going on; Peter and Emily had decided to tie the knot as they were both very much in love. Every one in the circus was invited and there was merriment and happiness all around. Emily gave up the job at the café to take good care of her new family.

Now Lucy was a beautiful young lady, with long light brown hair, and beautiful soft brown eyes she inherited from her late father. she learned all the different trades of the circus, but she excel as a trapeze artist. The crowd flocked from miles away to come and see her performing: she was the darling of the circus, and very much an asset to the circus. Robert liked her company and called her his darling little siss.

He was always present when she needed him most to protect her against unscrupulous young men, who would do anything to steal her love. But Lucy was not ready for commitment; her only love affair was the flying trapeze, and she lived for it.

When she was twelve tears old, Danny bought her a dog; now that he was in charge of cleaning the animals quarters he could afford to spoil his little Lucy and Robert as well. He carried his broom with him wherever he went around in the circus and he was proud to show that he was in charge of the animals' hygiene.

Lucy called her dog Toby, and no one but her was allowed to feed him; he was a pedigree spaniel, docile and affectionate. He went jogging with his mistress every morning. At sixteen Lucy was an accomplished artist and knew all the secrets of the trade; she was not afraid at trying her hand at anything, from climbing the ropes to sweeping the floor when necessary.

One day, when Lucy had some time to spare before a show, she told Danny who was brushing a horse a few yards away, that she was taking Toby for a run.

"We shall not be long, we are just going across the park and into the woods, and back: it will take us around half an hour at the most", said Lucy.

"Be careful Lucy, for there have been bad things happening lately in that area", said Danny.

"What bad things Danny?" said Lucy.

"Across the town, a teenage girl was raped and murdered last month only. Have you not seen the police notices all around the circus warning people not to walk alone in the woods?"

"Oh that, don't worry Danny, I can take good care of myself", and she kicked the air in a karate fashion; "I also have Toby to protect me: are you satisfied now?"

"I would feel more at peace if I came with you".

"No Danny", said Lucy, "you have some work to finish".

"Listen, wait for me for in ten minutes. I will have finished grooming the horse and I shall be free to come with you".

"I am sorry Danny, but I can't wait that long; we have to go".

"Promise me to be very careful especially if some one approaches you with a black sack in his hands".

"Oh Danny, grow up will you: a black sack…"

"Yes Lucy, a black sack; that is how the killer covers the head of his victims before raping them".

"O.K. Danny, I will be on the look out for the serial killer; don't worry anymore. Come on Toby let's go".

And off she went with Toby at a steady pace. They went through the park and she saw their old mobile home where they used to live. It was getting late and Lucy had less than half an hour before her show. Time was running out, so she took a short cut through the wood remembering Danny's warning: but she shrugged it off. These things happens to other people; Toby was trailing far behind sniffing at some trees. Lucy stopped for a moment to tighten her laces and sat at the foot of a tree. Suddenly, without a warning she felt a bump at the back of her head, and before passing out, she perceived a black cloud enveloping her. Toby arrived too late to find Lucy half naked and her head covered in a black sack. His arrival saved Lucy from being murdered; for the rapist panicked when he saw the dog running at him and barking. He just had time to flee. Toby cried and licked Lucy's feet hoping to wake her up, but without success: his mistress would not budge. So he charged through the woods and towards the circus, barking all the way. He found Danny sweeping the stables; he growled and snarled at him pulling at his trousers.

" What is it Toby?"

Toby was looking at him howling.

" What is it Toby and where is Lucy?" said Danny.

Suddenly it dawned on Danny, that things were not as they should be, especially when he saw Toby sprinting back to the woods. Danny followed him as fast as he could, but he was getting out of breath. The dog stopped next to Lucy, barking and sniffing around. Danny saw a bundle lying on the ground; he knew that it was Lucy; "was she dead" he asked himself".

"Lucy, Lucy, get up: please God don't let her die, not my baby siss"; and he started sobbing and crying like a child: he saw the black sack covering her head and tried to undo the laces: but before he could untie the bag, he heard a scream behind him, and some one was hitting him with a walking stick; it was an old lady yelling at him and shouting abuses at him, telling him to let go of the victim.

She had a dog with her looking menacingly at him.

"You leave her alone", said the old lady, "do you hear me you murderer; help, please someone help". Danny became nervous and frightened by her screams. He looked at the old lady trying to plead with her, but she kept screaming and hitting him, making no effort to listen to what he had to say.

Danny saw two men running in his direction: they thought that the old lady was being mugged: so he panicked and raced back to the circus. Toby stayed back, keeping an eye on his mistress. He also made friends with the old lady's dog.

When the two men arrived at the scene, the old lady told them what she saw and that the murderer had made off in the direction of the circus. One of the men called the police on his mobile, and then the two of them headed for the circus. The old lady stayed behind trying to undo the black sack. The two dogs kept her company.

Danny had reached the stables by now, and was telling himself that he did not do anything to harm his baby siss. So why was this old lady shouting and screaming at him, and calling him names?

"I told her not to go alone; I warned her about the rapist: Why would she not listen to me? I told her to wait for me, why did she not? It is my fault, I should have gone with her: but she insisted that she could take good care of herself. Oh God, why did I let her go; now he was a murderer, the old woman said so". It was his fault that Lucy was dead now, he killed his sister, and he kept sobbing and blaming himself " Please Lucy come back to me, I need you now," kept repeating Danny, I am afraid to be alone.

Within minutes two police cars arrived at the scene of the

crime followed by an ambulance. A paramedic removed the black sack from Lucy's head and checked her pulse.

"She is breathing, she is still alive". He covered her face with an oxygen mask, while his colleague gave her an injection. A crowd was forming around Lucy and the police; they had to cordon the area not to lose some vital clues.

"Who saw what happened?" asked the inspector.

"I did and I arrived just in time, the murderer ran toward the circus…" the old lady said.

"Slow down maam, I have to write down your statement".

A few minutes later the inspector with a sergeant left the scene of the crime and headed toward the circus with the old lady and her dog sitting at the back: Toby stayed behind with his mistress.

"What do you think sergeant, is it again the serial killer?" said the inspector.

"Yes it is, but something is puzzling me…"

"What is it?" asked the inspector.

"Why he did not kill her this time, it does not add up".

"Maybe he was interrupted by someone, but who?"

"I saw him first, and there was a little dog as well"

"Do you mean the spaniel dog?" asked the inspector.

"Yes, yes, the one who stayed behind with the girl…"

"So the dog is the real reason why the girl is still alive: he saved his mistress' life".

"I always said that dogs are man's best friends". And she kissed her dog.

The two officers looked at each other smiling.

"What makes you think that the man you saw was the murderer?"

"He was on top of her".

"But may be he was trying to take the sack off her face: was her dog barking?"

"Oddly enough no: actually he seemed friendly with the man".

"So that eliminates him from our enquiries, don't you think so sergeant?"

"I agree with you inspector, may be he was trying to help"

"I saw him on top of her, and why did he run away when he saw me?"

"Were you screaming when you arrived at the scene?"

"Of course I was, I wanted him to stop; even my dog was showing him his teeth".

"What I think has happened is that the man who indeed was trying to help got frightened and alarmed by your screams and the menacing teeth of the dog; that is why he ran away".

"But I saw him, I swear…"

"Anyhow we are here now, and we shall find the truth".

When they arrived at the circus, they parked not far from the stables, and the three of them made their way to the big tent followed by the dog. There was so much activity in that tent, that the officers had the feeling of entering a bee-hive. Every thing came to a stand still when the inspector asked to see the manager. They were shown the office, and the crowd of artists followed them wanting to find out what was going on.

"Can we be of any help officers?"

"Why, are you the manager?"

- No, but we might be able to help you officer".

"Well I am inspector Brian Donell and here is my partner sergeant Collins. This lady here thinks she saw a man running away from the scene of a crime, and he headed towards the circus.

"What does he look like?"

The old lady gave an exact description of the man. "But it cannot be" said someone in the crowd; this is our Danny".

"Danny could not harm anybody" said some one else.

"We love him dearly" shouted the crowd:

"Why? What is he supposed to have done?", said another artist.

"A young girl has been raped not far from here and this lady saw the man you call Danny running away from the scene".

One of the clowns ran to warn Peter; he knocked at his office and went in without waiting for an answer.

" You better come quickly boss, something awful has happened".

"What has there been, an accident?"

"The police are after Danny and they have come to arrest him."

"What do you mean, the police are after Danny: Why? what did he do?" And the artist related to Peter what had been said beforehand.

"What, Danny a rapist, how ludicrous, what people would believe now; honestly: but first let me ring Emily and Robert. I want them to be present with me to hear that".

When they entered the tent, there was uproar going on, and everybody was trying to defend Danny against the old lady's accusations.

" What is happening officers? what is all this fracas here, we have a show to put on to-night; we have not got time for nonsense."

"Hi, I am inspector Brian Donell: this lady swears by almighty God that one of your men has attacked and raped a young girl in the woods: he could be our serial killer.

"Who is that old woman who dares accuse my son Danny of rape and murder ? Where is she hiding, let me get hold of her, I will make her change her mind right away; and who is the alleged girl who has been raped?

Robert who heard what had been said, left the tent in a hurry for he knew where to find Danny. Whenever Danny was in trouble, he always made his way to the stables and talked to the horses; so Robert made his way there to find a terrified Danny in deep conversation with his favourite horse.

"Hi Danny, there are some people in the tent who would like to ask you some question"s.

"I have done nothing wrong Robert, you know that I would not hurt my Lucy…"

"Lucy? Why, what happened to Lucy?"

"She, she, went all by herself to the woods, she, she, would not wait for me…"

"What happened Danny, what happened to our Lucy?"

"Well, Toby came back by himself after a while, and I…I started to worry about her…"

"Yes carry on: what happened to Lucy".

"Well … well,I ran back with Toby and found her…found her…"

"What Danny, what did you find?"

"Lucy is dead, Lucy is dead."

"No, it cannot be, you must have made a mistake, Lucy cannot be dead".

"An old woman looking like a witch, started shouting at me and called me a murderer: I am afraid of witches; so I panicked and ran as fast as I could, to be with my friends the animals. You do believe me Robert, don't you?

"Of course I believe you big brother; you cannot hurt a horse-fly even if you tried. Tell the inspector exactly what you have told me just now; he will believe you Danny, I swear" and he managed to drag Danny back to the tent, holding his hand.

As soon as they entered the tent the old lady shouted: "murderer, you are a murderer" it is him, I saw him with my two eyes putting a sack over her head, I saw you". And she tried to hit him with her walking stick.

"Will you stop this you old witch, or I will do something to you that I will regret later on", said Robert.

"Yeah, yeah", shouted the whole congregation menacingly.

"Go and change your glasses" said someone.

"Come on Danny, don't be afraid, nothing is going to happen to you. Just tell us exactly what do you know about it: we all know that you have done nothing wrong…"

"Yeah, yeah", shouted the crowd. "You have done nothing wrong Danny: don't be afraid now".

"Where is your sister? she should be here with you to hold your hand".

"Lucy, Lucy, is there, dead by the tree".

As soon as she heard that, Emily fainted and fell, but Peter was quick enough to save her from hitting her head on the ground. Two officers were already holding Danny's arms, while he was screaming and crying: "Lucy is dead, Lucy is dead." Inspector Donell came to him and said: "No, no, no one is dead; the paramedic arrived on time to save her: actually, it was thanks to your dog that the girl is still alive. She has been taken to hospital for observation."

"You murderer, you raped that girl, I saw you…"

"You get away from here you old witch, before I too, do something that I will regret later on" said Peter.

Emily who was up feeling much better, now that she heard Lucy was not dead, shouted at the old woman: "you leave my son alone, do you hear me old witch."

"Now Danny will you tell us in your own words what you did and why you were there?" said the inspector.

"Tell him Danny what has happened, exactly the way you told me before".

And Danny repeated word by word what he told Robert before hand.

A policeman came to the inspector and confirmed to him

that it was the work of the serial killer and rapist wanted by all the police forces in the area. "He has been hunted for the last two years without success; and he was the cause for the death of over ten women by now. Luckily for Lucy, this time and thanks to the dog, he never finished his work".

" I want a twenty four hours protection for that girl right now; I am afraid that evil man might come back to finish the job".

"Right away inspector: I will post one of my men at the door".

"Where is my daughter Lucy, I want to see her now".

"She is at the hospital right now and in good hands; but you can come with us to the station, as we have to bring Danny with us to fill some forms: We have to ask him some more questions, as he has been identified as being at the scene of the crime".

"What kind of questions inspector? He has already told you everything he knows, what else do you want from him?" said Peter.

"It is only a formality, but I have to do it: and you maam, you better leave us your address in case we need you again".

"He did it officer, he did it", said the old lady.

"You better leave now, before the crowd get mad at you. I shall not be able to protect you against their anger: so you better go".

"O.K. officer, I am leaving now with my dog; you know where to find us if you need me".

"I am going to see Lucy, and you Peter go with Danny".

"I am coming with you Emily, for I want to see siss".

"I am coming with you inspector, but first let me call my lawyer".

"I assure you Peter that a lawyer won't be necessary, it is only a formality".

"My boy is afraid of his own shadow, so be gentle with him".

"I can assure you maam, that no harm will come to him: I will have just to ask him some more questions in case he remembers something unusual".

"We must not forget that a girl has been attacked and raped: she was knocked out by a blow on her neck and covered by a sack…"

" Not a black sack? Oh God, it is the work of the serial killer; thank God she was not killed like the others. But what has it got to do with our Danny? He is innocent surely you don't…"

"That is why I have to take Danny with me to the scene of the crime; when he sees the place again, something unusual might jog his memory".

"I want to go to the hospital and see me Lucy" said Danny.

"I am afraid that you are coming with us sir".

"I will come with you son, and I hope our lawyer will be there waiting for us" said Peter.

"We are on our way to the hospital to see our little siss".

Peter told the rest of the team to carry on as usual, and replace Lucy and Robert's performance by a ballet show. One of the officer handcuffed Danny and took him to a waiting car. He looked so pitiful that some dancers were crying as well. The old lady had disappeared long before, without being noticed.

Chapter 15

At the hospital, poor Lucy was in a very bad shape. Her head was bandaged and some blood was still showing down her nose. She was complaining of having an awful headache and some parts of her body were very sore. She was in a state of shock and her eyes were fixed onto the ceiling: she kept repeating: "I am not a bad girl."

All that night Emily and Robert kept a vigil by her bed. After many long hours and at long last, Lucy came back into the world of the living; but she could not remember what had happened to her. She was complaining about pain almost everywhere.

"What has happened to me momsy and why am I here"

"It is nothing darling, you had a bad dream".

"What kind of dream momsy, and why am I in hospital?"

"You had a kind of little accident siss".

"What kind of an accident?"

Robert looked at Emily, but did not answer.

"Why Danny is not here, anything happened to Dan Dan?"

Suddenly, everything came back to Lucy: she remembered Danny warning her to be careful; she also remembered going for a jog with Toby, and then someone thumping her on the neck, and then complete black out. She let out a huge scream, when she realised what had happened to her. Emily put her arms around her to comfort her.

"Why did I not listen to Dan Dan, when he was warning me: Why have I been so big headed; where is he so I can tell him how sorry I am".

"There, there baby we will overcome this problem together; meanwhile try to have some sleep now".

"And I will be here to help siss, don't worry; we will catch whoever did this to you", Robert said.

"But why is Danny not here with me right now: I want him to hold my hand as well. I sense that something is not right with Dan Dan. Robert please tell me what is wrong with him: I implore you to tell me what is going on please".

Just as Robert was going to say something, the door opened and in came Peter excited and on edge.

"They are keeping Danny over night for interrogation: the lawyer could not help; there was too much at stake to grant him bail; too much. That old witch kept swearing that it was Danny..."

"What Danny, what did he do?"

"They reckon that Danny is the one who attacked you, and that he is the serial killer".

"What a lot of nonsense: my Dan Dan a rapist? Has the world gone mad?"

"Do not worry darling, tomorrow we shall have him out; meanwhile try to concentrate on getting better".

"There is no way that Danny would do such bad things to anyone, And especially not to his Lucy. No way, I want to go and see him now; I can feel that he needs me by his side right now; please Peter take me to him now: I want to tell him that I am not a bad girl, I am not" and she started crying all over again...'I'm a good girl I am'.

"I promise you that you will see him tomorrow: but first get better now please, and remember that we all love you".

"Yes siss, we all know that Danny is innocent, and that you are the apple of his eyes, so no way he could be guilty". And he gave her a big hug.

"Yes darling, please concentrate on getting better now", said Emily.

"Please bring him tomor ..." and she went into a deep sleep

without finishing her sentence.

That night Lucy had a nightmare. She dreamt that Danny was drowning in a deep pond and no one attempted to help him, although there was a big crowd watching him going under; and she Lucy was begging the onlookers for help but without success: then one giant of a woman, looking rather like a witch, came out of the crowd and into the pond, and pushed Danny's head under the water and kept it there. Lucy was maintaining his innocence but without avail...

Suddenly Lucy woke up screaming and covered in sweat: "He is innocent, he is innocent." The nurse on duty that night, and who rushed in trying to calm her, had to call a doctor who prescribed her a sedative as soon as he saw the state she was in; this had its effect immediately and Lucy fell asleep again, but this time she looked relaxed.

Next morning the family came to visit her and were told about Lucy's bad night. Emily took her in her arms while Robert held her hands. She was told how much she was missed at the circus.
"The crowd is complaining at not seeing you on the trapeze: they love you and missed you; so please get better and come back. Everybody needs you".
"What happened to you last night, was it a bad dream?"
"Yes momsy, it was: I dreamt about Danny".
"Do you want to talk about it?"
"No, for it was too awful, and I do not want to be remembered of it"; and she cuddled up to her momsy.

Peter arrived an hour later with a gloomy face.
"Where is Danny, and why is he not with you? You promised to

bring him back this morning: you have promised".

"Yes darling, I have promised I know, all this morning, the lawyer and I have tried everything to set him free: but the prosecution think that they have a very good case against him. They are going to keep him for another forty eight hours".

"Meanwhile, the killer is running loose and free to kill again. What kind of justice is that" said Robert.

"Danny called me last night; he needed my help" and she related her nightmare to the three of them.

Emily tried to calm her , but without success.

"I want to see him now, before it is too late; I know that he is in trouble. Please bring me my clothes and let me go and see him".

"There, there child, calm down now. If you promise to get better by this time tomorrow, I promise to take you there first thing in the morning: is that a deal or is that a deal?" And Lucy fell asleep in Emily's arms like a baby.

Peter was looking at them with a gloomy face again. Emily seemed worried now especially after listening to Lucy's dream. She did not like it at all, it was a bad omen and she knew that her Dan Dan was in danger. But why and who would hurt him? It did not make sense; she told Peter of her fears but he dismissed it as being nonsense and related to the stress that they were all under.

Chapter 16

That night while Lucy was having a good night's sleep at the hospital, Emily could not sleep a wink. Peter was snoring next to her and Robert's room was quiet. She was still disturbed by Lucy's nightmare: what if Danny harmed himself? She got up quietly, went to the kitchen and made herself a hot drink. While sipping her hot chocolate she picked up the phone and dialled the police station. It was two o'clock in the morning.

Br.. Brr.. Br.. Br..

"This is officer Sam, how can I help you?"

"I am sorry to disturb you so early but it is very urgent..."

"What can be so urgent maam that cannot wait till the morning?"

"My son Danny is in one of your cells; could you tell me how he is?"

"What do you mean how he is? he must be asleep right now, it is two o'clock after all".

"I know officer what time it is right now; but could you do me a favour and find out how is he doing?"

"Do you mean that you want me to wake him up?"

"Not wake him up, but make sure that he is asleep all right. I have such a dreadful feeling about it right now; so I beg you to go and check his cell..."

"I understand maam, I have a kid of my own; so wait there for a moment, it will take a few minutes, I have to go downstairs". He placed the receiver on the desk, took the key to the cells and made his way downstairs. He found Danny lying on the floor face down; his eyes were wide open and his mouth was covered by white foam. Sam rang the alarm bell and opened the door to the cell, calling for help. Bob rushed quickly downstairs and told Sam not to move him; and he called the doctor on his mobile.

"Is he breathing Sam?"

Sam put his fingers on Danny's neck to check his pulse, but there was none: he panicked when he remembered that he left his mother on the line. "Oh my God, what am I going to tell that poor psychic woman" said he.
"Wait a while, for the doctor will be here at any moment". Sam left Bob with Danny and ran upstairs to the office: "how on earth am I going to tell her the bad news?", and he picked up the phone.
"Are you still there maam?"
"Yes, yes, what took you so long to come back?" said Emily.
"Well maam, well maam…"
"Yes, yes, what is it: is he not well?"
"I am sorry maam, you better come as quickly as possible…"
"Why, what happened?"
"I would rather not tell you on the phone, but something awful has happened. I am sorry I can not tell you more, but I have to hang up now for the doctor has just arrived" and he hung up.
"What is it officer, what is wrong with my son?" But it was too late. the phone went dead.
"Peter, Peter, wake up right now: something must have happened to poor Danny"; and she pushed Peter so violently that he fell on the floor.
"What on earth is going on, why are you not asleep, and why are you in such a state, trembling and shouting, and what on earth am I doing on the floor? Then he got up quickly and tried to calm her down.

Robert who woke up as well after hearing all the noise, rushed into their room and enquired: "What is it Emily, what is all the fuss about?"
"Danny, Danny, something happened to my Danny. Robert quickly drive me to the station, we must not waste a single moment".

Peter, still half asleep, slipped his trousers over his pyjamas, put on his slippers and ran to the car where they were waiting for him. At the station, there was an unusual activity going on for that time of the night. An ambulance was stationed with all its warning lights on; a doctor's car was parked there as well. Emily ran to the station shouting.

"What has happened to my Danny, I want to see him right away, where is he?"

"Hi, I am officer Sam, I spoke to you on the phone earlier…"

"And you put down the phone on me, where is your superior?"

"The inspector arrived a few minutes ago, and he is with the doctor, they are checking Danny."

"What do you mean checking Danny, what is going on officer?"

"Well", and he scratched his head, "well, there has been a kind of accident…"

"What do you mean a kind of accident, is he hurt? what did you do to my baby? I want to see him now".

"I am afraid that it is impossible right now, the doctor is with him: there is nothing we can do but wait; I am so sorry, please take a seat".

"Take a seat, take a seat, what do you expect me to do when you tell me that there has been some kind of accident, how long do you think I can wait I want to see my boy now?.

"He is not dead?" whispered Peter.

Sam lowered his eyes and kept quiet.

"Please maam, let me get you a cup of coffee".

"What for, I would rather prefer you brought me my son."

At that moment a door opened and a doctor with a grim face entered the office with the inspector; "It is a nasty business, I am afraid that he is gone, we were too late, the poor devil did not stand a chance, why was I not called earlier?"

"Who are you talking about Doctor?" asked Robert.

"A young man called Danny".

"What Danny my son is dead? It cannot be, you must be mistaken" said Emily. And she ran through the door and down the stairs calling his name: "Dan Dan…" Peter and Robert followed her with all the officers behind; Emily found the cell with officer Bob, sitting on the floor next to Danny: he was covered from head to toe by a blanket. Emily took the cover off Danny's face , and what she saw made her faint.

"Why is he covered with vomit?"

"The doctor said he must have suffocated in it …"

"But how and why?"

"Well he was crying and coughing and making himself sick: he kept asking for his momsy and Lucy, and we could not calm him. We left him crying, not knowing what to do. He refused the coffee we brought him, so we locked the door and came upstairs. But I assure you that he was alive when we left, I can swear to that. We never dreamt that it will end in such a tragedy".

"When he fell asleep, he must have been sick from crying so much and suffocated by swallowing his own vomit: what a waste" said the doctor.

"You told us inspector, that we had nothing to worry about, and that is was just a formality".

The inspector did not reply for he was saddened by Danny's death.

"It is an awful mess I am afraid to say" said the doctor. "If I were notified an hour before, I would have been able to save him: I am afraid that I need your signatures on some forms: what a loss, I can not believe that such a strong man can find his end that way. The autopsy will take place this afternoon before the inquest".

Emily, who had recovered from her loss of consciousness, was crying and lamenting; "What did you do to my boy, why he had to die so young, he would not harm anybody for he was such a gentle giant: why did you have to lock him up." But for the moment, those questions stayed unanswered.

"It was meant to be, mom" said Robert.. And he supported her for she was in such a pitiful state.

Peter came to the rescue and they all left the cell. In the office upstairs, they signed some forms and left.

"What are we going to tell Lucy; how is she going to react?" asked Robert.

"She is already in such a bad state; let us keep it quiet for a while".

On the way home, while Robert was driving, Emily who was in Peter's arms kept repeating: "It is a bad dream and nothing else, and soon I shall wake up and Danny will be here with me." But alas it was not meant to be.

At the circus, in the big tent, there was not the usual hectic activities, for the rumours spread that Danny had died. No one felt like working. They felt somehow lost for they had come to love and understand that giant of a man with a soft heart but with a low I.Q. He was always ready to help whoever asked him. He did not only kept the stables clean, but also the whole circus: now they realised how invaluable he had been and he was gone forever.

That day the circus did not perform at all as a mark of respect, and they all stayed indoors. The inquest confirmed the verdict of "death by distress" and that Danny choked in his vomit, but that could have been avoided. And no one remembered seeing again the old lady who had accused Danny of being a murderer; she had just vanished with her dog.

After the inquest, Peter contacted his lawyer ordering him to sue the police for negligence.

"I think that you have a good case here but it will take some time, said the lawyer.

"It does not matter how long it takes, but the police have got to pay for the loss of a fallen angel".

Next day Robert went to visit Lucy in hospital. She was getting better, and seeing Robert's face appearing through the door made her happy, but it was for a fraction of a second, for Danny was not with him.

" What happened to my Danny, why is he not with you Robert?" asked Lucy.

"Well, well…"

"What is wrong Robert, something happened to my Dan Dan"

"Well, well, I do not know how to tell you", and he started crying.

"Robert please tell me why are you crying?" asked Lucy.

"Well siss, there is no other way but to tell you what has happened lately: sooner or later you will find out…" said Robert.

"Find out what? Robert."

"Well, it is like this" and he related to Lucy all the events of the night before. Lucy did not utter a word: she knew that Danny was asking for help in her dream when he was drowning, and indeed he drowned in his vomit.

"Why was I not there for him when he needed me the most? now Toby and I are going to live without him: will we survive him? Oh God, why did I not take notice of him when I should have: he would be still alive now. What a mess I have made of my life".

"No siss, you have got me: and together we will pull through: We all have to be strong for the sake of Emily".

"You are right as always my dear brother; you are a pillar of strength, you are my rock."

"Thank you siss for I know that is what Danny would have wanted. So promise me to get better from now on".

"I do Robert, I do: as a matter of fact ask the nurse to bring my clothes in, so I can leave with you right now; I want to show Danny how strong I can be for his sake. I also want to be present at his funeral".

Everyone was pleased to see Lucy back; she had lost some weight but she was getting much stronger emotionally. At the funeral, everyone came to pay their respects, even the inspector who could not accept what has happened. Danny was missed by all, and Toby followed the cortege behind the coffin. He knew what had happened to Danny and that he was gone forever; he stayed behind and kept a vigil long after the coffin had been lowered to the ground.

With nature helping, slowly but surely life became more bearable for the family: time went by, and new challenges had to be met. A few months later , Peter received compensation from the court and the money was spent on buying a horse which was named after Danny.

After a while life went back to normal and bad souvenirs were buried deep under.

Chapter 17

Lucy was eighteen and growing ever so pretty. Robert replaced Danny and he was always by her side, taking care of her slightest whims. the police never caught the serial killer who managed to elude them at the very last moment. They were playing a game of cat and mouse, but for the moment, he was on top. One day, while watching the news on the television, once again they showed his latest victim; she was number seventeen and the law was at the end of its tether; they were warning young girls not to walk alone after dark.

"If I catch him, I will strangle him with my own hands", said Lucy.

"So would I", said Robert.

"I will make him pay for our Danny's death", Emily said.

"God will make him pay for all the pain he is causing to the girls; do not worry, for retribution is always a step behind", Peter said.

Meanwhile the circus was doing very well indeed; but one of the catchers in the trapeze team was leaving to get married and was moving to live in New York to open a restaurant. So a replacement was advertised for in the local papers. It was just past nine o'clock when a long queue of would be catchers was forming outside the circus; there were at least twenty young men waiting for the audition to start.

"That is far too many for me to deal on my own. Robert, will you share the load with me?" said Peter.

"O.K. dad, I will take half of them but I would like Lucy to be by my side; for I value her opinion very much".

"Fine by me if she is willing to do so. Go and fetch her".

Lucy was very delighted to be of some help and actually was flattered by the idea. They took their consecutive seats and divided the would be artists into two groups. After almost three hours of questioning and watching them swinging on the bars, they took a break.

"I am giving up on all of them Robert; none of them would do well: how about you Peter?" said Lucy. "Have you got someone suitable?"

"No, not yet: actually none of them could fit in. I think we ought to postpone it for another day and advertise in different area".

As the three of them were discussing the matter over a cold drink, a young man approached them in a very unusual manner: he was walking on his hands, and insisted on answering all the questions upside down. Lucy laughed her head off when Robert agreed to it. The crowd was laughing and cheering at this unusual audition. After answering all their questions in this unfamiliar manner and showing his prowess on the trapeze, he won everyone's approval apart from Lucy.

He was tall, dark and handsome. He was well built and one could tell that he took good care of his physique: His hair was very black and curly but what surprised Lucy most were his very dark eyes set deep into their sockets. He must have been in his late twenties or early thirties. When he fixed his eyes on her she was as if hypnotized and a shiver ran along her spine: she became frightened and gripped Robert's arms. He was a mixture of Mexican and American and walked very proudly.

He introduced himself as Damian and he was a descendant of a long line of acrobats; actually his father had owned a circus in Mexico, but ran into debts and had to sell it. After much consideration, Peter and Robert decided that Damian would fit in very well to the disbelief of Lucy, who seemed worried about it.

" What have you got against him?" asked Robert.

"I cannot explain it , but there is something about him that makes me shiver: it is a kind of power, but sooner or later I shall find out, and then you will not like it".

"If he ever steps out of line or upsets you in anyway, he will have me to answer to: do not worry Lucy: we are both here to protect you". Against her will, they signed him for a year and he was introduced to his new partners; when Lucy shook hands with him a fear gripped her, and her legs were like jelly; but what was it, she could not tell. it was some kind of fear, but why? She had never seen him before.

She promised herself to find out more about him. It felt as if someone was warning her of an impending disaster, and to be prepared for any eventuality. Her apprehension lasted quite a while and she could not shrug it off.

"I hope the two of us will make a good team Miss Lucy", and he gave her a lingering look which would have melted the heart of any other girl, but not Lucy.

"Are you all right siss, what is it? you look so pale suddenly; here let me get you a glass of water. Did Damian upset you somehow? If so I shall get rid of him right away".

"No, Robert, it is nothing, just a misgiving; he did nothing to upset me, on the contrary, he is the perfect gentleman; just when he held my hand, I had such an awful sensation which I cannot put my finger on: I cannot explain it Robert".

"Don't let it worry you my dear Lucy, I shall always be here to protect you. by the way siss, I think that you are becoming a witch, but a good one". Lucy laughed and kissed him: "I have the best brother in the world" said she.

"The feeling I get Robert, is as if I have been hit by an electric current"

"I think that seeing your old partner leaving makes you feel sad and lonely; but that feeling will go, you will see".

"I hope so, because tomorrow I shall have to rehearse with him and that is what scares me to be honest".

"You will be all right, just think positive". That night Lucy opened her heart to Emily and told her about her fears.

"I shall have a look at him tomorrow and tell Robert to keep an eye on him for a while; but please try to let go and not to get too upset about it".

The next morning was another beautiful day. The sun was already high above and hot; it was hardly eight o'clock when the three of them climbed up their respective platforms, Peter was sitting in a corner watching them with interest. First Robert swung on the bar, then did a somersault in the air, and was caught just on time in Damian's grip: surely enough Robert felt secure and trusted Damian. When Lucy's turn came, she did a double somersault to impress Damian, but at the last moment she panicked and missed his grip and fell on the net down below. Peter jumped out of his chair running toward Lucy:

"What is the matter darling, it is not like you to miss the catcher's grip, what is going on?"

But Lucy did not look good. Robert jumped on the net and came to her "are you all right siss?" and he put his arm around her. Damian who followed Robert said: "I am sorry Miss Lucy, I was just on time to catch you, but for some reason you have missed me."

"It is.. it is not your fault Damian, I made a mistake; actually I do not feel up to it to-day".

"We better call it a day: we shall start all over again tomorrow. It will give us time to reflect and recuperate".

Emily, who was standing quietly in a corner without being seen, could not understand Lucy's behaviour; she looked frightened: somehow. She came toward Peter pensive.

"Have you got an idea what is worrying our Lucy?" asked Emily.

"To be honest Emily, I have the feeling that she is falling for Damian: it is becoming interesting…"

"Is that what you think Peter, I would have thought that she is rather afraid of him"

"Afraid of him? nonsense, she hardly knows him, I think that my first guess is correct…"

"And what do we know exactly about that new man? I pray God that you are right, for I would not like to see my Lucy getting hurt in any way.

"Nor would I, Emily".

Lucy left the tent and changed into her jogging gear; she was followed by Toby and together they went running along the beach; when she had worked up a good sweat, she made her way back. Half way back she came across Robert and Damian who were running the other way. As soon as Toby saw Damian he barked and snarled at him and tried to bite his feet.

"You too do not like him Toby, I am not surprised", said Lucy.

"What on earth is this dog doing" said Damian.

"I don't think that Toby likes you Damian", said Robert.

"Why not, I have done nothing to him".

Toby was getting into a rage and kept jumping menacingly at Damian.

"Here boy here, come to your Lucy", but Toby would not let go of Damian's trousers; he kept growling until Lucy picked him up.

"He must have a score to settle with you Damian" Lucy remarked.

"But I hardly know him , I swear I have never seen him before".

"Maybe in another dimension Damian, you did not get on well together", and she made her way back with Toby in her arms.

"What is the matter Damian, you seem as if you have seen a ghost suddenly. Do not take too much to heart at what Lucy said about the other dimension; somehow she is a witch, but a good one. do you want to talk about it?"

"Believe it or not, but in my country we believe in these things", said Damian.

"Honestly Damian, what next".

"Well, there is something else that I forgot, but now it is coming back to me: when I was around ten, I was bitten by an Alsatian dog who took a liking to one of my butt cheeks" and he showed Robert an awful deep scar. "The dog was put down although he pleaded for his parents not to kill him. But since then, I am afraid of dogs even the size of Toby; they don't seem to like me and I avoid them whenever I can".

" I accept this explanation, it is a much more plausible than the first one".

When Lucy arrived home, she related to Emily the incident between Toby and Damian.

"That man seems weird to me, and it is becoming more strange and bizarre. Something is not adding up. I better make sure that Robert takes good care of my little girl".

When Robert came home and was told of Emily's fear for Lucy, he laughed and told every one about Damian's story with dogs. Emily sighed with relief.

"In that case, tomorrow I shall apologise to Damian and show him what a good partner I can be".

"Yeah, Yeah," shouted Peter and Robert at the same time.

That night Lucy had the same nightmare she had at the hospital: but this time, she was drowning and Danny was trying his best to save her. The next morning at rehearsal, Lucy managed her double somersault without a hitch, and Damian caught her in his strong grip; while catching her, she felt and sensed his eyes piercing her heart and she was overcome by his strength and sense of confidence. On her return back to her platform, when their eyes met in the air, she felt as though hypnotized, her legs turned to jelly and she once again lost control and fell on the net. She came down shaken and dazzled; she could not understand what was happening to her. It was not in her nature to feel that way toward a man: usually, she always had the upper hand with them, so why not now?

"It cannot be, I will not allow myself to fall in love with this man"; but as soon as he looked at her, she lost her confidence. She kept repeating that all this nonsense would eventually go away, and that she must work a bit harder at perfecting her movement, and keep her emotions well under control. "I have to shake them off for good". She climbed up the ladder and on to the platform. Damian was swinging supported by his legs, and was smiling at her and stretching his arms ready for the next catch: he knew that she would be his whenever he wanted. Lucy raised her arm to signal that she was ready. Everyone down below stopped and watched, and when Lucy performed an excellent act, and managed to go back to her corner without any hassle this time, there was applauses and whistling all around. She was proud of herself for she had got rid of her apprehension. At the end of the session she felt relieved and glad that no one heard her heart pounding. Damian came to her and congratulated her and offered to buy her a drink.

"No thank you", said Lucy.

"How about to-night after the show?"

"I am busy and my friend would not like it".

"I did not know that you had a boyfriend, who is he?"

"You met him on the beach; it is Toby, and he definitely does not like you".

Damian turned pale but said: "He is only an animal after all, I am out of his league this time."

"Well, if you want to take me out, you have to make friends with him", said Lucy.

"Too bad, because I find you irresistible".

Lucy blushed, looked aside and ran away. That night Lucy could not go to sleep, for she was questioning her feelings towards Damian, but every time she did so, Danny's face kept coming to the fore with a warning. Why? said Lucy, what is the connection between the two men? I am being warned, but what about? And Lucy decided to give Damian a miss. she picked up Toby who slept at her feet, kissed him, put her arms around him and fell asleep.

Chapter 18

Lucy and Damian made a good team, but she still froze whenever he looked at her. He kept asking her out, but she always found an excuse not to accept; she kept reminding him that he had to be Toby's friend, before becoming hers.

At long last he came up with a peace offering: he bought Toby one kilo of rump steak and offered it to the dog while he was resting at the feet of his mistress. As soon as Damian put the meat on the floor Toby tried to bite his hand. Damian managed to avoid it, and Lucy who was watching laughed her head off.
"Well Lucy, Toby and I are not meant to be friends: but what else could I do to be yours?"
"Nothing at all, we are just meant to work together and nothing else".
"Anyhow Lucy you know where I live; if you ever change you mind please drop in at any time that suits you".
"Thank you Damian but I doubt it very much".

And life at the circus kept its pace; Damian gave up on Lucy and stopped asking her out.

One evening while Lucy was relaxing reading a book. A thought crossed her mind: she suddenly realised that almost three months had gone by, since Damian had last made a pass at her; quite a record she thought: "I wonder who is he with right now? Maybe he found himself a friend". She remembered a pretty dancer with red hair called Milly who had been trying to befriend him and making advances to him ever since Damian arrived on the scene. She could not take her eyes off him: every morning before starting work, she would bring him a cup of coffee with a muffin, and try to steal a kiss from him, to the annoyance of her colleagues. She talked about him as if they were close friends, and Milly loved to give the impression to whoever wanted to hear that something was going on and even that they were an item. But Damian never mentioned his love life to anyone; for he was a very private individual. Some of her team mates seemed to be envious, for Damian was quite a catch. "I am getting jealous as well" thought Lucy. "I wonder what he is up to right now: is he with Milly? and what if I were to find out and knock at his door? what would be his reaction: would he ask me for a drink? He did say I could drop in whenever I felt like it: those where his exact words and I am going to do just that".

She looked at her reflection in the mirror, and was pleased by what she saw; she was tall and slim, with long light brown hair, and her beautiful brown eyes were warm and inviting. She could still see the glances the young men gave her at the circus, and followed their eyes wandering all over her body as if undressing her. But that was as far as it went, for she discouraged anyone who would dare to try their luck. Her encounter with the rapist always came to the fore, to warn her about any new encounter. Very gently she glanced at her breasts, and very slowly her hands felt their contours: she was proud of them for they were firm and of medium size. her hands went further down to her flat stomach, and still further down along her thighs where they lingered for a while. One day, she thought, she would find a man who would be very proud to have her as his wife. Meanwhile her thoughts went to Damian: Would she allow him to caress her beautiful body, and if so what would be her reactions. Would she freeze in his arms after her bad experience? Suddenly she felt afraid of her own feelings, took a deep breath and left.

She walked toward Damian's home and found it well lit; she

was not very sure of what she was doing or why she was there; but for some unknown reason something was pushing her forward: it could have been curiosity or fate, but she was there now. It was almost dark and there were not many people walking about. She was on the verge of knocking at his door when at the last minute she hesitated; she heard what sounded like moans and sighs: she panicked and quickly ran away. Half way back she stopped to recover her breath and she said to herself: "Whom am I running from, and why am I so afraid? Is Damian so frightening? surely not, and I am going to prove it: I have no reason to fear him, and to show him, I am going back." And she turned back heading for Damian's.

The lights were still on, she went to a window and was stunned by what she saw: there was Damian's body naked and beautiful, entwined and enlaced in Milly's body which was exposed and attractive. He was holding her so tight, that she was screaming and panting for breath. She was gasping for air when her whole body surrendered to his embrace. At long last he released Milly who was still trying to catch her breath, but was nevertheless evidently lying there hoping for more. He got up and lit a cigarette; he took a few long puffs and gave the rest to his partner.

Lucy, who had never seen a naked male body before, could not take her eyes off Damian. She admired his figure which was sculpted like one of those Roman statues; but this one was moving and alive: she yearned and wished that it was she that was in his arms, and not the red haired dancer. At long last and with much effort, she recovered her senses and moved away from the window.

She felt hurt and annoyed at the same time that Damian had chosen Milly. She was under the impression that he liked her and wanted her: why would he make advances to her if it was not the case? she was to blame for rejecting his advances, but that was no reason to play with her feelings; yet why on earth she was making all this fuss? Had she not ignored him?

The next day while training, Damian noticed that Lucy was unusually cold and distant towards him.
"What is the matter Lucy, have I done something to offend you?"
"It is nothing at all; I am just tired because I had a bad night".

As a matter of fact, when Lucy went to bed that night, she was crying and hurting, for she was envious of Milly. She dreamt that she and Damian were making love in a lake, while being watched by a very jealous Milly who was waiting for them to come out with a knife in her hand. But what enraged Lucy was that Damian was pleading with Milly to preserve his life and only take that of Lucy, as it was her fault and she was the culprit who took him away from her. Lucy was the guilty one in this case and she had to be eliminated. She woke up in a sweat and calling him names… Damian moved nearer to her, and went to hold her hands when she shouted; "don't touch me, do you hear me, keep away from me or I will tell Milly about you, and she will cut your throat." She ran away hiding her tears. Milly who was dancing with her team near by and was eyeing them, heard the wrangle and came to Damian:

"What is happening and what is all this outcry about? What did you tell Lucy to upset her, are you trying to flirt with her? If so don't you dare, for I warn you, don't you play with me, do you hear me".
"No one is flirting" said Damian perplexed. And he walked away.
"why was Lucy crying" thought Damian, "what does she knows about me and Milly? Did she see us together, if so when and where?"

All that day Lucy was in a bad mood. She vented her resentment on Robert and Toby. Robert seemed worried about her: "Whatever is eating you Lucy, give you no right to take it out on Toby, because that dog has got no one but you. I do not mind being shouted at, but first tell me what have I done to deserve it. Who has upset you, is it Damian again? if so I shall have a word with him". "No Robert, it is not your fault and I am very sorry to have upset you. I just feel very low to-day, please forgive me".

Robert gave her a hug and told her to have a rest, for in a few hours she would be performing. Lucy went to her room trying to hold back her emotions. "up to now, I would have sworn that Damian had a crush on me" thought Lucy, and all that time he has been dating Milly, what a swine and how silly have I been. I shall have a word with him after the show, and tell him where I stand, there will be no more nonsense between us: we are just professional colleagues and nothing more". That evening and throughout the show, Damian kept staring at her; he never took his eyes off her.

"Why are you looking at me that way?"

"Come to-night to my place, just after the show; I will organise something to eat and I have plenty of things to tell you. Will nine o'clock suit you?"

"Maybe but I do not promise".

"Please say that you will come, and I shall have some Chinese take away ready for you", said Damian.

Lucy never answered but she left the tent in a hurry heading for home and a shower. "at long last" thought Damian, she is coming to my way of thinking: to-night she will be mine and nothing will change that , not even Milly; but first I must have a word with her. Milly was talking with friends, and discreetly he attracted her attention. She ran to him and landed him a kiss on the lips.

"What have you got in mind for to-night Damian?"

"That is what I want to talk to you Milly".

"Are you going to order a chinese for me then, or is it a surprise?"

- Not exactly a surprise Milly, to-night I will not be able to see you; I have got to be in town and attend to some business".

"Let me come with you".

"I will be gone for a couple of hours or so, and I can assure you that you will get bored".

"O.K. then, have it your way: anyhow I have some washing to attend to"; and she went back to her group slightly annoyed.

About eight o'clock Lucy was ready and made her way to Damian's place; she was dressed to kill, and she knew it: he would not be able to resist her. when she arrived, she was half an hour early, and she noticed that his bedroom was lit. Very carefully and doing her best not to attract any attention, she looked through the window and saw Damian sitting on the bed, sniffing some white powder in an envelope. Lucy did not know what to make of it: was he on medication? What was wrong with him, unless it was drugs that he was taking. So many questions and not a single answer she thought. "I shall have to be very careful and on my guard. I will watch him like a hawk if I have to".

She knocked at the door and without waiting for an answer entered the living room; quickly Damian left his bedroom and shut the door behind him, while wiping his nose with his sleeve; he seemed to be spaced out but still managed to smile at Lucy.

"I thought that our rendez-vous was for nine o'clock, but I am still pleased to see you", and he looked at his watch.

"I know, but I could not wait to find out what you wanted to tell me".

"Now that you are here, come to the kitchen and help me get the table ready; the food is already here and I have an excellent bottle of wine".

"I would rather have some white wine if that is possible".

- Do not worry, I can accommodate you with white wine, and I have a bottle of champagne for starters".

Lucy was flattered by all this attention: certainly he knew how to impress his guests, but was far from knowing what was going to ensue. While she was laying the table, Damian brought the food which was on a slow burner.

"My goodness Damian why so much food, are you expecting some guests?"

"I hope that you are hungry", and he poured her a glass of champagne.

"Before sealing our friendship, I want to hear what you have to tell me".

Damian fixed her in the eyes without a word, and Lucy found herself unable to take her eyes off his; she could not move and was transfixed by his stare; she could feel his animal magnetism while his eyes were piercing her soul. she was far too weak to resist his mental onslaught and was at the same time fascinated and captivated by his eyes. From that moment she knew that she was his whenever he wanted her; he just had to snap his fingers and she would be his. She had never felt that way before, and could not tell if it was love or something else. A minute later Damian said: "Can you not guess Lucy, don't you know that I am in love with you, and I want you right now?

"Do you Damian?"

"Yes I do, and I cannot take my mind off you".

While he was uttering these words, he came so close to her that she felt the ripples of his muscles and smelled his breath.

"Do you really love me and want me?"

"More than anything on earth"

"Would you do everything I say…"

"You name it and it will be done".

"Even giving up your best friends?"

"I will give up whoever you want."

"Even Milly if I asked you to?"

"I don't know any Milly"

"You liar", and she slapped his face, "so tell me if you don't know any one called Milly?" "Who was that red haired dancer who was in bed with you the other night; do not deny it, for I was watching you making love to her through the window of your bedroom".

Damian was taken aback by her questions: for a while he stood there speechless.

"So that's what it is, that is why you have been in a bad mood all day, you are jealous Lucy: I am flattered indeed".

"I am not jealous at all, and I could not care less".

"So why are you here if you did not care about me?" and he grabbed Lucy in his arms and kissed her.

"What do you think you are doing, let go of me, you are hurting me".

"You know that Milly means nothing to me, and it is you that I want".

"Do you mean it Damian, do you mean it?".

"Oh yes, more than anything in this world; It is you that I love and want".

Lucy felt intoxicated by Damian's declaration, and when he kissed her again, her legs turned to jelly. Yes she did want him at long last. He started kissing her neck and face and she offered him her lips; but suddenly as he tried to undress her, she panicked and shouted at him to stop; "not yet" she kept repeating: but without warning she felt her hair being pulled and she fell on the floor. She was disconcerted and did not know how to respond; she realised that she was under his spell. She froze when Damian gave her a long and lingering kiss, then she noticed his arms running all around her body and touching her intimately. she was suffocating and could not utter a word. Before she knew it, she found herself completely undressed and entangled in a wild embrace. His body was twisted around hers, and she could not slow or stop the impetus of his assault. She wanted to scream and tell him to stop, but not a single word came out of her mouth. She felt like an onlooker watching her body being ravaged. She was devastated; this could not be what she imagined love was, and when at long last he possessed her she imagined that a demon had over powered her, and lost consciousness. When she came back to her senses, she saw him standing there with a glass in one hand and a tablet in the other. "How do you feel, for some reason you fainted".

Lucy could not believe her ears: this man enquiring about her well being had just raped her a few minutes before and was not bothered about it. She was wary of him now.
"Here take this tablet, it will relax you".
"What is it?"
"It will make you feel better, especially after passing out. It will not harm you I promise, on the contrary, you will feel good.
Again he gave her such a look, that her mind went blank: she obeyed his mute order and swallowed the drug.
"Let us have a shower before our meal; from now on, you will be no one's but mine: do you hear me Lucy; you are my woman. It will be our secret, let no one find out about it".
Lucy was not bothered about the shower or the meal, she looked at him mystified, got dressed as quickly as she could and was about to leave when he caught her arm and pulled her once again into his arms; she was pale, trembling and haggard.
"What is it Lucy, why are you crying: for God's sake stop that, will you. I am sorry, all right. I thought that you loved me?"
"I do, but it did not have to be like this; I was not ready for it yet, and you have just raped me: and that reminded me of a very bad experience that I had to endure earlier in life".
"What was it , tell me".
"No, it is too painful for me to relate; and she opened the door and ran away. She ran and ran all the way home, feeling guilty and dirty.

How could she had been so gullible to believe that a man like Damian could ever love her. He was just craving for lust and had to gratify his senses .It did not matter to him whether he subjected his partners to violence or rape. He lived in a world of fantasy and it was not relevant if they suffered. She swore that she would never let it happen again; how stupid had she been to believe in love.

When she arrived home she was in disarray and desperate. She ran straight to the bathroom and stayed under the shower for quite a while. She scrubbed and scrubbed her body in the hope of getting rid of Damian's touch and smell; then she sat under the shower crying and asking Danny to help her. "Why have you left me Danny, I missed you so much and need you right now; so please come back to me." Then she came out with an idea: if Danny could not come to her, what stopped her from going to him? Especially now after the events of the day. She searched in the medicine cabinet and found some razor blades. She picked one and went back under the shower where she slashed her wrists and sunk into oblivion.

Chapter 19

San Francisco was basking in the sun. Holly's career was escalating steeply in the world of ballet. Every living choreographer wanted her for their shows and offered her very advantageous contracts, but she stayed loyal to the San Francisco ballet society. She appeared on films as well as shows; she performed all over the world where she was very much in demand. It was especially at home where she was adored the most, and her husband was complaining at not seeing much of her. Whenever she was free and had time to spare, she would run to her old ballet school and say hello to Imogen, her former teacher: she never lost touch with her. She offered to give lectures about the world of ballet, to the delight of Jane and Marion who made sure to attend as well.

Holly too, would have liked to see more of Henry, but they had their careers to think of. Henry had become a professor in the neuropsychiatry department of a well known private clinic down town. He loved his job and was dedicated to it; it was not unusual for Henry to spend some fifteen hours a day at the clinic and never complain, for it was his life and he lived for it. As for Holly, she was working for weeks on end touring the country. When at long last she came home, she found herself rehearsing for a new show. This was why Henry and Holly never bothered to move away from their grandparents' home. Actually Georges and the two old ladies organized their lives around the young couple. They were all happy and when Henry was delayed by his work, he spent the night in a near by hotel, where he had his own suit reserved.

One evening Marion and Jane kissed Georges good night and retired early to bed.

"Do not stay too long watching television", said Jane.

"There is a famous circus from San-Diego on the screen to-night, it will be on, in half an hour Jane and you know how much I like circus: I must watch this one; it will remind me of some happy times in my childhood. So sleep well and keep the bed warm".

"Good night then: why don't you make yourself a cocoa as you are staying up late".

"I will do just that, good night and sleep well darling".

"A cocoa indeed" muttered Georges under his moustache. He got up and went to the cabinet where he kept his drinks. He took a bottle of brandy and poured himself a good measure in a glass; he took a sip and switched on the box and flopped in his armchair. He took another sip and another one again, and waited for the circus: his eyes were getting heavier and slowly closed. Suddenly he was awakened by very loud music on the set; he woke up startled and on time to see dancers and acrobats parading in a huge tent; but what attracted him the most, was the flying trapeze artists. One of the girls seemed familiar; she was tall and slim with light brown hair: she was wearing a two piece suit leaving her stomach bare. But what puzzled Georges was her likeness with Holly, especially the way she carried her body. Georges felt confused, he got up and put his spectacles on, and kept repeating to himself: "it cannot be" I cannot believe it, this brandy is playing tricks on me, I am too old to believe in miracles". He watched the girl climbing the rope to the top platform, still in a daze. Georges saw her doing a double somersault in the air and was caught up on time by the catcher; who seemed to be of Mexican descent; she hung onto him for a fraction of a second then twisted and caught the bar which was coming at her from behind and landed back on the platform. The crowd was applauding her as she stood tall and waving at them: When she was still waving, her body was shown in full on the screen, and it was then that Georges noticed just above the navel, the same birthmark as Holly's. He suddenly remembered years ago, his late Sarah telling him how the two sisters had the same birthmark just above their navels.

He jumped up as if bitten by a wasp and screamed: "Jessica" but the excitement was too much for the old man, for he collapsed on the couch with a fatal heart attack. Marion who heard him screaming got up from bed and came knocking at Jane's door. She entered the bedroom to find Jane sound asleep and snoring; she shook her hard to wake her up.

"Why are you not asleep, what is it Marion?".

"Wake up Jane, wake up, for I heard noises coming from downstairs"

- Is that you Marion? what are you doing here and where is Georges?"

"I am not very sure, but I heard him shouting the name of Jessica".

"What? Jessica is back, it is a miracle".

"No, no, I have just heard him calling her name for some reason".

"He must be drunk; maybe he took a glass or two while watching the telly.

Don't worry too much about it, I am sure that it is nothing; just go back to sleep and tomorrow we shall ask him what was all the fuss about". And she went back to sleep. Marion went back to her room puzzled. She was too nervous to go downstairs to find out what was going on. "But I swear I heard the name of Jessica".

The next morning as they came down, they saw Georges collapsed on the couch and an empty glass on the floor.

"Look at him Marion, he spent the night on the couch drunk, and she came to Georges trying to wake him up: she lifted his arm and quickly let it fall and screamed".

Marion, who was already in the kitchen, ran back and said, "What is it, why did you scream?"

"Oh my God, Marion; he is cold and stiff: I think he must have passed away in the night, while watching his circus".

"But I heard him shouting Jessica's name…"

"When was that?" asked Jane.

"Last night when I came to your room to tell you that I heard noises downstairs…"

"You came to my room? Then why on earth did you not wake me up?"

"I did and you told me to go back to bed…"

"I don't recall you waking me up last night: anyhow what are we going to do right now?"

"We ought to call the doctor, he might not be dead".

While Marion was on the phone, Jane went back to Georges hoping that she could wake him up. You know that you cannot hold your drink Georges, and now look at the state you are in: come on, get up and I will help you up the stairs" but there was no sign of life in Georges. His eyes were wide open as if he had seen a ghost. "Come on and get up Georges, the doctor is on his way; I am sure that he will make you better".

But there was still no sign of life: Jane was rubbing his hands hoping to revive him; she slapped him very gently to bring some colour to his cheeks, but without success . At long last, she realised that it was too late and he had left her for good. She felt lonely all of a sudden and realised it was an end of an era for her; she felt the loss. More than half of her life has been spent with him and he was gone without saying good-bye. How could he do this to her; may be he did not love her enough. While waiting for the doctor, Marion tried to get in touch with Henry at the clinic; he was already in the theatre operating, but his secretary promised to let him know presently. The doctor arrived a few minutes later to confirm that he had died of a massive heart attack.

"What was he doing to put him in such a state?" asked the doctor.

"He stayed up late to watch a circus…" replied Marion.

"A circus, a circus; the excitement was too much for the poor old man".

He rang for an ambulance on his mobile and was going to give the two old ladies a sedative to calm them, but they refused for they wanted to stay well awake and be with their companion for as long as possible. Jane wanted to ring Holly who was in Los Angeles but gave up the idea, when she realised that she would be in the middle of a rehearsal.

" Don't worry Jane, Henry will let her know as soon as he finds out about Georges: I told them how urgent it was. Surely enough a few minutes later, Henry called to say he was on his way. he notified Holly as well who had left the rehearsal as soon as she heard the news, and was flying back home.

Georges was cremated a few days later, for that was his wish. Holly who worshipped him was so distressed by the loss that she cancelled all her engagements for the following two weeks. Her grandpa was always there for her whenever she needed a shoulder to cry on, and he was also the father she never knew. But now she had her husband to fall back on; while she was having all these thoughts; she felt Henry's arms around her and as if he read her mind, he said: " I am sorry for your loss darling I liked the old man as well, and I am here to take his place for you, and I will do my utmost to try to replace him and be as supportive as I can for you and the two old ladies".

"I know all that sweetheart", said Holly and she kissed him.

Two weeks later Holly went back to her rehearsal in Los Angeles, and tried to catch up with the rest of the team. Jane and Marion were at a loss for a while.

"He said that he wanted to watch the circus, I wished now that he came up with me to bed, I should have insisted".

"I wonder what made him call the name of Jessica?"
"He always dreamt after all that time, that one day we will be all reunited again somehow; I wonder what life would have been like, had we not lost Jessica: would it have been different? I wonder".
"Would Holly be what she is now, had she had a sister to play with: I wonder as well".

That night they lit a candle for Georges, and reflected on the meaning of life and the beyond: they pondered if there was any.

Chapter 20

That night when Lucy slashed her wrists, Toby was waiting outside the bathroom for his mistress to come out. All of a sudden he jumped up and started sniffing around; he could smell the blood that was pouring out of Lucy's wrists. He managed to push the door open and saw Lucy lying in the tub; he barked at her to wake her up but without any success; then he quickly rushed to Emily who was busy in the kitchen and barked again.

"What is it Toby, why are you so loud, have you missed Lucy?" But Toby kept on running to the bathroom and back yelping harder: at long last Emily felt that something was not as it should be: Toby was trying to warn her of some danger.

She followed him to the bathroom and there she saw Lucy in a pool of blood.

"Lucy, Lucy, what have you done?" Hearing no reply, she panicked and yelled for help. Peter and Robert who were playing a game of chess rushed to the bathroom and were stunned by what they saw. Robert who was calm and composed quickly got a bandage from the medicine cabinet and wrapped it around Lucy's wrist to stem the flow of blood, while Peter rang the local doctor who lived on the premises. He has been working for the circus for years and married an acrobat He arrived within minutes and praised Robert's measures for stopping the bleeding.

"What you have done here Robert may have saved your sister's life: you ought to be congratulated".

"I have always been proud of my son", said Peter and he hugged him.

"It is not me who needs thanking , but our hero here Toby who found her". "Make sure that Lucy takes her medicine that I prescribed and she should have plenty of rest, especially after she lost so much blood. I shall come first thing in the morning to check on her progress; but the main thing is that she is out of danger now. He checked her once more to make sure that she was asleep.

"I wonder what made her decide to take her life, why? Do you know something Robert?"

"Right now and for some reason she is going through a very tough time".

"She never confided in me, but I would not be surprised if Damian is involved in it.

"Damian, the catcher, why is there something going on between them?"

"I am not sure, it is just a hunch that I have", said Robert.

"From the very beginning Lucy never liked him; she was wary of him", said Emily.

"But she never said a word…" said Peter.

"She never wanted him , in the first place".

"Why? He is a good catcher, I watch him at work".

"Whenever he comes near her the poor girl freezes and she cannot explain it".

"But she never mentioned it, not a word".

"She did not want to worry you, anyway I asked Robert to look after her and keep an eye on her".

"From now on, I am going to be extra vigilant, I promise".

"Well done son and good for you", said Peter.

It took Lucy a whole week to recover, for she felt very tired; but with all the love she received from her family she soon felt better; but she was too weak to go on the trapeze yet, so she concentrated on staying flexible. She felt betrayed by Damian and realised a bit too late that she was being used for his own selfish gain. But now she was at his mercy; because of him, she became addicted to drugs; Damian made sure to supply her generously, but at a price: and she knew it; there was nothing she could do to get away from him; he had to possess her not only physically but mentally and emotionally also. When she fought back and refused to satisfy all his whims, he just cut her supply of stimulants. She did not know where to turn for help. The work that she loved most was becoming very demanding. Once she missed Damian's grip and fell painfully on the net; another time she failed to reach the bar. Robert noticed the changes in her performances and became suspicious.

"What is happening to you Lucy, you are not yourself lately, you seem to be dreaming or in a trance most of the time, do you want to talk about it?"

"It is nothing Robert I assure you that it will pass".

"If Damian is the cause of your problems, I want to know and you better tell me before it is too late; I will sort him out".

"No, no", said Lucy angrily; it has nothing to do with Damian, "I am telling you, there is nothing wrong with me, I am just a bit tired, I am telling you again there is nothing wrong with me. There."

Robert stopped questioning her, for he did not want to upset her any further. At meal times, she seemed to have lost her appetite and was losing weight; her zest for life was fading and the smallest thing upset her. She took it out on Toby who kept his distance now and refused to sleep on her bed: instead he chose a corner of the room and was unhappy. Emily and Robert spoke to Peter about it.

-"Do you know what is bothering Lucy lately? She is not herself any more" said Peter.

"She refuses to confide in me", said Robert.

"Could she be in love?..."

"If that is what love does to people, I will want nothing to do with it. I am better off without it. But in my opinion, she is heading for a breakdown rather than falling in love".

"I wonder if I ought to have a word with her, for it is starting to affect her work seriously: One day she could have an accident and even now some of her team appear to be affected by her change of mood", said Peter.

"No Peter", said Emily, "I think you should wait a while I am sure it will disappear of its own accord".

"I hope that you are right darling".

One evening, Lucy was at Damian's place and as usual they were enjoying a smoke and a drink; then they started having sex when the door flung wide open, and there standing in front of them was a very mad Milly. She was angry and hurling abuse at them both; her face was red with rage when she got hold of Lucy and punched her a few times on the face, then she threw herself at Damian, punching him and scratching his face; when she had had enough, she pulled his hair and kicked him in the groin. Damian was desperately trying to protect his face from Milly's madness, he was grimacing with pain. Meanwhile Lucy got dressed as fast as she could and ran away, leaving Milly yelling and kicking.

After much struggle Damian managed to get the upper hand. He overcame and calmed Milly.

"Why, why do you have to cheat on me? Don't I give you everything you want? What has she got that I cannot give you: is it because she is the boss's daughter?"

"It is just a fling Milly and nothing else, I swear…"

"That is why you were kissing like mad…"

"I swear to you again and again, that she means nothing to me and that you are the only one for me".

"If I see you once more with that tart, I swear to God that I will kill you; do not tempt me: you are mine and mine only…"

"Yes Milly you are right, I am yours and no one else; but right now let me tempt you with something you have always liked".

He went to his bedroom and came back with a tablet that she swallowed pretty quick while he poured her a glass of wine. The effect worked straight away for she felt it immediately. She started to smile and even apologised for her bad behaviour: he pulled her toward him and carried her to the bedroom where they spent the rest of the night in each other arms, as if nothing had happened a few minutes before.

When Lucy reached home, she ran straight to the bathroom, and what she saw in the mirror made her scream with horror. Her right eye was closed and swollen and her nose was bleeding. She looked and felt awful: she wondered whether her nose was not broken, for it was very painful. How on earth was she going to explain what had happened. No one would believe if she said she walked into a door. What would happen to her performances? She could not appear in that state: she already could hear the gossips. "Oh God what a mess have I made of my life" she said loudly. Then she heard some footsteps and someone wanted to use the bathroom. "Oh God, not now" said she.
"Is that you Lucy, will you let me in, will you be long?"
"In a minute momsy," said Lucy.
And she wet her head and face and wrapped her head in a towel hoping to hide her face.
"Come on Lucy, please open the door, for I cannot hold it much longer".

While opening the door, Lucy turned her head the other way as if she was drying her fair: Emily never saw her face. She wished momsy a good night and rushed to her room where she collapsed on the bed, covered her face and cried: "what is going to happen to me?". Next morning at breakfast Emily called her but there was no reply.
"Please Robert, go and wake your sister, for her breakfast is getting cold".
Robert knocked at her door and turned the knob, but it was locked

from the inside.

"Come on siss", said Robert, "it is time to get up; your breakfast is getting cold"; but there was no answer.

Robert went back to finish his breakfast. after a while Emily said that she hoped Lucy did not do something silly again. She hardly finished her sentence before Robert jumped to his feet, went to her bedroom and forced the door open: but the room was empty. "Emily", said Robert, "come quickly, Lucy is not in her room". "What do you mean she is not in her room? where could she have gone so early", and she looked around puzzled; the window was wide open.

"Peter did you have a word with her last night?" asked Emily.

"No, I did not see her after her performance either, as a matter of fact".

"So where is she?"

"I will go and find her, may be she is practicing" said Robert.

He went to the big tent and looked around, but she was not at her usual spot: he called her but there was no answer. There was a complete silence for a while, then he heard what could have been a kind of lament, which was hardly perceptible. He could not make out where it came from; he looked up and around, and there was Lucy sitting high up on a bar: her face was covered by her arm. "What on earth are you doing up there at that time of the day?" asked Robert. "Come on down". But there was no reply.

"Come on down siss, what is the matter with you this time?"

There was still no answer, but Lucy was sobbing loudly now. Robert was worried: it was not like Lucy to be so depressed; something must have happened to upset her so much, but what was it? and he did not like it at all. He wanted to protect her but did not know how, so he climbed up the rope and reached the bar where

Lucy was sitting: she saw him coming and quickly turned her face the other way.

"What is the matter with you, we are all worried about you; especially momsy, when you did not turn up for breakfast; so what is it, please tell me; you know that we all love you, don't you?"

But Lucy kept on sobbing louder and louder.

"It is nothing Robert, it will go", said Lucy.

"You call that nothing; you are crying and upset…"

"What is the matter with me Robert, look at me, I am a failure, and I have let my family down as well as you, yes I am a failure and I keep worrying every one: you will all be better off if I disappeared". And she kept crying louder than before and hiding her face. "Stop talking soft" said Robert: "come into my arms and let me take good care of you"; while he put his arms around her and she turned to rest her head on his shoulders, which was when he noticed her face and was taken aback:

"What on earth happened to you Lucy, have you been in a fight? look at your face, and who gave you that black eye?"

"Leave me alone will you: I am telling you, that it is nothing. Why can't you accept it; it was just an accident".

Robert was very worried and said: "You have a black eye and your nose might be broken, and your upper lip is cut, and you want me to swallow your story as if nothing happened? What is the matter with you: don't you think that I care for you siss? So now tell me who did that to you and I shall sort him out".

"No, no one did anything to me; I am just a bitch and I deserved what was coming to me at long last".

"No, you are not a bad girl Lucy, you are just going through a bad patch: you want to grow up too quickly, that is all: but you do not deserve what you have got. You cannot be a bad girl, for you are my sister. Now tell me who did that to you".

Lucy kept on sobbing and reluctantly told him about the

row she had with Milly the night before, and how it all turned out sour at the end.

"Do you mean Milly the dancer with the red hair?"

"Yes that dancer, the one with red hair indeed."

"But what was the row about?"

"Oh, you don't want to know:"

"Oh yes", said Robert, "I do want to know, why don't you try me; I know Milly, and she is not an aggressive girl, I would say that she is rather sweet unless she is provoked".

"If I tell you everything, and I mean everything, will you promise not to tell anyone?"

"I must tell our momsy".

"It will kill her and she will chuck me out".

"Don't be soft Lucy, you know that we all love you and care for you: how many times do I have to repeat that."

Lucy nodded her head and wiped her face with her hand.

"Here", said Robert, "take my handkerchief, I always carry one".

Lucy related in detail all that had happened between her and Damian, and how he forced himself on her when she went to his place and how vulnerable she was that evening: she did not want it to happen, but he was too powerful and she was under his influence; she made the mistake of accepting the drugs he was offering so freely, and now it had become an addiction; he kept supplying her with the stuff, but at a cost to her health. Now she was at his mercy and he would never let her go: she had had no idea that Milly loved him; "but how am I going to get rid of him and my addiction? I do not love him at all Robert I swear, but he keeps pestering me for sex and if I refuse, he stops providing me with the stimulants; last night Milly caught us in bed together and she went wild and beat us both".

Robert was bewildered and baffled by what he heard. He

could not believe that his baby sister, whom he loved and adored, could have been so naïve as to get caught by a man like Damian. It was his fault for not looking after her properly: he had failed her because he had to spend most of his time worrying about the business which called for most of his energy. What would Emily say, for she had entrusted him to look after his little sister. He had promised her that he would, but failed to do so.

"Say something Robert, your silence frightens me; please talk to me Robert".

Robert was still looking at her with disbelief.

"Please Robert, don't hate me, for I can't stand the idea of you not loving me and caring for me anymore".

- No siss, you don't have to blame yourself, for it is my fault; I did not take good care of you as I should: I also promised mom, and I failed her. But all this is going to change from now on. I will be here for you whenever you need me".

"Oh Robert, you are the best brother anyone could dream of, and if it were not for you, I would be dead".

And they hugged each other:

"Now let me help you down and take you home for you are in no condition to fly to-day or this week as a matter of fact" said Robert.

He helped Lucy down the ladder and went home: as it happened Emily opened the door and was taken aback:

"Oh my God, who did that to you?" asked Emily.

"Take care of her mom, I am going to sort that out", said Robert.

"Where are you Peter, come and see the state Lucy is in".

Chapter 21

Robert rushed out and went searching for Milly: he did not have to look too far, for she was rehearsing some new steps with her group. He interrupted the drill, got hold of her arm and pulled her aside.

"Let go of me Robert, you are hurting me".

"How dare you punch Lucy, do you want to get fired?"

"The brat deserved it, she is nothing but trash and a drug addict".

"I could kill you for talking about my sister that way".

Seeing the disturbance and hearing the threat from Robert, some dancers and artists gathered around the angry couple and watched with curiosity. The argument was becoming serious, since Lucy was being called names and Robert was threatening to kill Milly. Milly realised the mistake she had made by calling Lucy a drug addict, and tried to retract her statement.

" I did not mean it that way Robert, not about the addiction, I was telling a lie, I swear".

But Robert was getting really mad and was shaking Milly with such intensity that she fell: Peter who arrived on time to see the commotion, stopped Robert from harming Milly any further.

" Have you lost your senses Robert, what do you think you were doing? Go home and cool it; I will talk to you later".

Robert left the tent angry with himself for losing his temper, Peter helped Milly up and asked someone to fetch her a glass of water.

"Come on guys, the show is over: carry on with your work".

"I am sorry Peter honestly, I did not mean to hurt Lucy I swear; but she tried to steal my Damian by sleeping with him".

"So that what it was all about, men: and you think that Lucy was after your boyfriend"

Reluctantly and without thinking of what the consequences would be, she recounted to Peter all the events of the night before without omitting the drugs. Peter was livid and said: "so that is why my Lucy is failing at performing in her usual manner." Where is that son of a bitch, where is Damian? Peter left in a hurry and headed home where he found Emily and Robert trying to contain Lucy who was becoming hysterical. She was screaming and raving mad; Robert was holding her in his arms striving to restrain her from harming herself. Emily was wiping Lucy's face and was crying in silence. Peter took Emily aside and told her, word by word, what Milly had said.

" Milly did not mean to hurt her, It was on the spur of the moment. She felt guilty about it and was apologetic", said Peter.

"What are we going to do about Lucy's addiction?" asked Emily.

"I don't know, but let me call the doctor, he will be able to advise us. Meanwhile she is not fit to work and she could kill herself. I shall have to train someone else to replace her".

"Any idea who it could be?" asked Emily.

"Not right away", said Peter, "but let me ask Robert".

Lucy was quiet now and seemed relaxed in Robert's arms: Peter spoke to him very quietly so as not to disturb her.

"Do you know off hand someone who could replace our Lucy for the time being?"

"Yes dad", said Robert, "there is a dancer who as soon as she finishes her dancing, comes and trains on the trapeze with Lucy; give me two days and I will be able to train her properly".

"Thank God for that, I will go right away to find her and she will start her training with you first thing in the morning: by the way what is her name?"

"I am not very sure but it could by Anya", said Robert.

After calling the doctor Peter went to the tent and straight to the corner where the dancers were working. As he approached the group, he saw Damian limbering up and swinging on the flying trapeze: his blood went to his head and he called for Damian to come down; " I want a word with you, come on down right away." Damian threw himself on the safety net and walked toward Peter. His face was covered with cuts and bruises.

"What is up boss…" said Damian.

But before he could finish his sentence, Peter landed him a right hand punch which threw him off balance and landed on the floor.

" What was that for boss, what did I do to deserve it?"

"Get up and I will tell you what you have done to deserve it, get up slimy drug dealer", said Peter.

When he heard these words, Damian went very pale:

"You have got it all wrong boss, I do not do drugs…"

"You don't hey, you low life animal", said Peter.

By then everyone in the tent was listening to the argument.

 "Milly", said Peter, "where are you: come here and do not be afraid, repeat to this coward what you have told me about him and Lucy. Go on admit it now Damian, you cannot lie now"

"It was between Lucy and Milly boss", said Damian, "it had nothing to do with me, I swear".

Milly was looking down, for she was afraid and could not face Peter.

" Tell me Milly, did he give Lucy drugs: I want the truth". Milly with a whisper said yes.

"Did he sleep with her?" asked Peter.

 "Yes boss" muttered Molly.

"Are you going to deny it now, you scum".

Damian did not answer but he gave Milly a sinister look.

"I know everything about you now, you are fired right now", said Peter, and don't you ever dare to show your face in my circus, for you will have to answer not just to me, but to the police also".

Everyone in the tent were dismayed at hearing of drug dealing and applauded when they heard Damian being sacked; for he was not very popular in the circus. Peter went towards the dancers and tried to find out which of the girls was Anya. A slim girl with short hair walked toward him and introduced herself; as soon as he saw her Peter liked her, for she had a sweet face people could trust.

" I am sorry if I used the trapeze facilities without asking you first, but Lucy was teaching me some tricks, and did not seem to mind at all".

"There, there Anya, you have done nothing wrong, and I am here to offer you a new job".

"What is it? Sir."

"First, call me Peter like every one else; now tell me, how would you feel about trying your hands at the trapeze?"

"But I already do it in my spare time Peter."

"No, no, I mean as a professional:"

"Do you mean with Lucy?"

"You will be replacing her for a while until she get better, and then you will work together…"

"But I cannot do what she…"

"Do not worry, because from tomorrow, you will be practicing with Robert who will show you all the tricks"

"Oh God, do you mean that I shall be working with Robert all day?" said Anya.

"Yes why", asked Peter, "do you object to that?"

"Object, me? on the contrary, I would love to…"

So, you do want the job?"

"Oh yes please, I wanted to work with Robert for a long time now, and never had the opportunity to do so before; so it is with a resounding yes, that I agree: it is a dream come true, oh boy, am I lucky".

"Go and find him and tell him what I have said."

"Thank you Peter, I will not let you down" and she kissed him.

Meanwhile, the doctor came to visit Lucy and gave some medication to calm her down.
"I would like to refer Lucy to a clinic to detoxify her and make her kick the habit; I am afraid that it will be a long and expensive process, if that is all right with you".
"How long will she be away for?"
"Three months at the most and then she will be like new".
"Yes doctor", said Peter, "please do what is best for her".

Next day Damian came to pick up his pay; before leaving he begged Peter to forgive him and take him back; but Peter would not hear of it.
"The sooner you leave, the better for all of us. You are an evil man Damian".
Damian left muttering horrible threats under his moustache. As for Milly, no one wanted to talk to her for a while; she pleaded her innocence in the whole affair, but no one wanted to listen to her; most of them kept their distance. Lucy agreed to go to a clinic for her own good, under one condition: that Robert came to visit her as often as possible. She wanted to keep in touch with what was going on at the circus. She kept quiet when she learned that Damian had been fired, and was happy to know that Anya was replacing her for a while; and that after her return they would be working together. She liked Anya very much, and knew that she had always fancied Robert , but she was too shy to let him know. Now Anya was in heaven, for she had Robert's attention for a full two days.

Chapter 22

Life with Jane and Marion went on with sadness and acceptance after Georges' death; it was hard at the beginning not to see him sharing their meals or sitting on his favourite chair. But nature took over, and everything got under way as normal as possible. They could not do enough for the pair. Sometimes Holly felt as if she was suffocating. Occasionally the two old ladies traveled with Holly whenever the ballet society permitted them.

" My lovely angels, you do not have to follow me everywhere for I can take care of myself", said Holly.

"Nonsense, nonsense, we love to help you", said the ladies.

"I feel that I am becoming a burden to you. To be honest, I would like you to stay at home as before and take care of me when I come home", said Holly.

"If you really insist and would like us to stay at home, we would do just that: but remember darling that we are always here for you", said Jane.

"It is all settled then, and I feel much better. I thank you my darlings", Holly said.

"But you promise to call us every day when you are on tour", said Marion.

"Have I ever missed one single day up to now?" asked Holly. As soon as I have a break, I will call you, and put you in the picture as usual. And she hugged the two old ladies, knowing that one day they would depart as well.

One week end Henry came home and wanted to see his wife urgently. When she arrived, he commented on how well she looked and after supper, presented her with a surprise little box.

" What is it darling and what is the occasion?" asked Holly.

"Must there be a special occasion to offer my beautiful wife a present?" said Henry.

Holly opened the box and saw a beautiful necklace.

" Oh darling it is beautiful"; and she gave him a long and lingering kiss.

That night they made love with renewed passion and fell asleep in each other arms. Around three o'clock, Henry woke up with a bright idea which he wanted to share with Holly right away.

"Wake up darling, said Henry, I have something important to tell you; wake up"

"What is it, what is happening, why are you not asleep, are you ill?" asked Holly.

"No, no", said Henry, "calm down, it is nothing of the sort I assure you; I came up with a bright idea".

"Why can't it wait till the morning? Can't you see that you are disturbing my sleep, I am tired Henry, go back to sleep. Surely it can wait till the morning".

"No", said Henry, "I have to tell you now before I forget".

"What is it then?" asked Holly. "Go on tell me about your idea, it better be good".

"I am sure that you will love it when you hear it", said Henry.

"Please Henry stop torturing me and come out with it", said Holly.

"How about having a baby, I would love a girl".

"What" screamed Holly, and she sat up: "a baby, and you are waking me up to tell me such a nonsense?"

"I think it is a brilliant idea; we should start a family right away".

"Do you know what are the implications of having a baby, and all the complications which come with it? Do you know what you are saying? just forget it and go back to sleep".

"But I want us to have a baby or maybe two or three".

"Go to sleep now Henry, we shall talk about it first thing in the morning, I am tired now and tomorrow I have to rehearse for a new show; so please let me have some sleep now".

"Good night then", and he held her tight; but he could not sleep now, for the idea kept on coming back to him.

So he went to the kitchen and made himself a hot drink. Soon he was joined by Jane and Marion who had been disturbed in their sleep by their shouting.

"What was all that noise you two were making?" asked Jane. Were you having an argument?"

"Well", said Henry, "not exactly an argument, but let's say that we did not see eye to eye on something of importance to me".

"May I ask what it was about?" said Marion.

"Of course you may", Henry said, "and I will be delighted to tell you both my dear loved ones, and also ask for your opinions; but first let me make you a hot drink as the water has boiled".

"Go on then", said the ladies, "but can you tell us what was the discussion about"

"One more minute and I will tell you everything; I am sure that you will agree with me", said Henry.

And he brought them their hot drinks; but the two old dears were more interested in what Henry had to say. They wanted to know right away what it was.

"Well it is like this: I woke up with an idea in my head"...

"What, what, ..." asked the ladies.

"Wait: I was saying that something of great importance woke me up in the early hours of the morning", said Henry, "and I told Holly about it".

"But what it is Henry", asked the ladies, "come on, tell us..."

"A baby, I want us to have a baby..."

"A baby?" said the ladies. "What a lovely idea Henry, you are a genius".

They got up, embraced him and held him so tight, that he nearly fell. They left the kitchen ignoring their drinks and humming: "A baby, a baby, spring is on us."

In the morning, Henry came down whistling.

"Why are you so happy this morning Henry?", asked Jane, "and she winked at him. Did you sleep well after last night's news Henry?".

Henry did not answer, but he was all smiles.

"Shall we talk about it now?" asked Jane.

"No", said Henry, "we better wait for Holly to come down first. It will be her decision".

Jane and Marion exchanged glances and could not stop muttering; Marion was rubbing her hands as if she knew in advance what had been decided. A few minutes later, Holly came down for breakfast and noticed an unusual aura in the room.

"What is going on?", asked Holly, "you are all smiles, anything up with my two sweet ladies?"

Jane and Marion looked at each other with a giggle. While Holly was sipping her coffee, Henry said with a smile; "shall I tell them then, or would you rather do it?"

"Tell them what darling?..." asked Holly.

"You know", said Henry, "what we have decided earlier in bed..."

"Decided what in bed", said Holly, "for I was sleeping: would you like to refresh my..."

"You know", said Henry, "about having a baby..."

"Having a baby", said Holly, "who is having a baby...?"

"Don't you remember earlier in the morning we have decided to start a family..."

"What", said Holly choking over her coffee, "a family now, what on earth gave you the idea?" Jane and Marion, nudged each other and left discreetly; but they kept the door ajar, so they could hear the conversation.

"We spoke about it in bed and..." said Henry.

"Having a baby now", said Holly, "do you know what is involved in having a baby, and who is going to look after it: I am on my way to Paris for a new repertoire, and you want to have a baby now; you must be mad or insane, you do not make sense Henry".

"I think that it is time for us to have a baby", said Henry.

"What about my dancing career, you know that it is what I live for, and it is my main interest in life…?"

"What about me, how do I fit in your plan?…" asked Henry.

"Oh Henry you have your career as well, and you know that I love you, what else do you need".

"There comes a time when a husband feels the need to be surrounded by a family, and a wife only is not enough any more".

"But you are never at home Henry, you are always in between… travelling from the clinic to your hotel…"

"That is because you are rarely at home Holly; if I had kids waiting for me at home, I would happily change my hours at work. Any how, while you are on tour in Paris, promise me to think about it".

"I will, but do not hold your breath for I do not promise anything. Let us wait and see how it goes in Paris".

Holly left the kitchen and went to her room without uttering a word. As soon as she left, Jane and Marion surrounded Henry to comfort him.

" Well done Henry, keep at it until she changes her mind".

"Yes, don't give up on the idea, it would be so lovely to see children running around, it will be spring all over again, and a whiff of fresh air: we will support you all the way".

Henry smiled, kissed them and left for work.

Chapter 23

At the circus, life went on as usual: Damian was gone and was replaced by an English catcher. Lucy was being treated at the clinic. She was a model patient. She religiously took all the medicines, that were given to her, and attended all the group therapy that was on offer: she knew that as soon as she kicked her habit, she would be discharged and go back to the world she loved most, "her trapeze and her friends" especially Anya who she liked as a partner, and maybe a sister in law one day. She knew that Robert liked her as well.

Louise was a young woman of twenty five with short black hair and green eyes; she was tall and slim, and was Lucy's therapist; she took a liking to Lucy and tried to help her as much as she could. Lucy found her unusual, not to mention bizarre: she dressed rather like a man and acted like one as well. One day the pair of them went jogging in the beautiful park that surrounded the sanatorium and Louise insisted on holding her hand; another time, while Lucy was having a shower, Louise came into her room unannounced, opened the cubicle door, and stood there watching Lucy's body.

" How long have you been in watching me?" asked Lucy.

"Just a minute or so" said Louise.

"What do you want?" asked Lucy.

"Now you mention it", said Louise, "I forgot completely; but let me tell you that you are a beautiful woman, and I like you very much".

"But you are my therapist", said Lucy, "and a woman on top of that".

"Does it matter Lucy?" asked Louise. "Here , let me wash your back".

"Thank you but I have just finished and I am coming out", said

Lucy.

While Lucy was drying herself and getting dressed, she felt Louise' hands touching her breast.

" What are you doing Louise?", asked Lucy, "what would people say if they saw you; they will get the wrong impression".

"Oh I am sorry I have made you uncomfortable and please forgive me but you are so beautiful that I could not stop myself".

"Anyway", said Lucy, "what did you come here for?"

"Oh yes", said Louise, "I forgot: I just wanted to tell you that you are doing well and if you keep progressing, you will be leaving us soon".

"Thank you Louise", said Lucy, "I value your opinion…"

"I tell you what Lucy" said Louise, "why don't you let me prepare you a nice meal to-night, just for the two of us; I am a good cook, and I would like you to know how much I cherish your friendship. shall we say seven o'clock to-night? I live on the second floor just above yours"; and she left.

Lucy did not know what to think or how to react. Would she be able to resist her advances; what would her reactions be? So she decided to forget about it: Just before seven o'clock, Louise rang her to confirm her invitation; Lucy forgot about her decision not to go, changed into a dress and left.

When she got there, soft music was being played, and the light in the living room was toned down. The table was laid for just the two of them, and a big bottle of champagne was in the middle along with two bottles of wine. "While we wait for the pasta to cook, let us sample a glass of champagne" said Louise and she offered her the glass.

" I hope you like pasta and salad, but if you prefer, I can fry you a nice steak".

"No, pasta and salad will do nicely, thank you", said Lucy.

"I drink to our friendship" and she emptied her glass, eyeing Lucy who sipped hers.

They ate and drank and talked about life in general; and Louise made sure to top up Lucy's glass whenever it was getting empty. Lucy talked about her unfortunate misfortune when she was a teenager and her disastrous love affair with Damian; it was he who had initiated her to drugs, and it was his fault that she had ended up at the clinic.

"So", said Louise, "I should be obliged to your friend for you being here". And unexpectedly she kissed her on the lips, but Lucy was too drunk to react.

"Let me pamper you Lucy, for you have had more than your share of suffering; and I want to look after you, and be your friend if you let me. I promise that you won't regret it". She held Lucy's hand and without a word took her to the bedroom: Lucy offered no resistance and was simply pleased to lie in bed and sleep it off.

She was alone when she woke up the next morning, and was rather surprised to find herself naked and in someone else's bed. She had an awful headache, and slowly realised what had happened. At that precise moment Louise came in carrying her breakfast in a tray.

"Did you sleep well Lucy, and how are you feeling this morning?" asked Louise.

"Why am I here and what am I doing in your bed?"

"Don't you remember what happened last night, you seemed to be enjoying what was going on".

"Last night", said Lucy, "oh my God, what have I done?"

"You have done nothing to be ashamed of Lucy: you and I made love, and I must say that you are quite a catch" and she tried to kiss her, but Lucy shied away and noticed that Louise was full of admiration for her. She realised she was not covered and pulled a blanket over her body.

"No need to be shy with me now", said Louise, "you have shown me everything last night, or have you forgotten as well".

"Last night was last night; I am sorry if for some reason I gave you the wrong impression, but I am not inclined to that kind of love: I would rather prefer a man. What would people say, seeing us together like that? I would still be your friend, but nothing else".

"I am awfully sorry Lucy that you don't feel the same as I do: I was under the impression that you cared for me; it is my mistake, and please forgive me, and let us be friend the way you wish".

"Yeah, Yeah," said Lucy and she got dressed at the double and ran to the door. On her way to her room, Lucy wondered why on earth Louise thought that she was gay. "Have I encouraged her in any way, if so when?"

At the circus Anya and Robert were becoming an item. They were seen together hand in hand wherever they went. Anya became a familiar presence at Peter's home, to the delight of Emily, who until now had thought that Robert was a loner. Together they put on beautiful shows which were very much appreciated by an audience who valued their talents. Three times a week, they drove together to visit Lucy who was excited at seeing them in love.

" I am so happy Anya, that at long last you have decided to make a move on my brother: he is so shy, that I thought he would end up marrying the circus".

"I heard that siss, and let me kiss you for caring so much about me; by the way, I have a surprise for you" and he opened the door of his car and there came Toby running, barking and jumping at Lucy. She picked him up obviously delighted to see her old companion. During all the visit Toby never stopped licking her face; he had missed his mistress and was not afraid to show it.

"If Toby carries on, there will be nothing left of your face Lucy".

"I am afraid that he is getting old my Toby: I dread the day when he will have to go: I shall be devastated" and she kissed him on the nose.

Two weeks after her experience with Louise, Lucy left the sanatorium. She was pleased and eager to go back to the circus and was delighted to be working once again with Robert and Anya, and got used to the new catcher as well. Whenever she saw Robert holding Anya's hand, Lucy would tease him and ask him when they planned to set the date. At long last, the couple announced their engagement to the delight of their families and the circus in general. Lucy was in her glory for she adored Anya; less than six months later, they tied the knot. For two days there was nothing but rejoicing and drinking at the circus.

Peter who was getting old and slowing down as was becoming all too obvious, turned over the deeds of the circus to his son:
"From now on, you are the boss Robert, and I shall always be here whenever you need my help. But of course you have been running this place all by yourself for years now, and I am very pleased to see you take over. It has been a dream come true for me" and he hugged his son for a long while.

One evening, Milly who had been very lonely since Damian's departure, arrived home and noticed that the door was ajar; she was surprised; she could have sworn that she had locked it that morning. She looked around her suspiciously, but noticed nothing out of the ordinary. "I must have forgotten to lock it" said she loudly as I was in a hurry"; but she noticed that the lock had been tampered with: as she went in slowly and cautiously, a hand covered her mouth from behind and she heard Damian's voice: "Shush, not a word, for no one must see me around here, do not switch on the light, and promise not to scream:" Milly nodded her consent, and besides, she was afraid of what he might do to her if she showed her fear. Damian released his grip and when she turned to face him, she was surprised to see a clown with red hair.

"I would not have recognized you in this disguise…" said Milly.

"Never mind that Milly,I have a job to do, and I need your help".

"What kind of help do you need from me, after such a long time: Where have you been", and she looked him straight in the eyes. "I have missed you so much, don't you know how much I love you?"

"It is simple, I want you to get in touch with Lucy for me…" said Damian.

"What: after all that happened between you two, why? what is she to you? Have you not had enough trouble with…"

"I can swear to you that it is not what it looks like, I assure you it is only business…" said Damian.

"Only business: who do you take me for, an idiot? Do I look that stupid? Anyhow", said Milly, "what is in it for me?"

"Shush, don't shout, people outside might hear us".

He took an envelope from his pocket and handed it to her.

"So it is drugs that you are selling her, and nothing else: am I still your number one woman, or have I got competition now that you have left".

Damian took her in his arms in an embrace, sat her on the bed, and begun to undress her.

"Do you still doubt me?" And he got up, took his trousers off and jumped into bed with her. Milly, who was madly in love with Damian, would have done anything for him and whatever he asked from her: she was under his spell and could not envisage her life without him. In the early morning he left her apartment making her promise to see Lucy and give her the letter. "Tell her that I live nearby, just across the woodland".

" And here is something for you too"; and he gave her a sachet. Milly took it and gave him a long and loving kiss. "I will come and see you too" she said.

"Yes", said Damian, "you do that: let's say to-night at eight o'clock, before Lucy shows up; so she would not see you…"

"How can you tell that she will come?" asked Milly.

"She will", said Damian, "she will, be assured of that; what I have put in the envelope will make her run to me…"

"But make sure it is only business, do you hear me"

"I promised, did I not?" and he rushed out and away in the dark.

In the morning, while everybody was rehearsing, Milly took a break from her dancing and went searching for Lucy. She found her working on the trapeze with Anya and Robert, he signalled her to come down, and showed her the envelope.

"Are you looking for me?" asked Lucy.

"Yes", said Milly, "I have a note for you".

"Who from?"

"Take it and find out".

"No, if you do not tell me."

"It is from Damian…"

"No thank you", said Lucy, "I want nothing to do with him…"

"But there is a surprise for you inside", and quickly and discreetly, she handed over the envelope and ran away.

Lucy seemed surprised, but she opened the envelope and read: "I have missed you a lot, come to me tonight around nine o'clock at the following address. Destroy the letter after reading it. and before you come, enjoy the two tablets that I have put in the envelope especially for you, they will relax you. P.S. keep it a secret, and make sure not to disappoint me;" And it was signed by Damian". After reading it, Lucy started to shake as she used to: she was wobbling and quivering all the way back to her team. Not again, thought Lucy; I am going to tell him off this time, and warn him to let go of me for good, and if he refuses, I shall have to call the law on him, once and for all.

"Where have you been Lucy?" asked Anya.

"I just had a word with an old friend for a minute".

"What did you talk about, for you are pale and shaky: do you want to talk about it?"

"No, it is nothing; I would rather start working instead. I have wasted enough time already". She hugged Anya and said: " I value your friendship very much, in case you do not know it yet", and she embraced her.

Chapter 24

That day Milly was very tense, she could not concentrate and kept looking at her watch while dancing. "What is it", asked a dancer, "you cannot take your eyes off your watch: are you not feeling well? or are you expecting someone to come through that door?"

"On the contrary", said Milly, "I am feeling on top of the world and I can not wait until eight o'clock to-night".

"Why", said the dancer, "what's special to-night".

"As a matter of fact", said Milly, "the earth will be moving for me to-night".

"Anyone I know?"

"No way, he is my Adonis; so no one knows him, there".

"You are a lucky one: as for me, I go straight to an empty apartment", said the dancer.

"Never mind", said Milly, "one day it will be your turn".

At seven thirty that evening, Milly was ready and looked a picture. She quickly locked her street door and walked quickly towards Damian's place. It was getting dark and she did not like to walk alone in the woodland; so she started running; half way through, she stopped for a moment believing that she heard steps behind her and thinking that Damian was coming to meet her; she smiled and slowly turned around, but it was too late for Milly: a blow hit her on the neck, she staggered around and fell flat on her face and into oblivion. During that time, Lucy was having her supper with the family; she had no appetite and seemed nervous and worried.

"Why are you not eating Lucy? Don't you like your chicken: I prepared it the way you like it best", Emily said.

"It is perfect momsy, but for some reason I am not hungry right now".

"Shall I make you a pancake? you know, your favourite, with honey and chopped almonds: what you like best".

"No thank you, I think I am going for a walk".

"Would you mind Lucy if I ate your supper, for I have to eat for two from now on", said Anya.

"What", said Emily, "did you hear that Peter, our Anya is pregnant".

"Why did you keep it a secret Robert", said Peter, "and why did you not tell us before?"

"I did not know myself Pa, it is new to me…" said Robert.

"I only found out this afternoon", said Anya, "I did not want to worry you in case of a false alarm; I wanted to keep it a surprise until I was certain, and now here I am, two weeks pregnant".

Robert took her in his arms and kissed her tenderly.

"From now on there will be no more flying for you darling…"

"It is too early yet, I can still work for another two months…"

"No way, I do not want you to take a chance with the baby, it is not worth it".

"I agree with what Robert is saying" said Peter. "Let us celebrate the occasion and open a bottle of champagne; it is not very often that someone in our family gets pregnant"; and he looked in the direction of Lucy. Lucy blushed, and went to the couple congratulating and hugging them both.

"Oh, I am so happy; I am over the moon for I am going to be an aunty: I am already getting used to the idea, it is marvellous" Lucy said.

"Are you still going for your walk Lucy, would you not prefer to stay with us and celebrate?"

"No momsy, all the same; I need some fresh air and exercise".

"Will you be taking Toby with you, for it is getting late".

"No momsy, poor Toby is getting old: look at him right now; years ago, he would have run and jumped at me, as soon as he would have heard the word go: but now 'go' does not affect him at all, he would rather sit in his corner".

"I understand Toby now, for I am in the same situation as him" added Peter.

"Nonsense Peter, for you have many years ahead of you yet; especially as a grandpa".

"Yeah, yeah", shouted the rest of the family.

"Let us go with you siss, for it is getting dark outside, Anya and I will keep you company".

"No, no, there is no need for it: you stay and finish your meal and enjoy the celebration. I need to be by myself right now and reflect on what I have achieved in my life up to now".

"That is really heavy stuff Lucy, just enjoy life".

Emily seemed worried and looked at Peter for moral support. he nodded his head and told her not to worry. Lucy left the table and went to her room. She stood by the mirror and looked at her reflection: she saw a pretty young woman with a solemn look on her face. She did not seem to enjoy life as other women of her age did: she looked run down and concerned. "What am I doing with my life" thought Lucy, "what have I achieved up to now? Looking all around me, I see people doing their best to protect me, but where are all my friends, and boyfriends for that matter. I have spent three months in a rehabilitation clinic, and what do I have in my pocket: drugs. It is all déjà vu and I am on the verge of making the same mistake all over again. Why can I not be lucky as Anya; and find myself a reliable man to love and be loved, why? I want a family of my own and children who could call me momsy as well. When at long last is my shiny star going to glow? Am I doomed for the rest of my life to be with that man called Damian? Why, why, why, oh why". She had just finished uttering these desperate words, when she swallowed the two tablets Milly gave her that morning, as she could not resist temptation. Still looking at herself in the mirror she said: "Look at yourself Lucy, and what do you see: the fact of the matter is you are a mess, and who on earth would want you. I am going to meet a man that I wish dead: the man who enslaved me and manipulated me for his own greed, is that what I want from life?" She kept psychoanalyzing herself, and decided to go and talk to him for the very last time, she would explain to him that she did not love him and never had as a matter of fact, and tell him to forget about her: but if he refused to let her go, then she would have to resort to an extreme procedure; and that would be to elliminate him altogether. She went to a drawer and found a pair of scissors which she put in her pocket. Would she be able to use them? she wondered; "but if he pushes me too far this time, I swear to God that I will make use of them, oh yes, for I'll never be called momsy, what's the point?". Once more she thought how foolish it was of her to try and see him again: even for the last time. What if he turned on his charms, would she be able to resist him? With all these thoughts and questions going through her mind, she changed into a pair of jeans and a jumper and looked at her watch thinking that it was eight thirty. She was expected at nine o'clock, so she had to hurry. She kissed Toby good night as he was lying comfortably on her bed, and shut the door quietly behind her and left in the dark. It was a cool evening and as she put her hands in her pockets, she realised that she had forgotten the pair of scissors; she thought of going back for them, but when she looked at her watch she noticed that it was getting too late; "never mind" she said to herself "I shall have to use my special power of persuasion, and if he still refuses to listen to the voice of reason, then I shall run away. He will not be able to catch up with me". She wondered if she would have been able to use the scissors if she was pushed to it; deep down, she was pleased to have forgotten them, for if she had missed her first strike, he would have been able to overcome her easily, for he was a very strong man and she was afraid of him.

She could see quite well in the dark, for there was a full moon and the sky was clear. She went around the woodland to be on the safe side. people were still talking about the serial rapist who had shown no mercy to his victims. She stopped for a while to admire the moon and was reflecting on how nice it would have been to be walking hand in hand with a loved one under the moonlight; but these things happen only to people in movies. While she was thinking what life might have been had she not met Damian, she arrived at his address. It was a log cabin not too big, but spacious enough for one person. What looked like the living room was lit discreetly. She was about to knock when she realised that the door was not locked; she entered and asked if anybody was there. "Hello" she repeated a bit apprehensively; she looked at the clock and it showed seven thirty only. That is funny thought Lucy, I could have sworn that I left home much later than that: the tablets I took earlier, are playing tricks on me already. She listened for a moment and thought that she heard the sound of water running in the bathroom. She opened the door and there was Damian naked under the shower. He was humming and scrubbing his body as if to get rid of some stain. How beautiful he is, thought Lucy, standing in a corner and admiring his exposed body; he was well proportioned and very proud of his muscles, even when he was showering. Damian was not an inhibited man; he used to say that since God had given him a beautiful physique, surely he ought to be proud of it and make good use of it; if not what was the use of having a nice body?

Soon Damian became aware of a presence in the room, turned around and caught Lucy's eyes in awe before him.
" How long have you been standing there Lucy?" asked Damian.
"I don't know, I seem to be in a trance…"
"How come, did you not take the tablets I sent you?"
"Oh yes, Milly gave them to me this morning…"
"And how is she doing, the dear girl?"
"You know how she is doing, for you saw her this morning…"

"You are right, I saw her this morning, but it was for a fraction of a second, just to ask her to give you the tablets. Anyway why are we talking, get undressed and come and join me instead. We have plenty of time, for I was not expecting you so soon".

"I am surprised as well for my watch is gaining…"

"Anyhow, now that you are here, come on in"

"I can't, I am feeling light headed…"

"But you took the tablets…"

"Yes, yes, I told you already, how many times do I have to repeat it?…"

"So you should be on top of the world…"

"But I am not, I think coming through the woods frightened me and made me shiver …the idea of coming across that killer, who is still at large. I wish he was caught and dealt with".

Damian gave her one of his looks that she dreaded most, and knew what it meant; for he came out of the shower and said: "let's leave the talking for later , because right now I have much more interesting things to attend to".

He did not bother to dry himself and lifted Lucy in his arms, took her to the living room and lay her on the floor; very slowly he undressed her and covered her with kisses, and possessed her there and then; Lucy was in no condition to resist Damian the beast, for some unknown reason she seemed to encourage him and want him. Gone were the vows of fighting back and trying to bring him to reason, and gone also was the idea of escaping from him and running away; for he was all over her, and she was suffocating. She wanted to scream and tell him to stop ravaging her body, but no sounds came out of her. While he was getting more aggressive towards her, she had the feeling that he was not being hostile to her only, but to all womankind.

Oh God she thought, it is happening all over again to me;

She gave up all resistance and once again she fainted. When she woke up, she was tucked in Damian's bed, and he was watching her with a question mark on his face. He was smoking and holding a glass of whisky in his hand.

"Here, have a drink and a smoke, it will do you good".

And she drank from his glass and smoked his cigarette.

"What happened to you, why did you faint?" asked Damian.

"I don't know and I cannot remember what took place".

"Can't you remember making love .."

"Do you call that making love, you son of a bitch, you do not know the meaning of it…"

"I love you Lucy, you know that I do…"

"If that is what you call love, then I won't have anything to do with it; by the way, can you tell me what kind of relations you had with your mother?"

"Why do you want to know that for? Oh no…"

"Well, when I was in therapy, we were told that most of our miseries in life came from some kind of lack of love in childhood; especially from the mother's side…"

"Is that so, what are you a kind of shrink now? you ought to stick to what you know best; and anyhow, I do not want to talk about my mother, is that clear: Drink that glass, get dressed and leave, I will let you know when I want to see you again".

"I think this is the last time that you will see me Damian, and I mean it this time…"

"We shall see."

Again and as always Lucy felt out of place after going with Damian. Something was telling her that it was not right, and they were not meant for each other, but why, she could not put her finger on: she was angry with herself at being so weak when near him and annoyed at not resisting his whims and impulses. On the way back she kept repeating to herself, that it was the very last time she would see Damian and hated herself at not resisting him; as soon as she was in his company, she was as if hypnotized and not in control of her faculties. It was like a cat and mouse game. Now the truth was facing her, she was a mouse and afraid of him. She knew that if she did not give in to all his whims, he would kill her, she had no doubts about it, and the thought frightened her: she tried not to think of it and to forget him all together. I will fight back from now on, she vowed to herself, I shall not be his sex slave anymore. With these thoughts, she arrived home depleted of all energy and went to her room where she collapsed on the bed.

Chapter 25

Next morning, everyone was rehearsing except for Milly. She was nowhere to be seen, and Linda who was in charge asked about her, but there was no reply. No one had seen her since the day before. "Maybe she is not well" said someone.

"I spoke to her yesterday, and she told me that she was having a kind of blind date..." said the dancer.

"Did she tell you that?" asked Linda.

"Yes, to put it in her own words, she was meeting her 'Adonis'"

"Her... what..."

"Her date."

"I will go and knock at her door after this session: maybe she is in bed needing help".

Later that morning, she made her way to Milly's place, knocked at the door and waited: but there was no response. She knocked again and again but there was still no answer; she called her name and looked through the windows, but there was no sign of life. "Oh well: it is too bad" said Linda. "She must have taken a day off without telling me. I shall have a word with her tomorrow". But Linda was somehow puzzled for it was not like Milly to miss a session; she was dedicated to her dancing and lived for it. Whoever she was going to meet must have been very special.

On her way back to the circus, she met Peter and still perplexed, she asked him if by any chance he had seen Milly.

"No why? was I supposed to see her to-day?" said Peter.

"No, no, Peter she has missed her session this morning and it is not like her at all; I thought that after the quarrel she had with you and Robert, you might have fired her..."

"It has nothing to do with it Linda and I know Milly, she is an exceptional dancer: I agree that we quarreled for some reason, but this did not reflect on her job. So here you are, you have got your answer Linda? I did not see her and did not fire her, maybe she was fed up and left on her own accord".

"Milly would not do such a thing, she would not run away, for she loved the circus" said Linda.

"Don't let it worry you too much, wait till tomorrow, I am sure she will be back with a good excuse".

"You are right Peter, my problem is that I worry too much about my people for no reason whatsoever; I love them too much".

Peter put his arms around her shoulders to give her more confidence and said "I am sure she will reappear tomorrow with a plausible excuse; so stop fretting now, there". When Peter arrived home, he asked Robert if he had seen Milly that day.

" No, Pa, and I don't think that I want to see her either, she is a wicked little madam. And you Lucy did you bump into her to-day? or are you still avoiding each other after the row you had"

"No", said Lucy, "not at all Peter, actually it did not come to my mind to look for her or to avoid her for that matter. I do not like her, that is all".

"Let us have some tea and let's forget about that girl, Shall we?"

"You are right as always Emily, let's have some tea".

Again, Milly did not appear for rehearsal the next day, and Linda was worried. "What if she had had some kind of an accident, or was maybe lying in hospital, how am I going to find out?"

"We ought to call the hospital or the police station…", said a dancer.

"Don't you think it is a bit premature for us to be worried so much? What if she met somebody and is spending a week with him" said a colleague.

"Yeah" said the rest of the team, "let's give her a few more days she is surely enjoying herself".

Around eleven o'clock, Robert came out of his office excited and out of breath; he rang a bell he was holding to attract the attention of everyone, they all stopped working and surrounded Robert to find out what was all the fuss about. Peter joined in, for he was curious as well. "My friends" said Robert, "come nearer for I have an excellent announcement to make: it involves everyone of us".

"What is it?" shouted the crowd.

"I have good news for all of us; I have just received confirmation of a contract, we are going to work in San Fransisco for a very long while. We will leave in ten days time; that will give us ample time to prepare - what do you think of that?.

"Yeah" cheered the crowd, "well done Robert; you have outdone yourself this time. Let us buy you a drink after the show".

"Yes, you are all invited for a glass of wine to-night, we all deserve it : so we shall meet outside my place".

They were all delighted and congratulated each other. They were all talking together, when Linda climbed on a bench and asked to be heard. "Has anyone of you seen Milly, for the last two days?" "She has disappeared and has not attended her sessions; have you seen or heard of her whereabouts?"
Everyone seemed puzzled by her disappearance but no one could remember seeing her lately or talking to her for that matter.

For the next few hours they were excited at the prospect of moving to San Francisco and it remained the subject of conversation for the rest of the day. The excitement could be felt all around. Linda kept pestering Peter about Milly's disapearance, so he decided to call the police. Ironically, it was the same inspector "Brian Donell" who was assigned to the case. He was the one who dealt with Lucy's rape, and he now felt ill at ease for being picked up to handle Milly's disappearance. Until now they had not come close to apprehending the serial rapist. The circus never forgave the inspector for failing to catch the killer: so when he showed up at the circus, he expected to be given the cold shoulder. He knew from the start that it would not be an easy assignment. As soon as he arrived he was surrounded by a hostile crowd.

"Who can remember seeing Milly last?"

"Well, the last time I saw her, was at the rehearsal and that was five days ago".

"And who are you?"

"I am in charge of the dancing team, and Milly was one of my best dancers who never ever missed a session."

"How did she seem to you when you saw her last, was she worried or as usual?"

" She had a big argument with Robert" muttered a timid voice at the back.

"Oh", said Linda, "it was nothing really…"

"She was pushed on the floor" said the voice.

"Do you mean that she was assaulted by Robert?" asked the inspector.

"I would not put it in that context, it was rather a misunderstanding", said Linda.

"She spoke to me before her disappearance" said a dancer.

"Can you remember what it was all about?" asked the Inspector.

"She was going to meet her Adonis; that was the right word…"

"To meet who?.."

-"In other words, she had a kind of blind date", said a dancer.

"Any idea who it was and where they were meeting?"

"Not at all, she was very secretive:"

"Thank you for telling us all that, we might have a lead to follow, but first we must find out who that stranger was". He sent one of his men to his office to report the involvement of a stranger in the case. Meanwhile he asked Linda where he could find Robert.

"He is at his office, I will go and get him…."

"Will someone go with one of my men and show him where Milly lives".

"I will go, she was a friend".

"Did you take everything down sergeant?"

"Yes, every single word up to now".

"Take their names as well, for I want a statement from those who saw her last".

Meanwhile, Linda returned chatting with Robert.

"I hear that you want to see me inspector, what about?"

"I understand that you had a quarrel with Milly before her disappearance, can you elaborate on it?"

"Of course inspector, I had a row with Milly, but it has nothing to do with her vanishing, and it was at least ten days before".

"What was the quarrel about?"

"Well", said Robert, "the night before, she had a quarrel or a fight if you prefer with my sister Lucy; it was a vicious one on top of that; so the next morning, I came to warn her about it, and she became abusive, so I lost my temper and pushed her and she fell".

"By the way, you mentioned your sister Lucy, I remember her quite well, how is she doing now"

"Well", said Robert, "she has healed from her ordeal if that's what you mean".

"By the way, I understand that you have threatened to kill Milly: is that correct?"

"He did not mean it literally inspector", said Anya, "it was a matter of speech and in the heat of the moment; surely, that does not qualify him as a murderer. If it did, we have all some time in our life time lost our temper and threatened somebody: so we are all murderers".

"And who are you if I may ask? You seem very intelligent".

"She is my wife Anya", said Robert.

"Congratulations are in order Robert; if one day I should need a lawyer, I will definitely ask for your help Anya…"

"And you will definitely get it inspector".
Robert gave her a hug and a kiss.
"So where were we?" asked the inspector.
"Well, said Robert, I told Milly that I would kill her if she harmed my sister again: between you and me, I do not think that I could have done it. It was nothing but hot air; that is all; you know inspector how it is when one gets mad".
"Yes I understand" said the inspector; "it could happen to an angel". Brian Donell was treading cautiously, for he remembered the experience he had with Danny years ago, and how it ended in tragedy. Surely enough he was not prepared to make the same mistake again. He could still remember how hurt were Lucy and Robert, and how sorry he was for listening to that old woman.
"I would like to hear from Lucy, her side of the story, if that is possible; may be she could enlighten us somehow".

Lucy who was not far away and heard everything that had been said, came forward and confirmed what Robert voiced beforehand. Sally, who was a dancer as well, came to Lucy and said:
" I saw you talking to Milly that same day when she disappeared"…
"Oh that", said Lucy, "it was nothing at all…"
"When was that Lucy, can you elaborate on it?" said Brian.
Lucy seemed a bit nervous now.
"Well, it was… it was nothing inspector, nothing worth mentioning I assure you…"
"I would still like to hear it from you, everything can help find Milly".
"Well, it was like that: she just wanted to make amends and be my friend all over again".
"Are you sure Lucy?" said Sally, "for when you came down the rope, I saw Milly giving you some kind of a note".
"Shush Sally, you do not know what you are saying…"
"But I swear that I saw Milly giving you something…"

"So what if she gave me a note of apology, she thought I would not listen to her: are you satisfied now? That is all what it was".

But the inspector was not convinced, for he could smell a rat; and surely enough, Lucy was hiding something.

"I think that you and I Lucy should have a private talk; is there some place where we could go?"

Peter who was listening quietly, came forward and told them to use the office.

"I will come with you to give Lucy more confidence".

"So will I" said Emily who had kept quiet up to now. "I want to be with my child as well, and I want to know what is she accused of:"

"We shall all come" shouted the crowd…

"I am afraid that will be out of the question right now. I just want to clear up a few points with Lucy, nothing serious".

"I shall come as well" said Robert.

"Let's have the whole family, it is fine by me" said Brian.

They all headed for the office, leaving the rest of the crowd pondering the issue. Emily prepared some coffee and offered some to the inspector.

"Milk and sugar inspector?" asked Emily.

"Just sugar Emily, thank you", said the inspector.

"It is true that Milly and I had a row" said Lucy.

"Can you tell me what it was all about?" asked the inspector.

"It was about a boy friend, it was really silly, you know women stuff, it is not really worth mentioning" said Lucy.

"Let me be the judge of it; it has been said before, that you were given a note, is that correct? and what was it all about? can you remember?"

Lucy was getting agitated by now and Robert noticed the change.

"What is the matter siss, we have nothing to hide, tell the inspector every thing he wants to know, for you have done nothing wrong", said Robert. "Well, well," said Lucy "it is like this", but she could not finish her sentence, for her emotions were too great and she broke into tears and cries and turned to Emily for comfort. Emily rushed to her and gave her a cuddle as if she was a baby.

"Hush, hush, my little lamb, calm down now, no one wants to hurt you; no need for all these tears" but Lucy's tears turned into tremors and she had to be laid on the couch, while Robert and Anya tried to calm her. Brian Donell was sipping his coffee somehow feeling uncomfortable with what Lucy was going through. He was trying to understand what was bothering her, and why she was having convulsions; was she taking drugs? Quietly and discreetly he whispered to Peter, asking him whether Lucy was on drugs:

"She was some time ago", said Peter, "but has been detoxified in a clinic for a few months".

"I am afraid to say", said the inspector, "that in my opinion,, she has had a relapse; she is showing all the symptoms".

"I hope you are wrong, for we have a circus to run", said Peter. Brian Donell did not reply; he was wondering if Lucy was involved in something and was hiding the truth. Did she know where Milly was? Was she hiding the whereabouts of Milly, if so, for what purpose? No, he must be wrong , it did not make sense. Lucy was getting calmer now, sat down and accepted a cigarette offered by the inspector: her hands were still shaking while she managed to take a few puffs; this seemed to have a calming effect on her".

"I am sorry Lucy if I have upset you, but it is my job to ask questions. Believe me that sometimes I hate myself for distressing nice people like you, especially after all you have been through: but I have a job to do, you can understand that, can't you?"

Lucy acknowledged by nodding her head: she was still smoking and looking haggard.

"Take your time, and let me know if you can carry on", said the inspector. "Here is a glass of water" said Emily. "Try to calm down now and see if you can answer some questions, unless you prefer to leave it for some other time: I am sure that the inspector here would not object".

"Not at all, as a matter of fact, I have urgent business to attend to".
And he looked at his watch; "good gracious me, is that the time? I
better leave now".

"Here is my card, give me a call whenever you can remember
something".

"Thank you inspector", said Lucy, and she took the card, glanced at
it and put it in her pocket.

      The inspector and his men left, and soon everything went
back to normal. That night Lucy and the family went early to bed:
Emily was baffled: Why, would she have something to do with
Milly's disappearance? not her little Lucy, she was harmless, she
would vouch for it: my little girl cannot be involved in any kind of
trouble, I would swear on the bible. Lucy is a kind and sweet person
and would not mix with wicked people. She had to protect her,
especially now that she is so vulnerable. Did not Danny, her only
son die to protect Lucy? She went to her room and knocked at her
door.

"May I come in Lucy?" asked Emily.

"Yes momsy, please do".

"How do you feel sweetheart; anything I can do to help? Do you
want to talk?"

"Please momsy, do not worry too much about me, and I am ever
so sorry to have caused you so much trouble in my whole life; I
don't know what is happening to me right now; it is as if I am
riding a storm and have not got a single notion how to get out of it.
I promise that first thing tomorrow morning, I shall go and see the
inspector and put everything in order; and I promise that you will
be proud of me as before".

"Darling Lucy, I am and always will be proud of you whatever the
circumstances; life is like a roller coaster, you have to enjoy the
'ups', and accept the 'downs'. Once you know how to do it, then life

turn into a dream.

"Will you show me how momsy, and always be here for me?"

"That is what a mother is for, darling Lucy: so now go to sleep and don't fret about it anymore" she kissed her and tucked her in.

"Good night momsy, I am proud to have you as my mother".

Emily left the room leaving the door ajar and wiping her eyes.

Chapter 26

Next day Lucy rang Brian Donell and made an appointment to go and see him.

"Come any time this morning Lucy, for I shall not leave the office till after lunch".

Lucy arrived just after ten o'clock and parked her car just outside his office. She never noticed a grey mercedes sports car drawing next to hers a minute later.

"Would you like some coffee Lucy?" asked the inspector.

"Oh yes please inspector".

Brian Donell poured her a mug of coffee and asked her if she took milk and sugar: "neither" came the answer.

"Well now Lucy, what can you remember?"

"Well inspector, I could not tell you everything yesterday in front of my folks…"

"I would have sworn that it was the case, but now, there is only the two of us; tell me everything you know".

"What I am going to tell you would have upset them enormously; they worry so much about me, especially my dear brother who has decided to protect me against the whole world if he had to. That is why inspector, what I am going to tell you now, will be confidential".

"I promise you Lucy that whatever you tell me right now, will stay our secret. Cross my heart. And hope to die" added Lucy with a smile.

"To my family, I am still their little Lucy: especially after the rape ordeal; they are trying very hard to protect me. I have the feeling of suffocating, especially with my dear Robert who is always around; he is my rock, I know, and I always come to him whenever I am in trouble. The inspector poured himself some more coffee and sat across the desk facing Lucy and said: "now tell me in your own words what happened, take your time and try to remember everything". And Lucy related word by word everything that took place between Milly, Damian and herself. She described in detail her argument with Milly, when she was found in bed with her boyfriend, and the punch up that followed. The next day, when Robert saw my face, he caused the incident at the circus and to protect me, threatened to kill Milly; but of course, it was only words on the spur of the moment. Robert is too sweet to do anything of the sort". She also told the inspector about the punch up between Peter and Damian.

"Why, what happened then".

"Well, in the heat of the moment, Milly told Peter how Damian was providing me with drugs…"

"Is that correct?"

"I am afraid so inspector", and she turned her eyes away.

"So Peter went into a fury, and as soon as he saw Damian, he punched him in the face and fired him on the spot".

While relating all this, Lucy's face turned pale, and the inspector noticed it;

"now calm down Lucy, you are not here because of the drugs. Let us carry on about Milly".

"well, after the row with Robert Milly went around apologizing to everybody".

"Why would she do that?" asked the inspector.

"Because she felt guilty at telling Peter about the drugs. Knowing that it would create trouble between my family and I, and she was genuinely sorry".

"Now, tell me about the note, Milly gave you the next morning, what was it about?"

"You might find it hard to believe it inspector, but I am such a stupid cow…"

"There, there steady on Lucy, you are not being judged here…"

"Well it is true, Milly gave me a note from Damian…"

"After all the problems he caused …"

"Well it is hard to believe, but after all this, he still wanted to see me that evening…"

"I wonder why Milly did not object to it; it does not make sense…"

"You do not know Damian, for he can be very persuasive, especially with women. So Damian made it clear that I come to see him that evening: and to make it easy on me, he put two tablets in the envelope".

"What were those tablets for?"

"They were drugs as a matter of fact, he said it would relax me".

"And did you take them?"

"I am afraid so…"

"How could you, you have just left the clinic, and what about your responsibilities to the circus? if Peter knew that, he would ground you, you are a danger to yourself and to your partners. What was the tablet called?"

"I know all that, don't I know it; don't you think that I hate myself for what I am doing to my family? they are so good to me, and look how I am repaying them; it was a one off, and I swear that it will not happen again".

"I hope so, for your own sake".

"Yes, yes, yes, I am not only stupid, but naïve as well; it took me no more than three months after my rehabilitation, and for Damian to reappear on the scene, for me to go back to my old habit…"

And she started crying…

"All right, all right now, relax will you; no one is judging you" and he gave her a tissue; "I am sorry, stop crying. Listen Luce, I am starving, let me take you to a coffee bar: what would you say to a bite to eat?

"O. K. inspector, but I am sorry that you think I am a spoilt brat and…"

"Stop calling me inspector, just Brian or Bri for you. I have known you for such a long time now, although in very bad circumstances, but I think that after all, we can call each other by our Christian names".

"Fine Brian, thank you."

They left the building and walked to the coffee bar across the road, where he ordered sandwiches and coffees. They never noticed the grey mercedes sport car pulling out and racing away. While eating her sandwich, Lucy added; " you have to understand Brian, that to me, Damian is overwhelmingly powerful, physically and mentally, and that he dominates me whenever I come across him. I do not love him or like him for that matter. I would say that I rather hate him for what he is doing to me, especially when he makes love to me: it is as if…as if…"

"What is it Lucy, as if what?"

"I cannot tell you, it seems so ridiculous…"

"Well Lucy try me, what seems so ridiculous?"

"Well Brian, it is like this …you see…"

"Go on Lucy, go on"

"Well, it is like this: when he makes love to me, he is like a beast, he does not make love in the real sense of the word, but he wants to possess me and dominates me, as if I were his slave and not a human being: it is as if he hates me for being a woman: every time that he takes me, I get the feeling of being raped all over again, and there is nothing that I can do to stop it or avoid it: and what makes it worse, it takes me back to the time when I was really raped: does that makes sense to you Brian? Do I enjoy being raped or am I a freak of nature: and I have to live with it. What have I done to deserve it?"

"There, there, Lucy: stop putting yourself down, and he frowned as if to reprimand her".

"Do you want to hear the worst…"

"What is it this time?.."

"Well Brian, when I go with Damian, I know in advance that he is going to violate me: and it is as if I welcome it in a sense I must be sick".

"That is nonsense, and you know it."

"Not at all, it is my punishment for being raped in the first place when I was a teenager. I must have been a bad girl then".

"It was not your fault Lucy, do not forget that you could have been murdered as well, was it not for your dog Toby. So how can you talk that way? Enough of self pity and pull yourself together".

"I know that you are right, but it is a psychological hurdle that I have to overcome myself".

"That Damian, does he sell you the drugs?"

"No, he offers it freely."

"So, he does not force you…"

"Not at all, but he just has to click his fingers and ask for sex, for me to drop everything and run to him it is as if I am under a spell of some sort…"

"You do not believe this hogwash, do you? You are like any other healthy woman who wants to be loved: but your time has not come yet. It is natural, and you have to be patient."

Lucy looked at him without response.

"Do you know where he lives?"

"Oh yes, I could take you there whenever you want me to."

"Not for the moment, there is nothing against him: he is within the law; but if he forces himself on you without your consent, then I will make an arrest; but for the moment, just let me have his address. I shall have to bring some of my men if I decide to take a warrant and pick him up, he could turn nasty. One more thing before we finish…"

"What is it Brian?"

"I have a friend who specializes in cases like yours, would you like me to have a word with him?"

"No thank you, I do not need a shrink: I will have to fight my way out all by myself: by the way Brian, I do not know what you are doing in the forces, you would have made a good psychoanalyst…"
"Actually, I was trained as such, but I was attracted to the crime side of life. That will be the end of our conversation to-day Lucy: you still have my card, so call me anytime, and I mean any time that you need me, day or night".
"Thank you Brian, I shall do exactly that: I promise. And she left feeling light and confident."
"How could I have told a stranger my deepest feelings" thought Lucy. "What is going to happen to Damian now, would he be caught and sent away? Would it be my fault? And what would he do to her if he knew that she spoke to Brian about him?" She kept asking herself questions, while driving her way home.

When Emily saw her state of anguish she was in, she asked her if everything went all right with the inspector.
"It is all right momsy, please do not fuss too much about me, for I told the inspector everything he wanted to know. He is definitely in the picture now. I have answered all his questions, but some of them really upset me and reminded me of the rape. I do not think that I will ever forget it, and that the real Lucy has gone for ever."
"We all love the Lucy we see right now darling".
"Did you know that his name is Brian? and that he trained as a psychoanalyst?"
"Oh, it is Brian now…"
"Oh momsy stop teasing me, and she came to Emily and curled up and cowered her head in her bosom".

Chapter 27

The circus was preparing to move to San Francisco and it was getting hectic and exciting, Milly was not seen again, and became just a memory. It did not matter much now , for they were too busy organizing the trip. She was replaced by a newcomer whose name was Sandra. The trip went ahead as planned and before schedule; they left their home base eager and excited. They stopped at the outskirts of San Francisco next to a field lined up with beautiful trees. A few metres away, there was a wood with a spring cutting through: the view was beautiful and romantic, and attracted many young lovers who came to relax and unwind in this beauty spot.

Lucy heard from the inspector that Damian had moved from his apartment the same day they had their talk:
"What a coincidence" said Lucy.
"Have you settled in your new place yet".
"Not yet", said Lucy, "we have just arrived."
"Have you still got my card?", said the inspector, "don't forget to call me if you need my help".
"I will not hesitate Brian, I promise. I must go now". And she hung up.

Sandra, the new dancer who replaced Milly, befriended Lucy and they started going for a jog every morning across the wood, followed by Toby who was getting old and trailed behind the two girls. Lucy tried to get Anya to join in, but she was getting big now and unable to run anymore. One morning, they left a bit earlier than usual, and Toby was feeling unwell, but still managed to follow Lucy and Sandra in their run, but he was dragging a long way behind.

"I think that Toby would have preferred to stay at home this morning".

"Yes, I noticed that yesterday, he seems to be under the weather lately. Something seems to bother him".

While talking about him and waiting to cross the road, Toby arrived and sat on the edge of the road. Thinking that he was following them, they crossed the road and as soon as they reached the other side, they heard the screeching of tyres and a car stopping abruptly with a bump behind them. Toby yelped for a second and lay on his side, under the wheel. Lucy heard Toby crying, but when she turned her head, she went white as a ghost. Both girls rushed back, and there was Toby lying under the bonnet of a car; he was inert. The driver of the car who looked upset came out to see if he could be of any help, but realised that it was too late; he saw the girls trying to revive him; one of them was crying and repeating: "Toby, get up, please get up now". Tears were flowing down her cheeks, and her companion was trying to comfort her.

"I don't know how it happened" said the driver in a very sombre mood; " I could have sworn that the road was clear, I do not know where the dog came from, he just ran under the car, oh God: what have I done."

Lucy looked at him prepared to shout, when their eyes met and locked: he looked so pale and upset that she calmed down. He was looking at her with amazement, as if seeing an old acquaintance. He had the feeling of having seen her before, but where or when? he could not tell. Her face was so familiar but he still could not place her; he could not remember meeting her beforehand. Was she one of his patients? As for Lucy, her heart melted when she saw the state of mind the driver was in. He was tall and handsome with black hair, black eyes soft and sweet; he gazed at her with such intensity that her anger disappeared and she felt disarmed. She knew the accident was meant to happen and it was somehow part of her destiny.

"My name is Henry" said the stranger, "holding her hands and still staring at her, captivated by her looks. "I am Lucy" she replied and this is my friend Sandra, and the dog was Toby, my companion in life.

"Hi Henry, I am sorry that we meet in such circumstances" said Sandra.

"I am pleased to meet you as well", and he was still looking at Lucy and still holding her hand.

"Now that we have been introduced to each other, do you think Henry that I can have my hand back?"

"Oh, hilarious, I am so sorry, let me put your dog in the car, and take you home".

"Thank you Henry, we accept the offer."

And they all climbed in Henry's car with Toby's body resting on Lucy's lap.

"Don't feel too guilty about the accident Henry, it was meant to happen; it is not your fault".

"Actually Toby was under the weather this morning and did not feel like jogging with us; as you can see, the fact of the matter is, it was destiny".

"You are all being kind to me to make me feel better, and I thank you for it. By the way, I am a surgeon; actually I specialize in brain surgery, and my main branch is the neuro-psychiatric side of it. Actually, I was on my way to an operation".

"I am sorry if we held you up…"

"Not at all, one of my colleagues will have to do it and he picked up his mobile and told the hospital about the accident".

"What do you do young ladies"

"We belong to a circus, I am a dancer and my friend here is a flying trapeze artist; the circus is a mile away from here".

"Wow, I am impressed; would you mind if I came one day and watch you perform?"

"Of course you can come Henry; our show starts every evening at seven o'clock. We also have a matinee at week-ends, so I look forward to seeing you". For some unknown reason Lucy did not know why she said it: she felt attracted to him like a magnet and could not take her eyes off him. Every time he looked at her, she felt good.

When he dropped them at the entry of the circus, once again Henry took her hand in his and kept staring at her.

"Once again Henry, give me back my hand I cannot get out of the car without it, and I need it for work as well"; and she gave him her sweetest smile; Sandra was smiling as well.

"I am so sorry Lucy, but deep down I do not want to let you go. I have the impression of having known you for ages, long, long time ago".

"Not to my knowledge Henry", said Lucy, "unless it was in another dimension: I don't think that I could have forgotten your face so soon".

She blushed and ran away carrying Toby.

They buried Toby at the foot of a beautiful tree at the back of their garden; although it was a sad day, Lucy felt that the sadness of Toby's death was replaced by a kind of floating feeling. She could not wait to find out whether Henry would turn up that evening for the show. She was not her usual self, and Peter who noticed it first said: "You seem to be in a cloud my Lucy, try to snap out of it, for the show will start very soon: I am very sorry for what happened to Toby, he has been your friend for a very long time now" and he gave her a hug. That evening, Lucy did not perform in her usual way; she was distracted by the thought of Henry: from where she stood, she looked at the crowd down below searching for the stranger who had mesmerized her, and with just one of his looks made all her worries vanish. But he was nowhere to be seen.

Robert, who was flying with her, noticed the change in her

face and asked: "What is it Lucy, you seem transformed, tell me what has taken place since this morning, for it looks like love to me."

"There is nothing to worry about Robert: to the contrary all my troubles are over and I feel so happy to be alive right now.

"I think siss that you have been stung by the bug of love: look at you, I have not seen you so happy for a very long time".

Lucy was not listening, for she was humming a happy tune to the surprise of Robert.

The show went on, but Lucy's heart was not in it. After the show she walked among the crowd, looking for Henry, but no, the stranger was definitely missing: her heart sank, and she felt abandoned, as if part of her was gone. "May be he was just joking then he said that he would come to watch the show, and I believed every word that he said: anyway, why would a brain surgeon want to come and watch a circus? He must have other things to worry about. Surely, he had no time for such futilities".

Her happiness had vanished suddenly and she felt lonely. She confided in Sandra:

"Maybe he has been prevented from coming due to an emergency, who knows? Remember that he is a surgeon. and they do not grow on trees: he must be very busy indeed: don't worry, he will call".

Lucy went home sad and sullen, and all that evening she hardly spoke.

"Now Lucy what happened to your good mood? Robert was praising you by telling us about a transformation, why the sudden change, were you expecting your love one to turn up? Would you like to talk about it?"

"Emily", said Peter, "do you have to tease the poor girl, can't you see she is in love?"

"Is that right Lucy, are you in love?"

Lucy looked at her momsy with despair, her eyes filled with tears, she got up and snuggled in Emily's arms.

"Oh momsy, if you only knew how lonely I feel".

"There, there sweetheart, what are all these tears for? Remember that you have got us; we shall always be here for you; don't you ever forget it.

Next morning a delivery boy brought a large bouquet of pink roses, meant for Lucy and she had to sign for it. She read the card that said how sorry Henry was for not turning up for her show, but he was detained at the last moment by an emergency; there had been some unforeseen complications during an operation, and he had to stay longer than expected. He was used to it, for that was part of his job; he was sure to make it for the next day. Lucy screamed with delight, Emily rushed to see what was the commotion all about, and when she saw the flowers and her daughter's face, she could not but rejoice.

"It is Henry momsy, he has not forgotten me, he is coming to-night, and he is ever so sorry at missing the show last night. Here, read the card for yourself".

Emily was over the moon for her little girl. In one day, her mood was transformed from icy cold to boiling hot: she got hold of Lucy and pressed her so hard against her , that the poor girl nearly suffocated.

That evening, standing on top of her platform, Lucy was watching Henry sitting in the front row and looking at her, full of admiration. He had a box on his lap and wondered what it was: was it an present for her? she was getting excited and could not stand still. She gave an outstanding performance to the delight of an appreciative and cheering audience. When she came down, she ran to Henry and gave him a long and lingering kiss, and could not hide her joy at seeing him. She held his arm so tight as to make sure that he would not run away. Henry seemed pleased at the welcome he received. They went outside the tent, and he placed the box on the floor and took Lucy in his arms cuddling her and kissing her. It seemed so natural to kiss this beautiful young girl, as if he had done it many times before; but where? He could not remember. As to Lucy, she enjoyed being caressed and embraced by the man whom she already knew as hers; she could feel it in her bones that they were an item, and no one would ever dare to separate them. Funny enough, the same kind of feeling was pushing Henry towards her; he could not resist her charms or take his eyes away from her. Lucy wanted him badly and waited for him to make a move when suddenly she heard a dog barking.

"Is that you Toby? But it can not be, for you are dead"

"I have a surprise for you darling, it is in the box…"

"Tell me what it is…"

"Open it and find out for yourself".

Lucy managed to lift the box which was quite heavy, heard a cry and a scratch, she quickly opened it, and there was a collier puppy jumping at her and licking her face.

"He likes you already; it does not surprise me".

"Oh Henry, what a lovely thought, it will replace my Toby, they look so alike, but this one is much younger".

Henry went back home with Lucy where he was introduced to the family; they all seemed to like him. She also showed them her new puppy.

"Will you call your puppy a new name or Toby?"

"No, Toby was my childhood companion, and I want his name to carry on. My new friend here is a surgeon".

"We are all pleased to make your acquaintance Henry, and from now on you are part of our family".

"And my daughter's friend is always welcome in this house."

"Thank you maam, I am glad to meet you and the rest of the family".

They had coffee, while Lucy was getting ready to go out with Henry.

"Have a good time you two, and please Henry don't bring her back too late".

"Do not worry Emily, she is in good hands, and I shall take good care of her, that is a promise".

Henry drove Lucy to his hotel where he was well known, as he spent most of his spare time there, especially when Holly was away on tour. They went to the restaurant and ordered champagne to celebrate their new friendship: half way through the dinner, he asked Lucy for a dance as they were playing his favourite tune; "You are always on my mind". They were so close to each other that they gave the impression of floating in the air.

As for Henry, it felt so natural holding Lucy so close to his heart, for he must have been with her all his life, not knowing it, she was so similar to Holly, that they complemented each other: to him, Holly and Lucy were but one soul with two different personalities; they were both his soul mate in two different bodies; that was why he did not feel guilty dancing with Lucy. It was as if he was dancing with Holly as well: he was pleased to know that he was not cheating on either of them. His life was near complete.

Lucy told Henry of her childhood, the agony of being raped and the death of her brother who died soon after, and the vacuum he left behind. She also told him of her unhappy liaison with Damian who enslaved her for his selfish needs, and how she could not get away from him mentally. While telling him the story of her life, he never took his eyes off her. He was holding her so tight against him, that he could hear the beating of her heart. "Listen Henry", said Lucy, "if you ease up your hold on me, I promise not to run away".

"Oh, how selfish of me I want you all to myself", and he kissed her tenderly. He was hypnotized by her personality which was so like Holly's and which he was at a loss to explain. It was as if he was married to two women who were but one; "it does not make sense" thought Henry; but that is how he felt, and he did not need to know any more.

After leaving the hotel he drove her to the outskirts of the town, to a peaceful beauty spot .The weather was mild and a myriad of stars were covering the sky. He put his arms around her and gave her a long and passionate kiss: she did not look surprised and returned his kisses. She knew how he felt about her, and his sentiments were reciprocated. At long last she felt that destiny was honouring her after so much suffering; and it was about time as well. It was such a deep feeling, she would have loved to linger a bit longer; she was prepared to lay her life down for him. They stayed in each other arms for a very long time until Henry felt strong enough to say: "I have something to tell you".
"Can't it wait, right now I am so happy to be just in your arms, that nothing else matters to me".

Henry felt tears welling up, and with an effort said: "What I have to say is very important and cannot wait".
"What could be so important that cannot wait? Don't you love me anymore?"
"Oh Lucy, if you only knew how much I love you, you would not believe it: now promise me not to get upset at what I have to say…"
"I promise not to get upset; there, are you satisfied now, and will you tell me what it is".
"And you will never stop loving me…"
"I will do anything for you Henry; I would walk the Sahara desert to find you if you were lost: are you satisfied now?"
"Oh my darling Lucy, what I have to say might be painful to you,

and you promised that you won't leave me". Lucy was mystified by his attitude, she sat up and looked at him.
"You want to break it up, is that it?…"
"No, not at all, on the contrary…"
"So for God's sake, tell me what is troubling you".
"I am married Lucy, I love my wife and I love you as well from the first time I laid my eyes on you: you two are so alike, that it is as if you were an extension of each other; I cannot explain it, but I love you both the same, I swear".

Lucy could not utter a single word, she was so confused by his revelation; for a moment, she had thought that at long last she had found the man of her dreams and hoped to spend their life together; but destiny had decided otherwise, and that it was not to be. It took just one sentence to destroy her illusion and a fraction of a second: how cruel life could be; she decided that in no circumstances would she be his second best.
"Take me home please, I want to go home now" and she started to cry quietly. Not a word was spoken on the way home, and Henry was despairing at seeing her sobbing, and he could not comfort her as she would not let him touch her. She froze in her seat looking like a lost soul, and nothing he could say would repair the damage; it was too late; gone were his dreams about Lucy and he felt the loss. As they arrived home, he had no time to get out and open her door, for she jumped out and ran to the door hiding her desperation.
"I love you Lucy", said the neuro-surgeon, "please forgive me for I did not mean to hurt you, I swear". But Lucy would not hear of it; she opened the door to her home and ran to her room and threw herself on the bed, and burst into uncontrollable cries. Little Toby who came to cheer her up by licking her face was rejected gently and pushed on the floor.

When she woke up, she was in an awful state and could not

tell how long she had been crying for ; she looked and felt awful, her hair was dishevelled and her eyes were red and puffed. She stared at the clock and it showed only four in the morning; again she looked at herself in the mirror and said loudly; " I thought he was my soul mate, why then is he married? Why could he not have waited for me?" She had so many questions but no answers. She took a cold shower and by early morning was ready to go for her training. Emily who was already up and preparing the breakfast, was surprised to see her up so early.

"Sit down and I shall get your breakfast in a minute: I suppose that with all the excitement of last night, you could not sleep; by the way, how did it go the two of you?"… She had hardly finished her sentence whenLucy burst into tears all over again.

"Oh my Lord, what have I done now to upset you, what have I said, what is it?"

Lucy as usual when she was upset, found refuge in her momsy's arms. She told Emily of the lovely time they had, and how it was spoilt by Henry's confession that he was already married.

"He said that he loved his wife as much as he loved me; what kind of a man can love two women the same? he should be put in prison just for his thoughts".

"There, there, Lucy don't judge him so harshly, at least he was honest with you and told you the truth before any more complications developed between you two; so be thankful he did not hide it from you. You could have been hurt much more than that later. That shows he is an honest man. Now just try to forget him, and remind yourself that there are plenty more fish in the sea waiting to be caught. One day you too, will find the right man like my Peter".

Lucy wiped away her tears and kissed her, thanking her mom for being so wise.

Chapter 28

When Lucy arrived for her training, the whole circus was in commotion, some artists were even crying:

"Sandra, what is happening, why all this confusion?"

"Don't you know", said Sandra, "haven't you heard?"

"Heard what?", said Lucy, "please tell me".

"They found a decomposed body in San-Diego, not too far away from our circus, and they reckon it is Milly's. The inspector is flying all the way out here to ask some questions".

"Ask questions? what for?"

"Wake up Lucy, questions about Milly's disappearance of course; what do you think: she was found raped and murdered with a black sack covering her head; there is a strong indication, that it is the work of the serial killer. It follows the same pattern..."

"Oh my God", said Lucy, "poor Milly what a way to die, I shiver just at the thought that it could have been me years ago..."

"There are rumours running around that the rapist is among us; it could be actually anyone of us, can you believe that? Everyone is being urged to be vigilant, and to report any suspicious character to the police, there might be a real threat to any of us at any moment..."

"But why can't the police catch him?"

"There is a huge police search going on right now, just look around you and you will see many strangers among us".

"Do you believe that Sandra, that it is one of us?"

As she was going away, Sandra called her back: "Wait a minute Lucy, I have something for you." And she gave her an envelope.

"Where did it come from?" asked Lucy.

"I don't know", replied Sandra, "some clown I have not seen before asked me to give it to you, he had red hair".

While taking the envelope, Lucy looked all around her and found nothing out of the ordinary; she thanked Sandra and went to a quiet corner where she opened the letter and read: "I have missed you and want to see you to-night after the show around nine o'clock; don't make me wait too long or disappoint me: here is my new address", and it was signed: your Damian. As she was going to tear the letter up, two small tablets fell on the floor, she quickly picked them up and put them in her pocket. "Who does he think he is that Damian" thought Lucy, "ordering me round to his place whenever he feels like it. I am going to put a stop to all that and give him a piece of my mind altogether. Enough is enough" and she joined the rest of her team.

A few hours later the inspector arrived and without wasting any time, started questioning people and making notes. When it was all over, he came to Lucy.

"Have you had a nightmare last night Lucy, you look like if you could do with a good rest right now".

"That is right Brian, I did not sleep at all last night."

"Why is that", said Brian, "are you feeling guilty about…"

"What do you mean by feeling guilty inspector, am I being accused of something?"

"I did not mean anything of the sort Lucy I apologise…"

"Apologies accepted Brian, no harm done".

"Now tell me Lucy", said Brian, "in our last conversation I understood that you were the last one to have seen Milly alive…"

"I don't know, may be or maybe not", said Lucy, "how can I tell?"

"She gave you an envelope the last time, did she not?"

"Yes, as I said before, it was from Damian…"

"But did she confide in you…?" asked Brian.

"Confide in me; are you kidding or what? she hated my guts Brian and I told you why already".

"After our last conversation about Damian", said Brian, "I sent two of my men to find his apartment, but it was empty as if he had been warned before hand".

"What are you insinuating Brian, that I warned him of your arrival? That is nonsense, for if I remember well, you said to me that day that you had no reason to arrest him…"

"You are right Lucy", and he gave her a smile.

"Are you still in touch with him?" said Brian.

"Everything I know about him I have told you already, and that I would call you if he ever got in touch with me; have you forgotten?"

"Oh yes, I remember, by the way I shall be at the station down town, here is my new card, please ring me anytime if something crops up".

"I will Brian, I promise".

"Be vigilant Lucy, I think that the rapist is going to strike again and soon".

That day Henry rang every single hour, and every time he was told that Lucy was busy rehearsing and that she could not take his call. One evening, it was Lucy's turn to come on stage, and when she reached her platform, she waved at the crowd and there down below and on the first row, surely enough Henry was there watching her with a bouquet of roses in his hands. Their eyes met for a fraction of a second and she quickly looked away. At the end of her act, she ran away to avoid seeing Henry. She went to her car without changing her costume and drove away. She did not want to be followed, and without thinking she drove to Damian's place; it was an apartment on the ground floor in a small block; she rang the bell and was told to push the gate and enter. She knocked at his door nervous and apprehensive wondering why she had come here and what she was doing knocking at his door; she remembered Brian's advice to be vigilant: but surely Damian was not a suspect, it could not be. "Enter" said Damian's voice. As soon as she went in, she realised that she made a mistake, but it was too late; she wanted to turn back, but Damian had already locked the door behind her.

"I did not think that you would come so soon, have you missed me Lucy?", asked Damian, he tried to kissed her but she turned away.

"Not in a million years Damian, I would not miss you."

"So what made you come so early, if it was not my charms…"

"I just wanted you to know that Milly was found dead."

"That is a pity."

"Is that all you have to say about Milly who loved you?"

"What else do you want me to say, I have got you and it is you that I love now…"

"You selfish son of a bitch, that girl has given you all her love", and she went to hit him: but Damian got hold of her wrists and forced her to sit on the bed.

"Let me go, you are hurting me", said Lucy.

"Not before I get what I want…" said Damian.

"I need to talk to you…"

"What about?"

"About us, it is finished between us and I don't want to see you or hear from you ever again; do you hear me?"

"I decide when it is over and when you can go, do I make myself clear? You are mine and you will do what I tell you to do: now take your costume off".

"No, I will not, I have just told you that it is over between us, are you dumb or plain stupid…"

Before she could finish her sentence Damian slapped her so hard that she staggered and fell on the floor: she was surprised by his unexpected reaction, felt vulnerable and frightened. She lost all that remained of her confidence and started shaking and crying.

"Nobody calls me stupid, do you hear me, nobody. Not even you Lucy".

"I am sorry, I did not mean to insult you, please calm down now. I have just come to tell you about Milly's body which was found in San-Diego not far from the circus, and that an inspector wished to question you…"

"What for, I have done nothing wrong and I know nothing…"
Damian's face had turned pale; he quickly regained his demeanour; but it was too late,for Lucy saw his face and wondered what he was afraid of, he looked so worried all of a sudden.

"Anyhow, what could the police want from me, as I said before, I know nothing about it."

"So why are you so afraid to tell them…"

"I am not afraid, why should I be?"

"They just want to ask you a few questions about Milly."

"Why me, I have done nothing wrong."

"Yes but she was your girl friend and they know it…"

"That is not true, you are my girl friend."

"I have told you already that I have never been your girl friend; I am afraid of you as you are of your mother".

"What did you say about my mother? How dare you talk about her? You know nothing about my mother".

And the expression on his face changed; he became like a baby and sought Lucy's arms to find refuge; she was surprised and did not realise what she was doing, for she put her arms around him trying to comfort him. To her complete amazement he was sobbing like a child in her arms; he was muttering something about his mother and how he would have liked to kill her. "Don't let them take me" he kept repeating again and again. Suddenly, he got up and regained his old composure. Lucy thought that she had been dreaming: He was a man with double personalities, for when she looked at him again, the new Damian had disappeared.

"Anyway, what do I know about Milly's murder, when did this happen?"

"She disappeared on the day you sent her to give me a note, do you remember?"

"But as far as I can recall, you were with me that night, have you forgotten; you came early and we went to bed that evening..." Lucy nodded, she was trying to forget that night when he forced himself on her.

"Anyhow, it has nothing to do with us right now: have you taken the tablets in the envelope?"

"Yes I did" said Lucy with a whisper, although she knew quite well she had not taken the tablets, and did not want anymore.

"Good, I am glad, now take your clothes off, we have wasted enough time".

"I don't feel like it right now, let's have a drink and talk instead".

"What is there to talk about, have we not lost enough time already? Come on and hurry up: take your clothes off, I said". Seeing that Lucy was reluctant to do so, Damian went to her and tore her shirt. He was going to do the same with her trousers when she threw herself at him with fists and kicks scratching his face and pulling his hair. At first Damian was taken aback; he was disconcerted by her reactions, but quickly responded by punching her and knocking her until she gave up; then he undressed her and threw her in the bed where once again he raped her. As usual Lucy gave up while watching her body being ravished by the demon Damian. When he had had enough, he fell asleep on top of her snoring and breathing heavily. she was disgusted with herself and feared for her life. She had the feeling that he was the serial rapist the police were hunting, but she had no proof, and somehow the real killer was too clever to elude the police for so long. She tried to move away from him, but he was too heavy for her to shift, she waited a while not knowing what to do, and as if destiny answered her prayers , Damian turned to one side giving her enough time to leap out of the bed. she got dressed as fast as she could, and ran out of the apartment.

It was still dark outside, she drove away rapidly to keep as much distance between them as possible. She stopped a few kilometres away to check whether she was being followed. But there was no sign of traffic. she looked at her watch, but it had stopped and the glass was broken. It showed two o'clock. She drove to a nearby café open all night and packed with truck drivers and ordered a coffee. she was still trembling while she drank her coffee and lit a cigarette. After a while, she calmed down and went to make a phone call. She searched for the inspector's card, but it was not in her pocket: it must have fallen out during her fight with Damian. So she rang the police station.

"I need to speak to Inspector Donell urgently" she said with a quiver in her voice.

""He is off duty right now" said the officer in charge, "do you know what time it is?"

"It is imperative that I speak to him right away; it is very urgent."

"You might catch him at home sleeping, do you want his number?"

"Yes please, but wait a minute, let me fetch a pen". She ran to the bar and asked to borrow one.

"Here you are miss", said the waitress, "you can have mine:"

"Thank you", said Lucy, "I will bring it back in a moment".

"Hi officer, I am back", and she wrote the number down on the palm of her hand, and hung up quickly to redial the inspector's number.

Brr... Brr... Brr...

"Who on earth is calling me at this time: Hi, this is inspect..."

"Inspector, this is Lucy."

"Lucy, Lucy, Lucy who?"

"Oh, come on Brian, this is Lucy from the circus. I am in dead trouble".

"Do you know what time it is , should you not be in bed?..."

"Wake up Brian, I am telling you that I am in dead trouble... in dead trouble..."

"Why? What has happened since this morning Lucy..."

Lucy was too excited and interrupted him and said: "I think I know who the serial killer is: actually I am sure of it. But you have to hurry before he disappears". The inspector jumped out of his bed and switched on the light.

"Where are you calling from?" asked Brian.

Lucy told him the name of the café.

"I think I know where it is; listen carefully, order yourself something to eat, I will be with you in less than thirty minutes, you wait for me: do you hear me?"

"Yes Brian, I hear you well but I am frightened, will you hurry up?"

"Make sure you sit near the bar where it is well lit, and also make sure that everybody can see you clearly, do you hear me?"

He hang up and got dressed quickly, then he called his partner to come and join him with some men at the café.

Twenty minutes later he parked his car by the entry and rushed inside. He found Lucy in a terrible state: her shirt was torn and she was covered with bruises all over her body and she had two black eyes. Her body was shaking like a leaf in the wind.

"What on earth happened to you Lucy and who is the son of a bitch who did that to you?

She was going to relate everything that took place that evening when he stopped abruptly and ran to the door. He thought that he had seen the face of a clown looking through the windows and staring at them: but it was all peaceful and quiet outside. When he told her about it, she grabbed his arms and started shaking worse than before. He ordered two coffees and whiskies from the waitress; as soon as they were served Lucy took her glass and gulped it down immediately. She heard the inspector say "Not so fast, take it easy young lady," and he pushed his glass towards her.

" Now I will tell you who did that to me and who beat me up so badly". And she recounted everything about that evening with

Damian.

"But you told me that you did not know where he lived".

"Please Brian forgive me for telling you a little lie…"

"Do you realise what you have done, you could have been killed like Milly; that was not very clever of you…"

"I realise that I have been very stupid indeed, and I am really sorry about the whole affair". She carried on telling him the rest of the story, when two of his colleagues walked in.

"You are just on time guys and you Lucy drive ahead of us with one of my man, and show us the way; we will follow you."

"I would rather not go if that is all right with you Brian, I need to run to momsy; here is his address."

They made sure that she drove straight back to the circus and made their way to Damian's place. When they arrived, no one answered the ansaphone; then they knocked at the door very loudly: "Open up this is the police". At long last a tenant from upstairs came down and opened the door; they rushed to Damian's apartment and banged on the door. As expected there was no sign of life inside, so they smashed the door open and went in. It was empty and whoever lived there had left in a hurry. They were joined by two officers in uniform. They searched the apartment inside and out, but found nothing unusual, until one of the officers looked under the bed and stretched his arm underneath and called: "Inspector, I think I have got something here".

"What is it?"

The officer pulled out a box very similar to that of a shoe box. The inspector opened it, and what he saw made him yell; "The son of a bitch, we have got him, at least now we know who he is;" and early tomorrow we shall have a photo of him to circulate in all the newspapers. "We also have the instrument of the crime"; and he took a black sack from the box very similar to that used to cover the victims. He also found a truncheon made of rubber and around twenty centimetres long with which the killer hit his victims from behind. "We have got him now, it is only a matter of time, before he realises that he cannot hide any longer and gives himself up". "Sergeant, will you ring headquarters and let them know about our findings and ask them to get us a warrant for the arrest of a certain Damian; he is over six foot tall, dark hair and brown eyes, deeply seated in their sockets: at least that's what Lucy informs me. Tell them as well to be cautious because he could be armed and dangerous. I am on my way to the circus to try and get a photo of him; Carry on looking for some more clues, we must catch him at any cost now, and we must not let him slip through our fingers this time. I have to rush and warn everybody at the circus to be on the lookout, as they could be in real danger".

When the inspector knocked at Lucy's home, Peter opened the door and said: "Does no one sleep anymore in this town? What is it now?", and he looked up and saw the inspector.
"Oh it is you inspector", said Peter, "you better come in, for our Lucy arrived earlier and she is in such a state right now actually. I suppose you want to question her and find out what happened".
"I was with her earlier actually", said Brian, "where is she now? I would like to see her, she has suffered a lot lately".
"Go through, the whole family is with her, they are trying to find out what exactly has happened. Meanwhile I shall make some fresh coffee".

The inspector knocked at the door and went in; a small light was on, enough to show poor Lucy in Emily's arms and shaking like a leaf. Robert and Anya were beside her wiping her face and comforting her: the doctor had arrived and given her something to quieten her".
"We did not find Damian in his apartment as expected, he must have left in a hurry, for the window was wide open. But we found something very relevant, which will incriminate him beyond any

doubt for the death of so many innocent lives. Until he is caught, I want you Lucy to be always on the look out; he could be very dangerous right now; so promise me that from now on, you will not leave this place alone. Always tell somebody where to find you, until he is behind bars".

"She promises, I will make sure of that", said Emily.

Meanwhile Peter brought some coffee and made some toast which he offered all around.

"By the way Robert could you provide me with a photo of Damian as soon as possible, I want it to appear for this evening's news flash".

"I know where to find one, said Robert, it is in a drawer at the office, I will go and fetch it for you right now. I want that son of a bitch to hang for what he has done to my siss".

"When I think that we have been employing a murderer in my circus", said Peter, "I get the shivers".

"And Lucy was right not to want him in", said Robert, "do you remember Pa?"

"I wish now that we had listened to her then", said Peter.

"And I remember how dear Toby was barking at him trying to warn us", said Robert.

Chapter 29

"You seem moody to-night Henry", said Holly, "anything the matter?"

"No, not at all, it is my work, it is getting hectic lately".

"Are you sure that you are not brooding about this business of the baby?"

"Not at all", said Henry, "as a matter of fact I think that you were right, it was really a bad idea".

"Why? I have been thinking that we could work on it soon", said Holly.

"How about our careers: are you going to give up dancing? And what about the clinic?"

"My dancing career could slow down for a while, and you could cut your hours at the clinic. I am sure that others would like some extra money darling. Well, you were right the first time so think about it, but don't leave it too late" and she kissed him.

But Henry's mind was somewhere else, preoccupied with the thought of Lucy. She had not been seen at the circus for a whole week now, and for some reason she had been replaced by another artist. He asked some of her colleagues the reason for her absence, but no one seemed to be able to give him the right answer: he seemed really worried and a few times he picked up the phone to talk to Emily, but at the last moment he changed his mind, as he did not know what her reactions would be. Most evenings he sat at the front row hoping to catch a glimpse of her, but without much success. Was she ill? or away on holiday? He wanted to tell her how his life had changed since he met her, and that nothing was the same without her. Although he had Holly, he was a special case, and needed both loves in his life. He could share his affection with both women, they were so alike that to him, they complemented each other. They were only one, so he was not cheating on either of them, how could he be? And they both represented his only love. He promised himself to knock at her door the next day, come what may. That day at seven o'clock he arrived on time for the event and to his surprise, here she was, making her appearance to the delight of the crowd. She ran towards the rope and climbed it eagerly, while everyone applauded her; Henry threw his bouquet of flowers at her feet for he could not hide his feelings towards her any longer. Lucy saw the flowers and her eyes fell on his; before starting her performance, she waved at him in such a way as to tell him that this presentation was dedicated exclusively to him only. Henry's face changed, he understood the message, stood up and blew kisses at her. Deep down he knew that his sweetheart was coming back to him. Lucy smiled at him and he never took his eyes off her for the duration of the show.

At the end of the performance and as soon as she touched the floor, instead of her usual bow to the crowd as was her habit, she ran into Henry's arms who gave her a long and tender kiss to the delight of the cheering spectators.
"Keep me in your arms darling and never let me go".
"You bet Lucy that I will never let you go, for you are mine, and mine only, and by the way I have missed you so much lately; it has been dreadful without you".
"I am yours Henry and I don't mind being your second best."
"My darling Lucy, it is not like that at all: you and Holly are so much alike in every way, that I love you and adore you both the same; so it is not a question of being second best. You two are my soul mates and the three of us are one item: can you feel that?"
"So your wife's name is Holly, I like it."
"And you two seem to have so much in common; it is as if you two have been two sisters in another world. It is beyond belief how

identical you two are. When you see her, you will know what I am talking about".

"Let's forget it right now, I want to be alone with you", said Lucy.

"After you change, I will take you to that same hotel where we danced last time. I found it so romantic being there with you and playing our tune as well".

"Which tune is that Henry?"

"The title is exactly what I feel for you right now: it is called "you are always on my mind".

"That sounds so charming; wait for me while I go and change."

While Henry was waiting in his car, a grey Mercedes sports car pulled in a few metres away: the driver wore dark glasses and a baseball hat. His eyes were fixed on Henry as if to memorise his face. Lucy came out of the house resplendent with beauty and smiling at Henry who got out to open her door and give her a big kiss at the same time.

"Take good care of my siss Henry", said Robert, "especially now."

"Don't worry Robert, I will take good care of her and protect her with my own life if I have to", and he drove away with Lucy glued to his side. She felt so happy and all the stress of the past few days seemed to have evaporated. Emily who saw them driving away, noticed a grey sport car pulling out at the same time; she thought nothing of it and soon forgot all about it.

Lucy and Henry enjoyed a lovely meal at the restaurant in the hotel; they emptied a bottle of champagne and danced to Henry's favourite tune; but most of all, they were just happy to be together. They were made for each other and Lucy at last realised that he was the man for her. Nothing would ever separate them again. Henry looked at his watch and noticed that it was past midnight.

"Please Henry, don't let it end to-night; let's stay together."

"Are you sure it is what you want".

"Oh yes, more than anything in the world; I am yours for the rest of my life: that is if you have me".

They left the restaurant and took the lift to his suite. He had been a guest of the hotel for such a long time now, that the suite was reserved for him, and him only. As soon as they found themselves alone, they fell into each other arms in a long awaited embrace: slowly and with loving care they undressed; at long last they found themselves naked in each other arms She was being caressed and cuddled like never before: she felt his kisses all along her body and his fingers exploring the outline: she was so surprised by the gentle and soft approach that she felt as if floating on a cloud, a white and warm cloud, and Henry was in it. She was so used to being handled roughly by Damian, that she was apprehensive at the beginning that he would be the same: forceful and wild. But when she realised how gentle and caring Henry was, and how refined his approach was all her inhibitions disappeared at once. His moves were so engaging, that it felt like caresses from heaven. She felt her body responding to every advance he was making, and when he took her ever so gently and slowly, she realised that Henry was not taking, but she was giving, and all of a sudden she felt, as if the gates of haven were opening under her feet and she surrendered completely and willingly to him. She had never felt that way before and knew that it was real love with him and went into a deep sleep.

She woke up hours later still in his arms; he was asleep. She looked at him surprised and with admiration; she was so accustomed to being abused and assaulted, that she had thought all men were the same, and here was a giant of a man proving her wrong; she was pleased and kissed his chest and lips until he woke up.
"How do you feel sweetheart?" asked Henry.

"I feel like I have never felt before in my entire life: I am in a beautiful dream and I do not want to wake up from it".

"I am starving, shall we have breakfast here or downstairs?"

"Oh no, let's stay here for I am so cosy in your arms".

He gave her a long kiss, then picked up the phone and ordered a big breakfast with champagne.

"Champagne", said Lucy, "at this hour of the day?"

"Yes, it is to seal our bond for ever and into eternity."

She got up to take a shower and he followed her: they teased each other under the water and again they found time to make love passionately. They left the bathroom still kissing and cuddling each other, and slipped into their dressing gowns. When they went into their living room, breakfast was awaiting them. They devoured everything that was on the table and emptied the bottle of champagne before helping themselves to coffee.

When they left the hotel, he drove her to the circus and stopped by her place. She ran in but before closing the door behind her she blew him a kiss. Henry drove away without noticing the grey Mercedes behind him.

"Where are you momsy", said Lucy, "I have so much to tell you; where are you?"

"What is it?" said Emily, coming from the kitchen.

"Momsy, I am in love with the most beautiful man in the world, he is all mine, mine and mine only, and I am all his. I am so happy; it is such a beautiful world", and she put her arms around her inviting her to a dance.

Emily was so happy for her child that they kissed and cuddled and danced like two school children.

"All right Lucy", said Emily, "all right let me go darling for I have work to do". She was out of breath; "I am very happy for you, at last you have found happiness, but who is that most beautiful man on earth?

"It is Henry momsy", said Lucy, "can't you tell?"

"But you have told me that he was married, and he loved his wife..." said Emily.

"And he loves me as well, and he has enough love for the two of us, he told me so and I do believe him; he is mine as well".

"Are you happy with this arrangement? Why do you have to complicate your life with a married man; for sooner or later you might get hurt".

"He is my soulmate momsy, why can you not be happy for me?"

"If this is what you want, so be it; I am very thrilled for you darling: but one thing he is not..."

"What's that?" said Lucy.

"Well, you told me a lie just now; because he cannot be the most beautiful man on earth".

"Why is that?"

"Because my Peter is the most beautiful and handsome man on earth, and the most wonderful too; there".

"Oh momsy, how can you be so mean."

That day Henry was absent minded and he found himself delegating one of his colleagues to attend to his lecture: he drove home early and was in the process of putting the key into the door when it opened and Marion was waiting for him excited and happy: Jane was behind her smiling as well. He kissed them both and enquired the reason for their joy.

"We cannot tell", said Jane, "we promised Holly not to..."

"Promised what exactly?"

"Aha, you are fishing now" said Marion.

"At least give me a clue", said Henry.

They got hold of his arms and went into the living room.

"What we can tell you is that it is excellent news", said Marion.

"Not only excellent but fantastic as well" said Jane.

"Please my two lovely ladies, put an end to my misery and tell me; I will not tell Holly".

They shook their heads.

"Is Holly appearing in a brand new show?" asked Henry.

"Very cold" replied the ladies.

"I give up then", said Henry.

"You will have to be patient", said Jane, "that is all. We have promised not to spill the beans…"

At that very moment the door opened and Holly came in. She looked at the two old ladies with a question on her face and they signalled negatively: she ran into Henry's arms and kissed him passionately and went to a cabinet and brought a bottle of champagne, while Jane and Marion fetched the glasses.

"What are we celebrating to-day?"

"Be patient and let me fill the glasses first".

When each had a glass Holly made the announcement: "here is a toast to you Henry, for you are going to be a father; I have just come back from the clinic, and they have confirmed that I am ten days pregnant". They emptied their glasses congratulating and kissing each other.

"Are you happy now Henry?" asked Holly. "How does it feel to be a future father?"

Henry took her in his arms and said: "I am the happiest man in the world, if you only knew how blessed I am". He felt so ecstatic that he danced with her around Jane and Marion who were jumping with joy, they kept repeating to each other: "We are having a baby around".

Henry sensed that a new era was dawning on him, and to crown it all, he had come across Lucy as well: he was being blessed by his lucky star and wanted to proclaim his happiness to the whole world. He wanted to tell Holly about Lucy, but would she understand in her present state: Would she understand him? Would she accept that he could love two people at the same time? Would she be as tolerant as Lucy? Of course she would, for Holly was above all that, and she would understand that the three of them were one. To him it made sense.

"How about your dancing career? it is going to take a knock".

"I shall have to take it easy for a while, But I will not give it up altogether, for I will dance till I drop", said Holly.

"I am so happy", said Henry.

"So are we, a new life in the family, how fantastic!", said the ladies. "We shall have to start shopping for the baby."

Chapter 30

Henry managed to adjust his life and accommodate Holly and Lucy at the same time; thanks to his job, he always found some excuses to meet with one or the other. He still could not understand why they were so alike in every way. When he left Holly to go and meet with Lucy, it was as if he had not left the other one: it was just an extension of the same personality. They both radiated the same magnetism and he loved them equally and dearly. As for Lucy she never asked for any special favours from him; she was happy that he was there for her whenever she needed him. And that was enough.

One day as she was practicing on the trapeze, there was a phone call for her in the office: a secretary took the call and went looking for Lucy:

"Come on down Lucy there is a call for you in the office", said the secretary.

"Do you know who it is?" asked Lucy.

"No he has not given his name, he just wants to talk to you".

Lucy, thinking that it was Henry, came down and ran to the office; as soon as she picked up the phone, she turned white and felt dizzy. She sat down and took a deep breath.

"You have got the nerve to call me, how dare you, after what you have done to me; you know that the police are searching for you, for they know your true identity now".

"I want to see you in one hour from now, I have missed you…"

"You mean you want me for a punch bag…"

"I am sorry if I hurt you last time; but I cannot stand people talking about my mother: I love you Lucy and I want you right now; remember that you are mine and no one else…"

"That is where you are wrong, you see, I have got myself a

boyfriend who loves me and take good care of me, and you better not show up, unless…"

"So you think that you can drop me just like that: you are going to be very sorry, for you will say goodbye to your fancy man very soon".

"What do you mean goodbye?" said Lucy.

But there was no answer for Damian had hung up. Lucy was worried, what did he mean by "say goodbye…oh my God", and she started to shake. Robert saw her and ran to her rescue.

"What is it Lucy, who was that on the phone?"

"That was…that was Damian".

"Damian, the son of a bitch, how dare he call you, wait if I get my hands on him, he will never forget it for the rest of his life…".

"No, no, let the inspector deal with it, he will know what to do about it" and she rang the inspector who promised to come right away.

When he arrived she quickly put him in the picture and told him about the threat.

"Tell me exactly what he said in his own words: take your time and try to remember".

"Well in his own words he said that if I dropped him, I should be sorry and soon I could say goodbye to my fancy man".

"Where is your boyfriend right now?"

"Why, he is at the clinic, he is a brain surgeon there."

"Give me his phone number or call him for me", said Brian.

Lucy phoned the clinic and asked to talk to Henry.

"I am afraid he is not here; said a nurse, he has been called to an emergency at home".

The inspector took the receiver from Lucy who seemed in a state of collapse and introduced himself; he was told that less than an hour before the surgeon's wife was taken ill, and he had left for home. They gave him Henry's home number which he rang immediately.

"Hi, I am Marion, what can I do for you?"

"May I speak to Henry please", said Brian.

"Why, he is at the clinic…"

"Has he not been called home by his wife?"

"His wife right now is in the middle of a show, and I can assure you that no one made a call from here…"

"Thank you maam", and he hang up.

"What is happening, what is going on?" said Lucy.

The inspector told her not to worry, everything would be all right. He rang the station and asked if there had been an accident during the last hour or so. Indeed came the answer, there has been one less than thirty minutes ago; a surgeon was trapped in his car after hitting a lamp post, but was rescued by fire fighters who rushed to the scene; he came out of it with a small scratch on his forehead, but his car was a complete write off. Actually they gave him a lift to his clinic where he must have arrived by now. "Everything is all right" said the inspector to Lucy; "indeed Damian carried out his threat but has been unlucky this time. We better catch that rat before he kills again". That evening when Lucy met Henry, he told her about the accident and how lucky he was to have come out of it alive.

"I do not understand why the brakes did not respond, I had the car serviced only a few days ago".

"Damian must have tampered with it", said Robert.

"He is real nasty, that man…" said Henry.

"He is a real dirty piece of work, and the whole of the police force is looking for him, for he is the serial rapist". And Henry took Lucy in his arms to protect her and said: "You had a damn lucky escape my darling and I thank God that you are here with us right now".

A few days later, one morning, on a beautiful warm day, Lucy went for a drive down town: once again and without attracting attention she was being tailed by the same grey Mercedes. The driver of the car kept his distance so as not to be conspicuous. Lucy stopped at a florists and bought two bouquets of flowers, one for her loved one and one for her momsy. She noticed an advert on the wall about a yoga class, and to-day it was a drop in session, anyone was welcome. She looked at her watch and noticed that if she hurried up she could make the class. She left the flowers in her car and ran upstairs to join the class. The session had started and they were sitting crossed legs meditating. She sat facing a young woman with blond hair. Her eyes were closed and she seemed to be in deep contemplation. Lucy copied her posture and took a few deep breaths, then when they were told to open their eyes, she observed the young girl with blond hair facing her: she had beautiful blue eyes shaped like almonds, she was slim and tall, and when their eyes met they smiled at each other. Somehow they knew they would become friends; when they stretched they both moved the same way, as if they had the same body; and even made the same mistakes to the amazement of the teacher. They had the same physique and looked alike.

At the end of the session the teacher asked them: "Are you two, Sisters?". They both laughed and together they answered: "Not at all, we have just met". and they exploded into laughters. The teacher was dumbfounded, it must have been a coincidence or a trick of nature. The two girls shook hands and introduced themselves:
"I am Holly."
"I am Lucy."
They were happy to have met and hit it off straight away.
"I know a nice coffee bar called Mario's, just across the road, shall we go and have a drink?
"Oh yes, it would be nice, we could have a chat as well and get to know each other"
They gave the impression of being old acquaintances: while sitting

at the bar sipping their coffees. Holly told her how much she loved being a ballet dancer with the San Francisco society, and that she was on vacation for a week or so. They had just returned from a long tour abroad. She added that she had a twin sister, who had been snatched away from her very early in life; they never seen her again or learned about her fate. Lucy was sad and touched by Holly's story, she held her hands for a moment, and suddenly and instinctively with tears in her eyes said "Will you let me be that sister you have lost?" and she blushed, not knowing why she said it. Quite often Lucy could not control her feelings and had to come out with what was on her mind. To her surprise Holly looked at her with deep emotion and gave her a tender kiss on her cheek. Lucy felt the same and returned her kiss.

"I am a trapeze artist at the circus on the other side of the town. It belongs to my father but now that he is getting old he has passed it to my brother on his wedding. He is a trapeze artist and a partner as well. My show is on every night at seven o'clock.

While they were chatting and telling each other their secrets, they were holding hands and looking at each other not able to take their eyes away; they gave the impression of being old friends.

"I am two weeks pregnant, and married to a magnificent man".

"My boyfriend as well is exceptional, tall and handsome with dark eyes".

"If I did not know better, I would have sworn that you were describing my man", said Holly.

And they burst into laughter.

"Would you like, Lucy, to come to one of my rehearsals and sit and watch? I am sure that you will enjoy it: you could do the warming up with us and you will meet my other friend Kyle".

"I would love to, Holly, later that evening you could come and watch me flying".

"As a matter of fact I was going to suggest to you just that, so it will be all right for to-night".

"Great idea, you might be able to meet my boyfriend as well."

"That would be very nice indeed."

They parted company promising to meet that evening at the circus.

When Lucy reached her car, the door was not locked. She looked to see if something was missing, and yes one bouquet was gone; she was surprised. Why would someone take just one of them and not both? It did not make sense, not at all. She left the car and went back to the florist.

"Hi, do you remember me buying some flowers a few hours ago?"

"Yes I do, actually I wrapped two different bouquets, you said that they were for two different lovely people."

"So you do remember selling me two different bunches?"

"Why, I've just said it, is there a problem?"

Lucy stood there puzzled.

" Are you all right miss, you seem to be miles away:"

No, no, I am OK. Actually I need another bouquet."

On her way home she was so preoccupied that she took no notice of a grey Mercedes which overtook her and cut her off while speeding away round a corner. "Who in his right state of mind would steal one bunch only?", kept thinking Lucy; "it does not make sense, and I could have sworn that I locked the car before leaving. It is not like me to forget; why is this happening to me all over again?" said Lucy loudly. "Am I getting sick in the head?"

When she arrived home and parked her car in front, she looked all around her and saw nothing out of the ordinary: she went inside, kissed Emily and offered her the flowers.

"How did your day go? any thing special happen today?"

"Momsy, I have met the most beautiful girl on earth, and we have become very good friends. She is coming to-night to watch me work: she is a ballet dancer and belongs to the San Francisco ballet society. Isn't it something: we have so much in common, and so much to tell each other…"

"By the way Lucy and before I forget, Henry rang to say he will not make it for tonight; he is tied up at the clinic, and he sends all his love and kisses".

"Pity, I wanted him to meet my new friend Holly, he would love her like I do. By the way momsy, something strange happened to-day".

"What do you mean strange?" said Milly with a worried face.

"See what you make of it: I bought two bouquets of flowers, one for you, and one for Henry; I left them in the car while I went to attend a yoga class.
I swear that I locked the door, are you still with me?"

"Yes, yes, go on darling, what next?" said Emily.

"That is where it becomes weird", said Lucy.

"What is so weird about all this?"

"So, I locked the door and went to my yoga class…"

"Well, well…"

"Be patient momsy, I am coming to it: after the yoga class Holly and I went to a coffee bar, and when I came back to the car…"

"Go on Lucy, I cannot wait to find out what next, so please hurry up…" said Emily.

"Nothing happened, except that the car was not locked and one bunch of flowers was missing".

"Are you sure, because I saw you coming with two bunches…"

"I know, I know, first I thought that my imagination was playing tricks on me, so I went back to the florist who confirmed that I bought two bunches the very first time".

"Are you sure you did not make a mistake and forgot to lock the door?"

"Oh momsy, why can you not take me seriously, I am positive that I locked the door".

Emily was puzzled, what if that evil man was trying his wicked tricks on her again? "Why can't the police catch him. she will not be happy until that man is put behind bars."

"Tomorrow morning, take the car to a garage, and ask them to change the lock; remember what the inspector said: to have some one with you at all times. Take Anya, it will do her lots of good in her condition, she needs the exercise. I will always worry about you Lucy until they catch that murderer".

"I shiver just thinking of him", said Lucy.

"Should you not tell the inspector about the incident?"

That evening, Holly watched Lucy's performance, and was very much taken by it; she could not stop applauding her even when the show was over; she ran to the stage and kissed Lucy who had just time to touch the floor. Holly saw Robert coming down the rope as well, and enquired if he was Lucy's boyfriend.

"No, not at all, he is my brother: here Robert meet my new friend, her name is Holly".

Robert could not take his eyes off her, for she looked and behaved like his little siss: how could it be possible?.

"I am sorry Robert, I mistook you for Lucy's boyfriend".

"And I am so surprised by your resemblance to Lucy..." said Robert.

"Yes it is surprising, even our yoga teacher mentioned it this morning", said Holly.

"I am afraid my Henry could not make it to-night, he is busy at work", said Lucy.

"Another time maybe."

The two girls met each other every single day during the following week, and became inseparable. They seemed to have so much in common and so much to talk about, that Holly was horrified at the idea of not seeing her again for the next few weeks as she was going on a tour very soon.

Chapter 31

One morning, Lucy watched Holly playing Swan Lake at a matinee show; she felt exalted and wanted to dance with her. She imagined dancing a duo with Holly and at the end of the show the audience demanded to see more of them. They made a beautiful team, just the two of them. She imparted her thoughts to Holly who jumped with delight at the idea of dancing together in real life. "I will talk to my choreographer and ask him to write a dance just for the two of us: what do you say?" said Holly.

"I think that it is a fantastic idea, and after that I will ask Robert to train you on the trapeze", said Lucy, "I am sure that you will make an excellent trapeze artist, and together we will put on a beautiful show".

"But I am afraid of height, and remember that I am two weeks pregnant".

"That is nothing Holly, stop fretting. Once Robert takes you under his wing, you will find out that everything is possible, even if you are pregnant".

And so started for the two girls a very hectic week of training; in the morning they trained on the trapeze, and the afternoon was dedicated to a beautiful piece of contemporary dancing. They were so perfect and made such a lovely duo that the director of the dance company offered Lucy a job; as to Holly , Robert told her to come and work for them after the baby was born; they would put on a special act for the two friends.

At the end of the week, Holly asked Lucy to come and meet her two old ladies; they were anxious to meet Holly's new friend, and asked her for supper that day.

"Will you be our guest Lucy"".
"I would love too: and next day it will be your turn, to come and sample my momsy's cuisine, she is a cordon bleu. Only Emily has not seen you yet.

When Holly opened the door to Lucy that evening, Jane was in the kitchen preparing the meal and Marion was laying the table. She looked up at the newcomer who had just entered the room and dropped the plate she was holding, and stood still as if she had seen a ghost; actually, the ghost of Jessica. Jane ran in to find out what was the commotion about, and she was taken aback as well ; she could not speak either. Holly noticing the turmoil said: "See, I told you she was beautiful, now do you believe me? Look at you two, you can hardly take your eyes off her, and I don't blame you. Everybody has the same reaction when they see us together".
"Lucy come and meet my two angels, they like you already without any doubt".
"Hello" said Marion and Jane at the same time, "please sit down, dinner will be served soon". To their surprise Lucy came to them and kissed them on the cheeks. Without knowing why, she felt very comfortable with the two old ladies. Meanwhile Holly served Lucy with a cool drink.
"I am so pleased to have met your two angels; they are so sweet" said Lucy.
"And they have definitely fallen for you", said Holly.
During the dinner Lucy felt very much at home with all of them. She talked and laughed with them and teased them as well, as if they had known each other for years. Jane and Marion were quiet at first but soon started gossiping with Lucy: they wanted to know where she came from and where was she born.
"I was born in San Diego at least I think so, that is the only place that I know actually; apart when we go touring the country with the circus".

"And what does your father do Lucy?"

"My father is the master of ceremony, but now that he is getting old, most of the time he lets my brother Robert take over".

"Is your mother an artist as well?"

"No, momsy stays at home looking after our welfare, and I adore her".

"You must be a very happy family".

"We are very lucky indeed on that account, especially after all the trouble I have caused them".

"Why, what happened to you Lucy, tell us" said Marion."I want to know everything about you" and she held her hands in hers.

"Go on, don't be frightened" said the ladies, who were getting curious, "we are here to support you".

And Lucy, with tears in her eyes, described to them the ordeal of the rape at the hands of Damian, and how she was saved from being killed, by her dog Toby, and because of it Danny her dear brother died. She also told them how unlucky she had been in love, with a man who treated her like a slave rather than a decent human being, and even now he would not leave her alone. Holly was crying intensely and the two old ladies were trying their best to comfort them; they were upset as well, for they liked Lucy indeed and deep down, they wished it was Jessica. After staying for a few more hours with the family, Lucy kissed them good night and reminded Holly that it was her turn to come the next day.

"Come to the show first, and from there we will go home where momsy will be waiting for us. I wonder if my brain surgeon Henry will come as well, but I doubt it…".

"What your boyfriend's name is Henry as well" said the two ladies at once and somehow baffled.

"Yes, what a coincidence:"

"You can say that again"; and she looked at Marion with a question mark.

"Oh my God, we have forgotten to serve the dessert Lucy, please stay so we can share it all together; what kind of hostesses are we to have forgotten the dessert? Come on Jane, come and help to serve the dessert".
"Oh yes the dessert".

And they left Holly and Lucy to chat together, while once in the kitchen the two old ladies stared at each other…
"What do you make of it Marion, it is so weird this resemblance", "But you heard her story, she comes from a circus family and the proof is there…"
"Yes but…"
"Come on Jane, we have to accept it, Jessica has gone ages ago, it is a kind of a freak of nature and there is nothing that we can do about it but to bear it; come on and let us serve the dessert".
"Oh, the dessert, I forgot all about it, they must be wandering what is happening. But I still think that Lucy is Jessica…"
"It would be one in a million chance: now let's go back to our guest".

When Lucy left, she drove back slowly, thinking about the two old ladies. They made her so welcome and she felt something about them as if they had been part of her life once, but when or where, she could not tell yet. It must have been in a completely different world, for she was certain she had not seen them before, not even among the audience. Lucy knew that she was somehow psychic, she still remembered her dream about Danny when he was drowning, and the next thing she knew was that he was dead the next day; and also when Damian was being auditioned for the job, and she voted against having him, she should have paid more attention to these warnings. How right she was at not wanting Damian in her team. Would she have paid more notice, her life could have been different now?. She was so deep in her thoughts that she never paid attention to the car cruising behind her. When she got home, she told Emily about Holly coming for supper the next day.

"Do you know what is her favourite meal?" asked Emily.

"Not at all momsy, I leave it to you to think about it; but I am sure that she will like whatever you cook, for she is like me, she goes for simple and healthy dishes".

"Will Henry be present as well?"

"I don't think so, he has a very busy schedule this week".

The next day, Lucy performed brilliantly in front of a captivated audience, but what mattered most to her was that Holly was down there among them, watching her with awe. They walked back home hand in hand like two sisters, and Anya and Robert were following slowly behind them very much in love. When they arrived at the door, Emily, who came out to welcome Lucy's friend, stood still, dumbfounded by their resemblance; they really looked like twin sisters. After recovering from her initial shock, she managed to smile and welcome her guest.

"Lucy never told me that you were so beautiful Holly" said Emily, and she shook hands with her.

"Thank you, and you are Lucy's mother I guess , for she never stops talking about you".

"Come in and meet the rest of the family: you have already met Robert and Anya , and here is my husband Peter".

When Peter saw Holly, he too was taken aback: there was so much resemblance between the two girls, and had he not known better, he would have sworn that they were sisters. Emily was worried: who was that stranger who looked so much like her daughter? Unless it was her sister... No, it could not be... It was so long ago, and Lucy was definitely her daughter; she brought her up and took care of her: she was her momsy. It would be a miracle if they were sisters, and anyway miracles only occurred in the bible. They talked about ballet and circus, and soon enough two camps were set in motion: on one side the men wanted to prove that trapeze work was the hardest, and on the other the women were united that ballet was the most demanding. But what mattered most was that they all had a good laugh.

"You can sleep here with me to-night Holly, my bed is wide enough for two; tomorrow after breakfast we could go training together", said Lucy.

"It is a lovely idea, but I have to be up early for rehearsal tomorrow. Maybe another day". She bid everyone good night and kissed Lucy.

When Peter found himself alone with Emily, he said: "How amazing, they look so much alike, like two peas in a pod, how could it be?" Emily did not answer, but instead she went straight to her bedroom not feeling herself. That night, Peter and Robert tackled the washing up, while Lucy and Anya dried the plates.

"Did you like her Anya?"

"Oh yes, she has a lovely personality".

"And you dad, what do you think?"

"Oh yes, she is a wonderful girl, I hope that you will stay friends for ever".

"That would be lovely", said Lucy.

Anya felt tired and went to bed leaving them to carry on with the washing up.

That night Emily could not sleep. Her mind was working overtime. She tossed and turned restlessly in her bed, until at last she got up and went to the kitchen where she made herself a cup of hot chocolate. She sat at the table worrying and thinking, that sooner or later, the truth would come out: and then how would she explain what had happened so many years ago: she did not want to lose her Lucy, for she was all what she had in this world; and she lived for her only. For Lucy needed her, but how would she react if she knew the truth. Would she hate her momsy and Danny who died for her. Would she forgive them, for not telling the truth about her real family. She had so many questions going through her mind, that she failed to notice Peter coming in.

"What is it Emily, I heard you tossing and turning in our bed, have you got indigestion?"

"No Peter, it is nothing…"

"How can it be nothing? you look as if you have seen a ghost…"

"You can say that again, you are not far from the truth…"

"Do you want to talk?"

"Yes I do, but I don't know where to start: and also promise not to judge me, but to be sympathetic…"

Peter took her hands and said: "Have I ever let you down before, have I ever given you any reason to doubt me?, I love you Emily, and if you are in trouble right now, I want to share your problems. Emily got up and shut the door so as not to be heard by the rest of the family. Lowering her voice, she related to him word by word what happened so many years ago; how Danny kidnapped the baby and how she hesitated to turn him over to the police; and her decision to keep the child for the sake of Danny. If not he would have been convicted of kidnapping, and he would have spent the rest of his life in prison, although mentally and emotionally he was not responsible for his actions. She was in no doubt at all, that it would have killed him, that was why she took the decision to protect her only child and make a run for it. You tell me Peter what else could a mother have done? Peter was flabbergasted by Emily's revelations; all the time that he had lived with her and the children, he never knew the truth, and now a ghost from the past was coming to haunt the ones he cared for the most in this whole world. He kept quiet for a few minutes until he heard Emily say "I understand if you hate me right now, and if you want me to leave, I will do so without any fuss".

"How can you talk about hatred Emily. I would have done the same to protect my Robert: there comes a time when family comes first and counts above anything else"..

"You don't know what a relief it is for me to share that dreadful secret with you Peter. It has been weighing on my heart for such a long time, that I feel that I have been reborn".

And they kissed and cuddled each other.

"What would you suggest we could do?"

"Nothing at all darling, let's sleep on it and allow destiny to carry its course", said Peter.

"Thank you darling for your support, I knew that I could rely on you, and that you would understand".

And they went back to bed holding hands.

Chapter 32

"Hi darling, said Henry, how was your day?"
Holly kissed Henry: "Sweetheart, one day I want you to meet my new friend, she is a performer in a circus and she is the most wonderful person on earth…"
" I thought I was that person…" said Henry.
"Well, I should have said, the most wonderful woman: there you are, are you satisfied now?"
"Who is this angel I hear of, until now, you were the only one in town".
"Flattery will get you everywhere darling", and they kissed each other.

Lucy and Holly met whenever they could. One morning after a yoga session they sat at the coffee bar, sipping their drinks and talking about the future; they never paid attention to the man sitting at the next table reading the paper. He had dark glasses and wore a baseball cap. He appeared to be reading, but in fact he was listening to their conversation with interest.
"Will you be going on tour soon?" asked Lucy.
"As a matter of fact, the company is moving out in three weeks' time".
"This time it will be a tour of Brazil. But in my present condition, I do not think that I will join them" and she caressed her stomach which was still flat.
"Why not", said Lucy, "you are still at the beginning of your pregnancy…"
"Yes, I know that I could go on dancing for a few more months actually, but Henry insists that I should be careful and not take risks".
"I am so pleased that you will not be leaving: by the way, I have a

secret to tell you, and you are the first one to hear it".

"What is it, tell me quick" said Holly.

And Lucy, as if not to let the world know, leaned forward towards Holly and whispered: "Put your hands on my stomach and tell me whether you feel something unusual as well…"

"You are not pregnant, are you?" asked Holly.

Lucy nodded her head and Holly jumped with delight: "Oh, it is wonderful, and is cause for celebration, I am so pleased and I am sure it is a good omen for both of us." and she ordered a bottle of champagne.

"Not so fast Holly, I am seeing a doctor tomorrow morning" said Lucy.

"I want to come with you", said Holly.

"No, I prefer to be by myself, in case of a false alarm; I shall meet you here after the yoga session; I am sorry to have to miss that class, and please apologize on my behalf to the teacher; tell her that I will be attending as usual after".

"Don't worry Lucy, I will tell the teacher the reason and she will understand…"

"Please don't Holly, in case I am wrong."

Next morning as hoped for, the doctor confirmed Lucy's pregnancy. She was over the moon and could not wait to tell Henry; so she rang his office and waited to be put through.

"Is that you Henry?"

"Yes, what a nice surprise, anything the matter darling?" asked Henry.

"Actually I am pleased that you rang, as I have booked a table at a new restaurant for to-night; it was meant to be a surprise. Do you like Mexican food? So be ready when I come after the show".

"Listen Henry, I too have a surprise for you and for everyone the matter of fact, it is wonderful news: I shall announce it to everybody when you come…

"Can't you give a hint right now?" asked Henry.

"No", said Lucy, "you must be patient: it is excellent news, that is all".

"Well, I shall make it as soon as possible."

Lucy met Holly at the bar as promised and told her the marvellous news.

"This is definitely great news, and we must celebrate" she ordered a bottle of champagne.

The same stranger was at the next table; he seemed preoccupied and was taking notes. That evening Henry arrived at Lucy's home much earlier than expected, for he was on tenterhooks. He demanded what was so important that he could be not told on the phone when Lucy opened the door to him, but instead she jumped on him covering him with kisses.

"Now that I am here tell me the good news" said Henry.

"First, let me open the bottle of champagne that I bought for you this morning; and I want everyone to get a glass" and Emily and Anya brought the glasses, while Peter and Robert stood there smiling at the couple.

"Now, please raise your glasses and drink to Henry who is going to become the father of my baby. I learned this morning that I am pregnant: it has been confirmed by my doctor. Everyone screamed with delight and drank in honour of the baby, and emptied their glasses. Henry was ecstatic; only a few months ago, he was begging Holly for a family, and now, two babies were on their way: how lucky he was, God had heard his prayers and was in agreement with him: he kept silent for a while and then burst into laughter and shouted "I am going to be a father". He shook hands with everyone and picked up Lucy in his arms and held her so tight, that she was suffocating.

"Please let me go Henry, I cannot breathe".

Before releasing her he gave her another kiss and relaxed his hold on her.

"Thank you Henry and I promise you not to run away", said Lucy. "You have no idea how happy you have made me".

"This calls for more drinks" and he left to get some more champagne, and they filled their glasses again and this time they toasted the parents of the unborn baby.

"Here is to Lucy and the baby", said Anya.

"Yeah, yeah" shouted the family, and once more, they emptied their glasses.

The celebration lasted quite a while and Henry said: "I don't think we are going out to-night. Let me order a pizza for everybody" and he picked up his mobile and ordered the take away.

Next morning, they had breakfast and Henry left for the clinic a very happy man. At lunch time he rang Holly to find out if everything was alright.

"Yes darling I am fine and as a matter of fact, I am over the moon".

"Why", asked Henry," what is the good news?"

"Well", said Holly, "you know my new friend I was telling you about, the one I met at my yoga class, well guess what?"

"What?"

"No", said Holly, "you guess Henry…"

"She won the lottery…" said Henry.

"No, you are being silly, it is much more important than that".

"More important", said Henry, "what could it be?"

"Well", said Holly, "she is pregnant as well, isn't it marvellous?"

"Wow", said Henry, "what a surprise!" and to himself: "This is the third person who is pregnant, what a surprise, God works in very mysterious ways.

"Are you coming to-night darling, I missed you last night".

"No, not to-night", said Henry, "I have to catch up with very important work; but are you going to your yoga class tomorrow?"

"Yes darling, we finish at ten o'clock, why don't you come and join me and my friend for a coffee and a sandwich".

"Excellent idea; I shall be at the coffee bar waiting for you and your friend", said Henry.

Next morning, Holly and Lucy met at the yoga class and were both congratulated for their good work by their teacher. "You two must be definitely related somehow, for you have the same approach in your movements: it is as if you knew in advance how the other is going to move; it is unbelievable".
"We are just two friends who actually met here for the first time" said the girls together.

On the way to the café, Holly announced: "By the way, Henry will be waiting for us at the bar, it is about time that you two met" I keep talking about you, I know that you will like each other and that you will be good friends.
"How can I not like him, he is your husband after all?", said Lucy, "and I must add that you have taste in everything or almost everything".
"I am so glad, I can't wait for him to meet you. I am sure that he will like you: soon, we must go out all together with your friend as well".
"I am sure that we will make a good team. Listen Holly, go ahead, I have to powder my nose; I will be with you in five minutes".
"Fine, but don't be too long: I will order your coffee and a sandwich", said Holly.

Lucy went to the rest room and looked at herself in the mirror and noticed her red cheeks: she was excited at meeting at long last her best friend's husband; she had heard so much about him that she already liked him. She rushed to the coffee bar and as she opened the door, she stopped dead in her tracks: there a few feet away, was Holly holding Henry's hands and laughing; but it was the hands of her "Henry" that Holly was holding: it was with her

"Henry" that she was having an animated conversation. How could this be: They never noticed Lucy coming in until the last moment as Lucy was trying to run away; Holly saw her and shouted: "This way Lucy". As she walked to the table, Lucy thought how cruel nature was towards her, why could she not let Holly meet a different Henry, there were so many of them in this world; did it have to be hers? and tears ran down her cheeks. Henry looked up and stood there for a moment as if struck by lightning. He was so shocked and surprised that for a moment he did not know what to say: he was at a loss. Lucy noticed his disarray and quickly wiped her face without being noticed by Holly: she managed to change countenance and somehow put a smile on her face.

"Hi, I suppose you are Henry. Holly told me so much about you". Henry recovered as well and shook hands with her while looking her in the eyes.

"You two know each other?" asked Holly.

"No, not at all" said Lucy and Henry at the same time.

"I could have sworn that you two have seen a ghost. Why don't you sit and drink your coffee. It is getting cold."

The three of them sat around the table and started conversing like old friends.

"It is unbelievable how alike you two are. If I did not know better, I would have sworn that you were sisters".

"That's what people keep telling us" said the girls in unison.

A man sitting at the next table, and reading a newspaper seemed pretty interested in their conversation. As they parted company, Lucy said: "Tomorrow, I shall be late Holly, asI have to take my car to be serviced; wait for me at the bookshop, I promise not to be too long. Fifteen minutes at the most, I promise".

"I will", said Holly, "but make sure it is only fifteen minutes".

They shook hands and kissed goodbye. While driving, Lucy was crying all the way back; why was her best friend married to her Henry? Why could it not be someone else, so she could hate her, but she could not hate her Holly. She had accepted that Henry had a wife, but why Holly: Fate can be so cruel sometimes.

"How did you like my friend Henry?" asked Holly.

"She seems to be a very nice person".

"I am so glad, because she means so much to me", said Holly. Henry did not reply, for he was miles away, wondering how Lucy felt. He knew that she had been crying before seeing them and also that she was hurting. He wanted to take her in his arms, and tell her how sorry he was; he wanted to comfort her as well, and funny enough he felt the same things towards Holly. Right now, at this moment of time, he would have loved to hold both women in his arms, and tell them how much he loved them both, and whisper sweet nothings in their ears. But how could he? What would the world say if it knew? How could he love two women at the same time? Why should he not, came the answer, why could he not love them the same? He had plenty of love available for both of them and he did not want it to be a secret any more. Surely the world would understand; now that Lucy knew, was it not time for Holly to find out: "I have one heart, but there is no reason for me to choose: after all if God sent him the two women, surely they were meant to be all together. I am not going to choose, for this will destroy me; they both make the earth move for me".

That night, Henry had a disturbing dream: he saw himself making love to twins, and they looked very much alike like Lucy and Holly. He jumped out of his bed shouting: "It is not possible, it cannot be." Holly woke up and switched on the light.

"What is it darling, what is not possible, you had a bad dream, look at you, you are sweating; let me get you a glass of water".

"After he drank the water, she asked him whether he wanted to talk about his dream".

"No, I am all right now, thank you for the water and I am sorry to have woken you up. Go back to sleep, you need it".

"Good night then darling", and she switched off the light.

Chapter 33

That night Lucy had a dream as well; she was saying farewell to Henry and he tried to hold on to her; but she was too quick for him and gave him the slip, she was running as fast as she could, as if she was on a mission. He tried to hang on to her clothes but they came off her body. She was waving goodbye to him with tears running down her cheeks, while he was calling her name. As soon as she disappeared into the horizon, in came rushing towards Henry a figure she knew quite well, and as soon she reached him they went into a long embrace. She knew that it was Holly. She woke up frightened and knew it was a premonition, and meant that maybe she was about to lose both Holly and Henry. But how and why? She should try to stop it, and the only way she knew how, was to tell Holly of their liaison. She would understand and accept it, for she loved them both. "No said Lucy, how could he leave me, carrying his child" but so is Holly whispered a voice. Lucy went to the kitchen to make herself a drink, thinking how silly dreams are: she had some biscuits and gave some to Toby who followed her everywhere. When she had finished, she picked up the dog in her arms and went back to bed. In the morning she told Emily of her dream, who frowned and seemed a bit worried.

"It is only a dream, don't let it worry you too much Lucy. Don't forget that we are all here to support you in case of rainy days; by the way honey, keep your mobile with you at all times in case of an emergency; call me any time.

"I will momsy", said Lucy, "don't worry, and I love you too. As you said before, it is only a dream: and Henry loves me after all".

"That is right child, keep telling that to yourself, by the way Lucy, in your dream you talk about a girl who is kissing Henry: is it the same Henry that we are talking about? and who is that girl in the dream".

"Oh momsy, did I not tell you what happened to me yesterday" said Lucy.

"No darling it must have slipped your mind; but I am here now". And Lucy told her about their meeting the day before, how she realised that Holly was married to her Henry, and the way she felt about the whole thing; especially when they were kissing and holding hands in front of her.

"What was Henry's reaction when he was with you?" said Emily.

"He was speechless and looked like a lost soul…" said Lucy.

"So he was not expecting you…" said Emily.

"Not at all momsy", said Lucy, "he was as surprised as I. Are you all right momsy?, you look so pale suddenly, as if you have seen a ghost"

"No, No, it is nothing at all; I am just under the weather. Now have a nice day darling, and she kissed her and left".

Emily was on the verge of telling Lucy, that Holly was not only married to the man she loved, but also that she was her twin sister as well. Learning all this at once and in these circumstances would have destroyed both girls. That was why it had to stay a secret and she had to take it to the grave with her.

It was a hot day and the temperature was soaring. Holly was browsing through a magazine in the bookshop waiting for Lucy. "She will be here at any moment now"; she looked at her watch, when a tall dark man, who was well dressed and wearing a baseball bat on his head approached her and asked "are you Miss Holly by any chance?".

"Who wants to know?"

"My name is Jack and I work with Miss Lucy at the circus, I am a clown".

"For a moment I thought that you were Lucy's boyfriend" said Holly.

"Not at all Miss", said Jack, "I am actually married…"

"How come I have never seen you before?" asked Holly.

"I don't think that you would recognize me under my disguise. but actually Miss Holly I have just returned from vacation". Holly looked at him while he took his spectacles off; he had very dark eyes, but what surprised her most was that they were deeply set into their sockets. For a while, she had the feeling of having seen this face before, but where?

Suddenly, he looked at her so deeply, that she felt a shiver going down her spine which made her very uncomfortable. She could feel his animal magnetism and tried not to stare at him, but it was too hard and too late as well: she fell under his spell;

"Well", said Jack, "Miss Lucy was on her way to meet you, when she felt dizzy and had to stop her car by the roadside to take some fresh air. Lucky for her, I was driving that way and saw her being sick outside her car. I stopped to ask her if she needed my help; she told me that she was pregnant and it made her sick in that heat; she asked me to drive her back to the circus and told me that she was on her way to meet her best friend. As my apartment was just round the corner, with her permission I took her there, and now she is resting on the couch: my wife is taking good care of her. She asked me to come and see you and take you back there. I would drive you in my car if you wish".

Holly looked worried about her friend: was she going to lose her baby? She did not know what to think. She was wary of that stranger, but everything he said about Lucy was actually correct. so she felt silly at doubting him.

"By the way", said Jack, "are you feeling well - you look so pale; you are not pregnant as well, are you?"

"How on earth did you know that?" asked Holly.

"Well", said Jack, "you have the same symptoms as my wife, she is pregnant as well, and when she hears bad news, she turns pale like you. By the way before we go, let me get you a glass of water, it will do you lots of good in this heat".

And he went to the counter and asked the assistant if he could have a glass of water for his friend who was not feeling good.

"I am sorry but I have a long queue waiting, go to the office which is at the back, and help yourself."

"Thank you sir, I appreciate your help," said Jack.

He went to the office where he found a clean glass, and filled it half way, then he looked around to see if no one could see him, and took a white sachet from one of his pockets, he sprinkled the white powder in the water and stirred it with his finger, until it disappeared. He went back to the shop where Holly seemed agitated and impatient.

"What kept you so long" said she.

"I had to go at the back and wash the glass; here you are, drink and let's go; for Miss Lucy must be wondering what is keeping us".

"What about my car?" asked Holly.

"Don't worry Miss Holly", Jack said, "I will bring it back for you."

For some reason, Holly started feeling dizzy and relaxed; she got up, tripped and fell into Jack's arms.

"Steady girl", Jack said, "not yet, it is too soon, what would people say", and he smiled.

Holly gave him a funny look but it was too late, she guessed that she had been doped and was at the mercy of that clown; and there was nothing she could do to escape him: she tried to scream but no sounds came out; her eyes were closing. Very carefully so as not to attract the attention of the people in the shop, Jack, who was of course Damian in disguise, supported her and walked her to his grey Mercedes. As he was pulling out with Holly slumped by his side, Lucy's car pulled in and parked a few metres away. She could have sworn that she had seen that sports car somewhere before, but where or when, she could not remember: she had a very vague feeling of seeing Holly collapsed in the front seat next to the driver; but she thought for a moment that her imagination was running wild: "I imagine things" said she, "it is funny what pregnancy does to people". She entered the bookshop and looked all around for Holly, but without success; there was no Holly to be seen in the shop. She asked an assistant whether he had seen a tall blond girl looking around.

"Why yes actually, and a man came asking for a glass of water because his friend was not well; when I think about it, she was blond with blue eyes. They left a few minutes ago, in a beautiful grey car".

"That man, what did he look like, can you remember?" asked Lucy.

"Oh yes actually", said the assistant, "very well, it would have been difficult not to notice him, he was tall with very curly black hair but what struck me the most were his eyes".

"What was special about his eyes?" asked Lucy.

"Well", replied the assistant, "they were deep seated and piercing…I would say he had hypnotic eyes…"

Lucy turned livid: now she recognized that driver in the grey car who pulled out as she was coming in; it was Damian. And the woman who was slumped by his side, was definitely Holly. But what was Holly was doing in his car? Where was he taking her? She ran outside talking to herself: "Oh God, please don't let him hurt her, Please don't make it happen, please protect my Holly. Damian has got her and is going to kill her; please someone help". She remembered the grey car driving straight ahead, so she followed the same route; she picked up her mobile and phoned the inspector; it rang and rang, and then an answering machine said: "This is inspector Donell, please leave a message and I will get back to you."

Driving as fast as she could she left the following message: "Brian where are you, I need you very urgently, it is a matter of life and death, damn you inspector, why are you not there? I am on the highway and I just saw Damian in a grey sports car and he has Holly slumped by his side. She looked drugged. I am afraid he is going to do something very, very bad to her, please help before it is too late, please Brian. I am trying to catch up with him; please call." Then she called Emily and told her what was going on, she asked her to locate the inspector as soon as possible.

"Be very careful Lucy, I am very afraid, don't go near that mad man, do you hear me" and she hung up looking for Peter and Robert. She found them and told them what Lucy had said. They left Emily to do her best to contact the inspector while they drove to the police station trying to locate the inspector. Meanwhile, as Lucy was speeding on the highway, just around the corner, she saw the grey Mercedes: it was around three hundred metres ahead of her; she slowed down so as not to attract attention, but Damian did not seem to be in a hurry, he was cruising at a moderate speed in order not to attract the attention of any police patrol. Damian was talking to someone, and at the same time she saw him drinking from a bottle. "Oh my God" said Lucy, "he is drunk as well; he might kill my Holly in an accident".

As all these thoughts were going through her mind, without warning, the Mercedes accelerated and disappeared around a corner; but when Lucy turned into that corner, the car had vanished: the street was empty and she was the only driver. She started to panic: "Where on earth has he gone and what is happening to my Holly, is she still alive? Did he rape her like the others, oh God I have so many questions and not a single answer. Damn you inspector, why don't you ring me? can't you see that I need you?" While she was near despair and turning a corner on the brink of abandoning the search for the car, she saw a grey car stationed by a small house. Lucy parked behind a tree and cut off her engine. She was just a few metres away. The driver got out of the car and she recognized Damian immediately. He walked to the other side without bothering to look around, opened the door and carried Holly on his shoulders as if she was no more than a sack of potatoes: She seemed asleep, for she did not try to resist him. Damian went up the few steps and into the house. "He must have drugged Holly the same way he did me", thought Lucy. "Let me try once more and see if I can raise the inspector". But this time, the line was busy.

Damian, who had emptied a full bottle of whisky, and was almost drunk, laid Holly on the bed, tore her clothes off and without wasting any more time, raped her there and then. Holly did not know what was taking place; she was in a stupor. When Damian finished with her, he just slumped on top of her and fell asleep. As soon as Damian went in, Lucy drove her car behind him, and waited a few valuable minutes, hoping that the inspector would get in touch with her: "Please ring now Brian and tell me what to do". Without waiting any longer and not realising what she was doing, she found herself walking towards the house and to her utter surprise, the door was not locked. She entered a room and what she saw made her sick. Holly was naked and her legs were covered in blood, Damian was asleep on top of her, but she could still see Holly's body covered in bruises:
"Wake up Holly" whispered Lucy, "Wake up" and she tried to pull her out of the bed.
Suddenly Damian turned to one side, freeing Holly. Lucy got scared and laid flat on the floor by the bed, unable to move. Her whole body was shaking and she stayed there helpless and paralysed. After an agonizing time, she heard him snoring, she turned to one side and her eyes were attracted by a box under the bed. She stretched her arm and pulled out a black square box, she extended her arm once more and this time extricated what seemed to be a truncheon made of hard rubber and around twenty centimetres long. Still shaking, she recognized the instrument of crime used by the rapist; there was no doubt this time; she had slept with her rapist for quite a while and that was enough to make her mad and want revenge. He raped her and now he had raped her Holly. Now she knew why involuntarily she has been afraid of Damian and why every time

they were together, he was not able to make proper love to her but forced himself on her. For the first time she knew that her instincts had been warning her not to take him on at the audition, and not surprisingly, why Toby wanted to bite him. Everything was crystal clear, she had been playing with fire up to now.

She picked up the truncheon, and silently walked to Damian side,"So, you are the one who raped me in my teens" said Lucy loudly; Damian, half groggy, opened his eyes and looked up, but it was too late, for the truncheon struck his skull with such strength that Lucy heard it cracking under the skin and blood started oozing from his face: "and that is for my Danny who died because of you", and again the truncheon landed on his face: "and that one is for Milly", and again she hit him hard; "and that one is for my Holly, for raping her as well, and she raised her arm to hit him again, but this time her strength was gone, and all her energy left her. She looked at him and what she saw made her vomit; there was nothing left of what used to be Damian's face, his head looked like a squashed water melon: she slowly looked at his face but there was no sign of life of what used to be Damian, the evil who caused so much misery to so many innocent people. Suddenly she threw up over him. Looking at him, she became conscious of what she had done: her rage and anger left her while she felt relieved and exhausted. There was blood spattered all around her and Holly. The bed and the walls were covered with it and red was everywhere. she noticed her hands shaking much more than before and asked herself if these were the hands that had caused so much damage. Her whole body started quivering and she began to laugh as if possessed by a demon.

At long last she was free, free of Damian and also free from the fear he put in her; she had waited so long for such a time to see Damian punished, but it was worth the waiting. She went to the bathroom and cleaned herself as well as she could and got rid of a great deal of blood; she placed her head under the cold water tap for a long time to cool down; she took a towel under the tap and ran to Holly to wash her. " Please Holly get up, it is me Lucy: we have to leave quickly before Damian wakes up; get up Holly, get up".

At last, there was some sign of life showing in Holly: she opened her eyes and tried to get up, she saw the body lying next to her with the head smashed; she became hysterical and started screaming. "Stop screaming and let me clean you", but Holly's screams became louder and she fainted. Lucy was in tears and did not know what to do; she looked at Damian, but he was quiet, and nothing of him reminded her of her former lover; his body lay naked in a pathetic twist: "What a stupid man you are Damian, you look more stupid dead than alive." She took his wrists searching for a pulse, but withdrew her hand quickly for he was icy cold. "Anyhow, it was your fault for what happened, it would have been quite different if you were normal: so don't blame me." She realised that she had killed him and panicked; "Oh my God, please someone help me please". "Holly wake up, we have to leave, wake up now".

She wiped her face and arms for they were still stained with blood and tried to dress her as well as she could. It was slow and painful. At long last, Holly opened her eyes.

"Come on Holly, we have to leave as fast as we can:" Don't look at that object, we must not be found with it; I will explain later in the car, and she slapped her gently to wake her up completely. Lucy walked her to the bathroom and helped her wash; then they left the house in a hurry. Lucy locked the door behind her, and once outside threw the key away. She assisted Holly to the car and drove away.

"We have to leave this area at the double", said Lucy.

"Why, what is going on and where are we?", asked Holly.

"Don't you remember?"

"Remember what Lucy?"

"Wait a moment and let me ring the inspector"; and she dialled his number.

"What for, what have we done…?"

"What have I done rather…"

"We have done nothing at all…"

"Oh yes, we have done quite a lot, but just relax for a moment and let me…"

"At last inspector you are answering your phone…" said Lucy.

"Who is it, is that you Lucy?…" asked Brian.

"Yes Brian, it is me Lucy; why on earth did you not answer my calls? I left you a message; where are you? I need you very badly right now."

"I have also tried to trace you, but without success either. I spoke to Emily who said that you have found Damian with Holly, is that true?" asked Brian.

"Yes, yes, it is correct, but all that is over now…"

"What do you mean: over now: where are they now…?"

"Damian, or rather what used to be Damian, is in a small house on the highway, next to a gas station, around twenty kilometres from the circus", and she indicated him the right location.

"Where is Holly, is she safe?…" asked Brian.

"Holly is with me, but she has been raped, and just by a miracle I saved her from being murdered as well…"

"Where are you going now?"

"We are going to find Henry".

"I will call your family and tell them that you are both O.K".

"No, we are not O.K. Brian, send an ambulance to the house I mentioned, you will need it" and she laughed hysterically.

"What have you done Lucy, wait for me…"

"Will you call Henry and tell him we are on our way. We need him right away; tell him to wait for us. I will explain later when I see you" and she switched off.

"What is there to explain Lucy?" asked Holly.

"Why did you not wait for me at the bookshop? I told you that I would be late, and how on earth did you meet Damian?" asked Lucy.

"Damian? who is Damian", asked Holly; "I don't know anyone with that name".

"So who was the man you where in the car with?" asked Lucy.

"His name is Jack, and he works at the circus with you…" said Holly.

"I do not know any Jack, and this man's name is Damian…"

"Now I remember", said Holly, "I was reading a magazine waiting for you when that man came to me and said that he was a colleague of yours and told me you have sent him to find me…"

"I have done nothing of the sort…" said Lucy.

"He named you and said that you were taken ill, and that you were recovering at his place, waiting for me…"

"And you believed him?" Lucy said.

"He knew that you were pregnant as well…" said Holly.

"How on earth did he know that?"

"I don't know, but everything he said about you was spot on, so I had no reason to doubt him; maybe at the last moment…"

"What happened at the last moment… Try to remember:"

"Hearing that you were not well, for a moment I did not feel well either; so he offered to fetch me a glass of water…"

"That is how he doped you…"

"He didn't, did he?"

While they were talking, it was getting late, and the weather was getting nasty as well; it was becoming dark and smoggy and Lucy switched on the fog lights; the visibility was getting bad and she needed all her concentration; so she tried not to look at Holly.

"So you believed him…" Lucy said.

"Well I don't know what I believed now", said Holly, "he was so convincing and he looked so honest; he even spoke about his wife who was pregnant as…"

"His wife; he is not even married" said Lucy.

"How was I to know; well after drinking the water, I felt weak: that is when he said something like: 'Not yet or not now' which made no sense to me at the time; but I noticed a funny sort of smile in his face…"

"Oh God, he plotted everything in advance and to the last detail, and where he was going to take you to rape you and murder you as well like the rest of his victims. Can't you see the scenario?"

Holly once again became restless and said: "Oh, I remember now being dragged on to his bed and assaulted: oh God it is not true, please Lucy tell me it is not true." Lucy never answered, for she was crying and felt guilty for not being there for her.

"My baby, my baby, what is going to happen to my baby? Have I lost it?" asked Holly.

"We are going straight to meet Henry, he will know what to do…"

"No, not Henry, I feel ashamed by what I have done; I don't want to find out…"

"He is the best person to help us, and he also loves us" Holly in her excitement never heard the end of the sentence.

"No, I would rather die than let him find out: don't take me to him Lucy, I beg you"; and in desperation, she grabbed the steering wheel in the hope of getting control of it and changing direction. Lucy could not stop her and the car veered off the slippery road, crashed against a tree and caught fire. Lucy and Holly were ejected a few metres away by the impact, and were lying dead in each other arms.

Chapter 34

When the police arrived at the scene of the crash they found no survivors but two bodies mingled together. Meanwhile, inspector Brian Donell who with two other officers managed to locate Damian's house, knocked at the door without much success; so they broke the door with the help of a sledge hammer. One officer rushed in with his gun at the ready; he quickly came out sick and vomiting

"What is going on, what is in there?" asked Brian.

"It looks like a scene from a horror film, inspector".

Brian went in slowly not knowing what to expect: what he saw was beyond all his anticipation. There was blood spattered everywhere in the room; a body with an unrecognizable face was lying on the bed; he was covered in blood, but what was most horrifying was that his head reminded him of mashed potatoes.

"Look at that inspector: and he showed him a box with black sacks in it". Another officer leaned forward and found the truncheon. "At last we have got him" said the officer, that is him all right...

"You mean Lucy has got him, don't you?"

Another officer rushed into the room out of breath, "inspector, you are wanted immediately at the scene of an awful car accident... and you are not going to like it". The inspector looked at him and ran to the car. he picked up the receiver and said his name

"You better come as soon as possible", said a voice, "for there has been an awful car crash with two women involved..."

"Two women?..." repeated Brian.

"Yes two women", said the voice, "someone here said that you knew one of them..."

"Oh God no, it is not possible".

He ran back to the house and told an officer to call a crime unit team and an ambulance "I have to leave you and dash now, for there has been another death".

When he arrived at the scene of the crash, he recognized Lucy's body and guessed that the other one was her friend Holly. Their bodies seemed enlaced in an embrace. The inspector felt tears coming to his eyes, for he had come to respect this young girl who had everything to live for; it was his fault if she was dead right now, for he should have been there with her when she needed him. Damn this job he shouted, why is it that it is always the innocents who die, why? and he took her hand in his and kissed it. He searched Holly's pockets and found an address and a telephone number. He dialed the number and a sweet voice answered:" Hi, this is Jane, what can I do for you:"
"Hi, I am inspector Donell, who am I speaking to?"
"As I said just now, my name is Jane, what can I do for you Inspector?…"
"I don't know how to say it, but I am in possession of a wallet, and it belong to a certain person called Holly. Are you her mother?…"
"God no, Holly's mother died years ago in a plane crash, I am her grandma, but why on earth do you want to know, have you found that wallet?"
"There is no other way, but to tell you…"
"Tell me, tell me… what inspector? anything happened to our princess?"
"I am afraid that there has been a terrible car crash, and the princess was in it; I am afraid that two girls actually were killed in it…"
"Oh no", said Jane, "do you mean our Holly is dead?…"
"I am afraid so , I am so sorry: and there was another young girl with her called Lucy, do you know her?"
"Oh my God, they were two inseparable friends, is she all right?"
"I am afraid no, they died together in each other arms…"
"Hello? are you there?"

Jane had fainted, and Marion who was in the next room, heard the fall and rushed in to help.

"What is it Jane, why have you fainted, and who is on the phone". She picked up the receiver and said: "Hello, hello, who is this?"

"I was speaking to Jane, is she... all right?" asked Brian.

"No she is not: and it is thanks to you that she has fainted and is lying on the floor. Who are you and what did you say to upset her so much?, said Marion.

"I am afraid I am the bearer of horrible news; there has been an awful accident involving Holly and Lucy, around a kilometre from the clinic..."

Marion did not wait to hear the end, she hung up and quickly redialled Henry at the clinic.

"Hi, can I help you?" asked the secretary.

"This is Marion, let me speak to Henry:".

"Hi Marion, I am afraid that the professor is in the middle of a lecture; can't it wait, or shall I take a message?"

"No, no, it cannot wait; tell Henry there has been a terrible accident one kilometre from the clinic, and that Holly and Lucy are involved: it is very urgent and we will meet him there". And she hang up. The secretary was in a state, she rushed to the lecture room and discreetly opened the door and waved the professor, to come out: "What is it, can't you see that I am in the middle of a lecture..." said Henry "I am so sorry professor, but Marion was on the phone just now and in a very bad state, she said that Holly and Lucy have been involved in a car accident, one kilometre from here..."

"Is it serious?" asked Henry.

"It sounded terrible, she hung up quickly and said she will meet you there..."

Henry did not wait to hear the end, he put his jacket on and ran to his car. Meanwhile the inspector was still at the scene of the crash. He rang Emily to tell her about the fatal accident, but she would not believe him; her Lucy would not abandon her momsy just like that, she knew better. She wanted to see for herself; she called Peter and Robert and told them about the car crash; but she added that it definitely was a mistake. As for Anya she shown all the signs of distress. She loved the two girls especially Lucy who had trained her to be an artist. She got hold of Toby and nervously caressed him; she would keep him from now on, she was sure that was what Lucy would have wanted. Robert and Peter drove Emily to the scene of the accident. When they saw the two girls lying cold in each other arms, they could not hold their emotions any longer particularly Emily who broke down and fainted. Peter was crying as well and Robert went to Lucy and said "Why did you have to leave us so soon, we loved you so much, so why did you leave?" And he stood there crying in silence. When Emily recovered, she kept crying for her baby; she was as expected in a very sombre mood talking to herself. "I have lost my Danny, my only son, and now, I have lost my Lucy, my only daughter. Why is destiny so cruel? What was she being punished for?. Was it for the mistake that Danny made so many years ago? But why take the girls away, they had done nothing to deserve it; so why?"

The rain was still coming down steadily, and the visibility was getting worse: Henry was driving like a mad man. He wanted to be near his loved ones, they needed him specially now that they were involved in the accident. It was time for him to reveal the truth to Holly. But was the accident serious? He hoped not, maybe a scratch or two; why on earth Marion did not say exactly what has happened on the phone, he would not have had to worry so much; I know that she is an old lady, but still she should have told him everything. Is my wife all right? and what about my lover, is she all right? I know that my lover Lucy and my wife Holly will stay friends forever, it is written all over them. Oh God, I am such a lucky person to have found those two souls who love me as I do them. I hope they have walked out of the crash with a cut or a graze… or maybe they have been hurt badly? It can't be, for they love me, I will not allow it to be serious, they love me as I do them.

Suddenly, he screamed like a madman: "My wife, my lover, you are together but one: please wait for me; don't leave me, not now." Across the road and some four hundred metres away he could see the lights of an ambulance and some police cars flashing; he just had one junction to cross and he would be there with his two darlings. While his thoughts were with his wife and lover, he did not notice the traffic lights switching to red, and he went through the crossing as an oil tanker was coming across. Henry's car smashed against it and caught fire, while his body was hurled into the air and landed a few metres away from the first accident: He too was killed on the spot.

"What the heck is going on here" said the inspector, "not another accident, I don't believe it". Peter and Robert followed the officers to where the accident had just happened, and could not believe their eyes; for there lay Henry's body twisted on the road. Robert looked at Peter with disbelief, for the couple they loved so much, just left this world less than an hour from each other. "What a cruel world we live in" said Peter. Marion and Jane arrived in a cab a few minutes later to find that their loved children have been wiped out within an hour from each other.

The next day, Jane and Marion met Emily at the mortuary to identify the bodies.

"I am sorry for the loss of your daughter, she was a close friend of mine", said Emily.

"Thank you", said Jane, "we are also sorry for your loss as well".

"We knew Lucy, she came for dinner one day".

"I am afraid that they are together now and forever", said Peter.

They entered the mortuary together, where the three bodies were laid covered on a table.

"Are you ready for it?" said the coroner. And he pulled the cover off one body, then the other two. The three of them were lying naked on the tables. They seemed to be so much at peace. The three ladies looked at them...

"Do you se what I see Marion?" asked Jane.

"Oh God almighty", said Marion, "it is not possible, after so long..."

"What is the matter, what can you see?" asked Emily.

"Look at their navels Emily; they have got the same birthmark: they are our twins Holly and Jessica. Jessica was snatched away from us, and we have never seen her again before".

"Now it makes sense why my Georges shouted her name before his heart attack. While watching the circus he loved so much, he must have noticed Jessica on the trapeze and seen the birth mark; but he was unfortunate for he did not survive the shock; for if he had, we would have been reunited ages ago".

"Oh my God, so it is true, his last wish was fulfilled, and that was what he wanted, to find Jessica alive".

"And you Emily, can you tell us how you came about to bring up our Jessica as your Lucy?" asked Marion.

Emily was taken by surprise and for a while did not know what to say : Marion and Jane thought that she could not talk because of her grief, but a minute or so later they heard Emily say: "A friend of mine who worked with me, had to go to hospital for a tumour in her brain; she asked me to take care of her daughter during her stay there; but when she found out how serious her condition was, and she thought that she would never come out alive, she made me promise to adopt her if she did not survive. And that is exactly what happened, and we kept calling her Lucy thinking that it was her real name; and she was a companion to my son who died a few years ago."

"We are so sorry to hear of the loss of your son as well. It is so unfair that destiny lashed at you that way". Emily was not listening, for she was in tears stroking Lucy's hair. When it came to Henry and they saw his dislocated body, the three women started wailing as loud as possible with Peter not knowing what to do or how to behave, for he wanted to scream as well.

"He is our son in law", said Jane, "what on earth happened to him…"

"He is Lucy's boyfriend, why is he dead as well, and how…"

There was no answer, and the two old ladies collapsed on the floor. The coroner and his assistant helped the ladies out and offered them a cup of tea, and the women looked at each other with disbelief.

"What an irony, for here lie reunited in death, three young persons who cared so much for each other when alive, and now even in death they seem at peace. They should be buried all together in death as well".

"What an excellent idea; we will have them rest together in one single grave, with one stone on top".

When they left, the inspector told Peter and Robert, the atrocious end of Damian at the hands of Lucy.

"At least", said Robert, "this one got what was coming to him; and from one of his victims".

"There is a God after all" Peter said.

"You bet", said inspector.

The hearse which was carrying the three bodies in a special coffin, was pulled by four beautiful black horses, followed by all the artists from the circus. The acrobats were doing somersaults, while the clowns were playing the trumpets; and they were followed by all the ballet dancers from the San Francisco ballet society. Henry's colleagues and friends were doing their best to follow the procession. Although everyone was in a sombre mood, it had the climate of a carnival. They were convinced that Lucy and Holly would have wanted it.

On their way home, they ate and drank to their memories. The director of the ballet company asked the families whether it would be all right for him to make a film of the two sisters' lives. At the same time, Anya went into labour although she had two weeks to go. Emily with Peter and Robert rushed her to hospital in time to deliver her premature baby girl. Straight away they decided to call her: Lucy-Holly-Jessica, in memory of the departed.

They were put to rest together in one single grave and next to Georges who took them under his wing. Some time later, a stone stood on top of their grave with the following inscription.

'Into this world, two princesses arrived.
Together invited, and at the same time.
Very soon, separated they were found,
And into different directions they went.
Until again, one day they met;
Knowing not who they were,
Bosom friends they became.
Unknown to them, their love they shared,
With one man who both he loved.
Until one day, nature had her say,
And again reunited, the two princesses were;
Together and with their only love forever,
At the prime age of twenty five.
Please, bless them all on their way.

Chapter 35

The weeks after the funeral were heavy to bear for both families. The circus was in mourning as well and did not reopen until a week later. No one felt like performing, and they could still visualize Lucy swinging on the trapeze. Rumours circulated that the ghosts of Lucy and Holly were in the circus to stay.

The police seemed to have received a vote of confidence from the public, for young women did not feel afraid to stay out late at night, or walk alone. They knew that the serial killer was dead now, and they appreciated their renewed freedom until one evening a bombshell once again fell on the city. It appeared on the screen in a news flash: once again a young woman was found murdered with a black sack over her head. This time she was not raped, but just murdered the same way as the others. Was it a copycat murder or was the rapist not really dead, or still better as some would have us believe it was Damian who had come back from the dead to take his revenge. But whatever was the reason, it succeeded to bring back the panic, and once again the streets were deserted.

The inspector was summoned to the Commissioner's office and asked without ceremony to explain the situation.
"What happened", said the Commissioner, "I thought that we had heard the end of the murders, so tell me what is going on? Explain to me the latest murder".
"I do not understand it myself Commissioner", said the inspector, "I assure you that he was battered to death and clobbered beyond recognition by one of his old victims who survived his ordeal. I will go to the mortuary right away and see the body; it is a puzzle…and I hope that the body has not been disposed of".

"Do what you have to do Inspector, but I want answers and results fairly quickly for everyone above is breathing over my neck, and panick is back again among us.

The inspector and his sergeant went together to the mortuary. They spoke to the coroner who laughed when he confirmed Damian's death.
"Can I see the body?" asked the inspector.
"I don't think so", said the Coroner, "for it has been disposed of…"
"I want it to be exhumed and confirm that it was the man we were after…" said the Inspector.
"I am afraid you will have a job to do this…" said the Coroner.
"Why is that?", asked Brian, "what has happened to the body, has it been cremated?"
"One moment Inspector, let me think" and he went to another office and asked the clerk to find him Damian' death certificate with all the relevant papers.
A few minutes later the clerk came back with the papers, and the Coroner read some note to the Inspector, an old man claiming to be his father came to collect his body to give him a decent Christian burial.
"Do you have the old man's address?" asked the Inspector.
"Yes I have got it here", said the Coroner.
The Inspector took the notes from the Coroner and read the address and suddenly exclaimed; "The son of a bitch, this is the same house where Damian was found battered. Thank you, you have been very helpful" and he left quickly with the sergeant on his trail.
"Sergeant call the office and get some back up immediately: I want four men to meet me there in twenty minutes, we shall wait for them there".
The sergeant rang for the reinforcements while the Inspector drove

to the house in question. When they arrived at the address, four policemen in uniform were already there waiting for them. Inspector Donell looked at the house and frowned, for the place had an eerie feeling about it. It was quiet and no one seemed to be there. They walked to the block of flats while three of the men went to the back. Without success the sergeant knocked a few times at the door, then one of the men shouted from the back that there was a window leading to the basement. The inspector rushed there and ordered one of his men to break the window. When it was done, one man went through and found a way to open the door from the inside.

They switched on the lights and saw a coffin lying on the floor. Brian Donell opened the lid and fell backward due to the putrid smell emanating from the decomposing body. They all covered their noses and looked down at it; it was definitely that of Damian's. They replaced the lid back on and looked at each other with a question mark:
"So Damian was not the serial killer after all…"
"But he raped Holly, Lucy was there…"
"But why did he not kill her?"
"If I knew the answer to that question, we will have our killer".
Everyone seemed puzzled. They climbed a few stairs and opened a door leading to Damian's apartment. They entered the room where his body was found, and nothing had changed; no one cleaned the room: the walls were still stained with blood, reminiscent of a fight; even the bed had not been touched since then. But there was a sleeping bag wrapped on a chair. With a whispering voice the inspector said: "somebody is using that apartment and sleeping on that bag."
The sergeant, whispering as well, said: "Whoever it is, he must be a sick man" The inspector instinctively looked under the bed, and what he saw made him swear:" The son of a bitch, he still has got

that box, look at it sergeant:" and he opened the box and there it was; a truncheon and some black sacks. " But we took that box away inspector, I can vouch for it." The inspector did not reply for he was in a pensive mood. After a while, he said: "I think we have a new killer at large, and he lives here, thinking that no one will search this place anymore."

"Nobody touch a thing here, and let's leave the place the same way we came in. We are going to wait for him outside behind some trees. He must not see us, and we will surprise him when he comes home".

They parked their cars not far away and waited watching the building. It was getting dark when they noticed a car stopping a few metres from the house and a silhouette of an old man came out of it. To the surprise of all the officers, the old man walked slowly to the door leaning on a cane. He seemed cautious and every so often he stopped to look all around him. As soon as he opened the door of the house, he went so quickly in that he attracted the inspector's attention. That old man seemed so fast and supple when it came to entering the place: "Something is not right" he said to the others, "be on your guard for he may not be what he looks".

"We are going in, two of you guard the back door and the rest come with me, something is not right here, I can vouch for it", said Donell.

Brian Donell knocked at the door, but as was to be expected, there was no reply. He banged on the door with his fist and called out who he was, but without success. Running out of patience, they smashed their way in with guns at the ready. They opened the door to the room but it was empty. Two of them went upstairs but still there was not a soul to be seen. The inspector looked under the bed and took the box out.

" That old man could not have gone very far, I am going to the basement just in case" said the sergeant.

"Take a man with you, to be safe" added the inspector.

As the sergeant was about to open the door to the basement, he had the feeling that someone was gasping for air. He looked at his officer, and with his index finger to his lips, he warned him to be quiet and still. He tip toed to the end of the corridor: where he saw an old cupboard and all of a sudden he opened the door swiftly, and there was the old man crouched in a tiny space unable to breathe properly.

"Come out of it with your arms over your head".

"I cannot, for I have to use my walking stick".

Thinking that the old man was genuine, the sergeant and his man lowered their guard and were about to put their pistols back in their holsters when the old man jumped at them with such a force that they were knocked down on the floor. Not waiting for them to get up, he ran to the back door and opened it, only to be confronted by two other policemen; he tried to struggle with them, but they were joined by a furious sergeant who could not believe that he had been knocked out by an old man. The fracas attracted the attention of the inspector and his man, they rushed to the scene, and at long last the six of them managed to control the fury and rage of the old man. They immobilized him on the floor and handcuffed him. When he stood up, the sergeant had a surprise. In his hand he was holding what seemed to be a wig, and his beard was out of place. The inspector pulled it out as well as his false moustache, and there was standing in front of them a giant of a young man, handsome and athletic.

"What is your name?" asked inspector Donell.

But there was no reply.

"OK, you better come to the station and tell us all about yourself".

He was taken forcefully to the car while he was still struggling and kicking.

At the station , they sat him at a desk, and managed to take his fingerprints and took his photos.

"You are allowed a lawyer to be present at the questioning; do you want one?"

He nodded but looked away as if he had nothing to do with it. While waiting for the lawyer to arrive, he was offered a cup of coffee. One officer stood guard at the door while the inspector with the sergeant left to discuss the situation outside.

Unbelievably, rumours spread in the city that once again they had caught the serial killer, the real one. The paparazzi invaded the station demanding to see the killer and to take his photos.

After nearly an hour, a female lawyer arrived at the station; she was tall, young and pretty, with dark hair to her shoulders. She introduced herself as Liz, and sat next to the accused man. The inspector once again asked for his name, and there was still no answer.

"You must give your name, if not I will not be able to defend you: is that clear?"

"Fabian, my name is Fabian."

"What is your relation with Damian whose corpse is in your basement?"

"He is my twin brother, he is younger than me."

"So, why did you murder that girl, and don't deny it, you have left your marks all over her: and how come you did not rape her like the others?"

There was complete silence.

"I put it another way Fabian, you left your marks all over her, she was half naked, and the well known black sack covered her head, but why on earth you did not rape her this time: why? What made you change your mind; what is it this time?"

-"You must answer the inspector, Fabian", said Liz.

Fabian looked at her with such penetrating eyes, that she had to turn her head away quickly; but it was not quick enough, for Fabian's look pierced her heart and soul. She felt the power of his mind and for a moment she lost continence and felt wet and very uncomfortable.

"You want to know why the last victim was not raped, I am going to tell you why; I left it to my brother to fulfil this dirty job, for he was a romantic and wanted to do the work properly; on the other hand my job was a kind of spiritual, I sent them to their maker as gently as possible. From very young age I had this killer instinct, and I would slaughter any animal coming my way , and my parents were very proud of my prowess; as for Damian, he was just the opposite, and my parents were encouraging him to copy me but without success, so he was beaten up and put in a cupboard most of the time. We all called him sissy. But to prove us wrong, and as early in life as he could, he told me to come with him, for he was going to prove me wrong.

The officers were listening amazed by Fabian's change of heart; now there was no stopping him, for he carried on.

"When I asked Damian what he was going to do to prove us wrong, he said: 'Just do what I ask from you without questions, will you do that?"

"What did you reply?" asked the sergeant.

"I did not say a word, I was just curious to find out what he had in mind. So, he took me to a rich neighbourhood and we saw children riding their bicycles in front of their posh houses. He hid behind a tree and told me to do the same. I was getting excited, for it looked as if we were going to have some fun with the children. 'Now listen carefully Fabian; think of those children as the animals you like to slaughter and you are so proud of'. I nodded with my head this time wondering what he was about to do. 'I am going there among those kids and I will lure one of the girls to follow me; I know how, but when we reach behind those trees, I want you to jump her and do to her what you do to the animals'. "Do you mean that you want me to kill her like I do with the animals…" "Not exactly the same way, but when you see us coming to that tree, take a stone and hit her hard enough for her to fall…' "And what will you be doing meanwhile?" I asked'. "You will see, you will be proud of me", said Damian".

"Did you agree to it?" asked the sergeant.

"Of course I did, what else could I have done, here you are, my sissy brother was going to show off…"

"And how old where you then?"

"Around thirteen…"

"My God, that young: so what happened next?"

"So here I was hiding behind a tree with a stone in my hand, waiting for Damian to walk by with a girl; I don't know what he said or what he did, for surely enough fifteen minutes later, he walked by with a sweet little blond girl, chatting and laughing together. She seemed so sweet and trustworthy that I nearly cried when I hit her on the head with the stone. I am sure that I did not hit her hard enough to kill her, but when she fell looking at both of us with a surprise in her face I felt sick in the guts. Then to my utter surprise, I saw Damian undoing his trousers, then he lifted the girl's skirt, lay over her and to my amazement he raped her. I could not believe my eyes seeing Damian doing it. 'Where did you learn to do that Damian?' I asked. 'On TV of course', said Damian, where else; 'now it is your turn to rape her'. 'No, it is disgusting: I hate sex, I hate it, I would rather kill than do what you have done…' 'Who is the sissy now?' 'I can still remember the face of our first victim and sometimes I still feel sick. From then on, we graduated and became more sophisticated. We learned to refine our acts and we became a team".

One of the officers who was listening could not take anymore of it, and left feeling sick.

"So there were two serial killers and not one…" said the inspector.
"I was the killer and Damian was the rapist, it is not the same".
"You are a sick man, do you know that?"
"I had to shadow my brother for he did not care whether his victims saw his face or not, so I had to send them back to their makers, to make sure that none of us get caught. Are you satisfied now or do you want to hear more gory stories?"…
"You leave the rest to the judge, he will decide what to do with you", said the inspector".
"One more thing you ought to know Donell, we were a good team until Damian fell in love with that circus gypsy girl. I warned him about her, but he would not let me finish her; he was such a sissy my brother. Now that he is gone, all my dreams have been shattered. They suddenly came to a halt; I wanted to send more women away to their makers, and to be remembered for eternity…"

And without any warning, he turned to Liz who seemed petrified by his story, and butted her on the head and then hit her head against the table so hard that her skull seemed to explode and blood spattered all around and covered the face of the inspector and the sergeant. Seeing that they were blinded by the blood for a moment Fabian seized his opportunity and knocked both men flat on the floor. He punched them both unconscious. He went to the door and knocked gently; the officer who was guarding the door from the other side, and thinking that the inspector was trying to open the door, pushed it open enough for Fabian to pull him in and hit him with a karate chop. He ran along the corridor, pushing and shoving whoever came his way, opened a door into the street and ran across the road just as a taxi was speeding his way. He flew over the bonnet and landed on the pavement across the road with his body twisted into a grotesque shape. His eyes were wide open as if bewildered by his ill fortune.

When the inspector and his men arrived on the scene, they were horrified by the sight and said: "Even in his last moment, this wretched pervert, managed to take the life of another innocent victim who was there for his defence.

THE END.